PRAISE FOR

THAT WHICH BINDS US

"*That Which Binds Us* is an Appalachian love story with glorious twists and turns, longing and grief, and resplendent redemption. Elizabeth is an original character of strength and purpose. You won't be able to put it down!"

—**Adriana Trigiani**, best-selling author of *The Good Left Undone*

"*That Which Binds Us* is a superior work of Southern Appalachian fiction, marking the debut of a gifted writer to watch. Mining the rich literary terrain of authors like Lee Smith and Adriana Trigiani, while breaking new ground of her own, Cathy Rigg has written a heartfelt historical tale of a people and their place that resonates long after the last page is turned."

—**Amy Greene**, author of *Bloodroot*

"Cathy Rigg has come up with the liveliest, most interesting and compulsively readable historical novel I have seen in many a year—I love this book! Of course I'm a Virginian too...but these themes are universal and the writing is wonderful."

—**Lee Smith**, award-winning author of *Silver Alert* and *Dimestore*

"Rigg has written a historical novel of exquisite storytelling, with an ear tuned to the voices of mountain people."

—**Amy D. Clark**, coauthor and editor of *Talking Appalachian: Voice, Identity, and Community* and host of the *Talking Appalachian* podcast

"Cathy Rigg's *That Which Binds Us* is historical fiction at its best, showing us exactly what it meant to survive the Civil War as it impacted the old ways in Appalachia. Rigg's novel is a fine-tuned ballad made of strong women, lost love, and family secrets. The characters are ones I recognize via my own ancestors, and its setting—from Cumberland Gap to Pound—is a place I know and love. This is a novel I will long remember."

—**Karen Salyer McElmurray,** author of *Wanting Radiance* and
I Could Name God in Twelve Ways

"Cathy Rigg's ability to evoke place is special. While reading her captivating debut novel, one feels the mountains of Southwest Virginia beneath one's feet. The ridges and seasons fill the reader's eyes, nose, and ears—a literary feat made more astonishing by the equally dizzying ease with which Rigg transports her reader to a world nearly two centuries gone. Research and imagination meld with crack storytelling skills to make *That Which Binds Us* a brilliant depiction of the Civil War years in the Appalachian mountains and one humdinger of a read."

—**Robert Gipe**, author of *Trampoline, Weedeater*, and *Pop*

"Cathy Rigg's debut novel offers a rich patchwork of voices, all deeply rooted—and fiercely loyal to—the mountains of Southwest Virginia, and who will, in one way or another, be forever changed by the Civil War. *That Which Binds Us* is a heartfelt, hard won tale of devotion, endurance, and the inexhaustible resilience of those who call Appalachia home."

—**Allison Alsup**, author of *Foreign Seed*

"Cathy Rigg, with her historical novel *That Which Binds Us*, has laid firm claim to Virginia's Appalachian Civil War era. And to my heart. This is a story of loss, yes, but also of love—and that's what bound itself to me."

—**Bren McClain**, author of *One Good Mama Bone*

"Even a close-knit, isolated mountain community in southwest Virginia cannot escape the terrors of the American Civil War in this multi-voiced story told cleverly by Cathy Rigg. *That Which Binds Us* is unforgettable historical fiction about the saga and secrets of tenacious Elizabeth Young, her family, and neighbors whose realities are brought to life through Rigg's scrupulous attention to one small corner of Appalachia, documenting place, culture, and language with loving kindness."

—**Marianne Worthington**, author of *The Girl Singer*

"In *That Which Binds Us*, Cathy Rigg weaves a story rich in history, authentic voices, and a strong sense of place. The characters in this historical fiction are poignantly crafted, and the southern Appalachian landscape is captured in lyrical description. Like the mountains themselves, the storytelling lingers in the heart and imagination."

—**Jayne Moore Waldrop**, author of *Drowned Town*

"Rigg's love for the mountains of southwest Virginia resonates on every page, while her decades-long research immerses readers in the mid-nineteenth century through characters that are so well-drawn, they climb off the page and sit alongside you as their story unfolds."

—**Patricia L. Hudson**, author of *Traces*

"Rigg deposits us in an Appalachia we've all read about, but Elizabeth Young's journey through the Civil War provides a searing, personal exploration of the era. *That Which Binds Us* compels readers from the first page to the last."

—**Laura Leigh Morris**, author of *The Stone Catchers*

"Cathy Rigg's *That Which Binds Us* is the best sort of historical fiction, bringing real people to life to tell their stories. Every page lives and breathes, and the Civil War itself, in all its horror and loss, comes alive like the people. By letting the characters tell their own story in their own words, we are drawn like moths to a flame. We endure terrible times with them, but we're ultimately redeemed, as are they, by their love, strength, humanity, and reverence for the land and community they call home."

—**Rita Sims Quillen**, author of *Wayland*, *Hiding Ezra*, and *Some Notes You Hold*

THAT
WHICH
BINDS
US

THAT WHICH BINDS US

CATHY RIGG

KEYLIGHT
BOOKS
AN IMPRINT
OF TURNER
PUBLISHING

KEYLIGHT BOOKS
AN IMPRINT OF TURNER PUBLISHING COMPANY
Nashville, Tennessee
www.turnerpublishing.com

That Which Binds Us

Cover image: Robert S. Duncanson (1821–1872), *French Broad River*, circa 1850–1851. Oil on canvas, 17 × 24 inches. Courtesy Robert Alexander Boyle.
Cover design by Ryon Edwards
Book design by William Ruoto

Library of Congress Cataloging-in-Publication Data

Names: Rigg, Cathy, author.
Title: That which binds us / by Cathy Rigg.
Description: Nashville, Tennessee: Turner Publishing Company, 2025.
Identifiers: LCCN 2024034046 (print) | LCCN 2024034047 (ebook) | ISBN 9781684429936 (hardcover) | ISBN 9781684429943 (paperback) | ISBN 9781684429950 (epub)
Subjects: LCGFT: Novels.
Classification: LCC PS3618.I39386 T47 2025 (print) | LCC PS3618.I39386 (ebook) | DDC 813/.6—dc23/eng/20240809
LC record available at https://lccn.loc.gov/2024034046
LC ebook record available at https://lccn.loc.gov/2024034047
Printed in the United States of America

For my mother and grandmother

I can now say that I have verified the saying of an old
Indian who signed Col. Henderson's deed.
Taking me by the hand, at the delivery thereof,
Brother, says he, we have given you a fine land,
but I believe you will have much trouble in settling it.

—Daniel Boone
from *The Adventures of Colonel Daniel Boone* by John Filson, 1784

THAT
WHICH
BINDS
US

PART ONE: 1854

UNRAVELING

CHAPTER ONE

———

ELIZABETH YOUNG

MARCH 1854

IT WAS FIVE DAYS UNTIL THE HANGING WHEN IT CAME to me I needed to see Uncle Ruck one last time. Papa never would've allowed such a thing, me being a girl and one just only thirteen. But as it was a plan I made, it was a plan I carried out to the fullest and even now I am glad, even with all that's happened.

Provisions was something to consider, our ornery mountain skies liking to make their mind up as they go—might be rain, might be snow, might be a mix of both, it being March in the Appalachians. I stashed some things down at the barn though in truth I could've walked right past Mama wearing a heavy coat and boots and a wide-brimmed hat and she wouldn't have took no notice. I could've strapped a Remington across my back and paraded here and there and all around and still she wouldn't have asked what I was up to or where I was going. She was already soft by then, missing, her life set apart. But Papa, he was different. He'd be working at the Mercantile which meant soon as I got to Blackmore's Fort I'd have to stay out of sight. His store was a good ways from the jailhouse but with him you never can tell. He knows things, Papa does, things you never expect and somehow can't figure.

There was many occurrences of the journey I remember, like taking the shortcut up at Widow's Holler, that old granny witch watching my every move. Like Stony Creek running high and me still needing to cross it. I looked that situation over with a good bit of determination and decided my best bet was to cut over near the old Sycamore where the water rushed with a great deal of fortitude but the rocks, such as they were, made a good path to the middle.

I pulled off my boots, rolled down my stockings, and got myself to crossing.

It was *cold* when I first stepped, bare feet on icy rocks, and a tremble ran through giving me pause. Then the thought came: *Skin'll stick to things that's froze.* I ripped off quick and moved swift stone to stone, and in no time I'd got to the center where sure enough there was no more boulders. There was just me and before me, a big wide spread of winter water.

I would have to go in, this was obvious, so I took a good hard look down. *Where was that bottom?* Not where I could see it, that was the answer, so I raised high the hem of my dress and I stepped on in. Stony Creek ate my foot, my ankle, my shin. It was up at my knee time I first touched bottom: Hallelujah, *that's one.* I brought forth the other, hooray *that's two. Three* it got deeper, *four* it got colder, *five six seven* then *eight nine ten* and I was out, delivered to the other side.

My body was shaking, and my breath was coming in shivers. I dried off best I could using the sleeve of my coat, but as an idea this was not that great. Finally I just pulled on my boots heaved myself up, and got myself to walking. It wasn't gonna do one bit of good to fret over this chill, so I turned my thoughts to the jailhouse and just what I was gonna say to Uncle Ruck.

Why did you do it? would be a good thing for starters.

THIS I HAD BEEN WONDERING SINCE THE DAY LAST week when the fateful news got delivered. I was down at Papa's store, on toward the back and wandering the racks when I heard the big wood door scrape across those crooked pine slats up front. It's one of those things Papa always said he was gonna fix but never got 'round to, which was fine by me since I liked it the way it was, letting you know somebody'd come in to trade and all. On this particular day, though, Mister Red was there for a whole other reason.

"They found him guilty, Jonathan," Red said. "He's sentenced to death by hanging." I couldn't see neither of them, blocked as I was by the big bolts of fabric between us. "Don't come as a surprise, I reckon. Still I figured it was best was you to hear it from me."

I peeked around to catch a glimpse of Papa's face, which had drooped like a sad little flower gone too long without water. His skin was the color of ashes and sagged loose from his bones, his back hunched over like it couldn't hold up his shoulders anymore. He stood the longest time not saying a word nor doing nothing at all but only looking down. Then he raised up his head and cast his eyes toward the Compton Hotel. "Well then. That's that," he said.

That's when Mrs. Theda Thorpe shoved a bolt of fine fabric back into the rack giving me a start. "I'll get this another time, Jonathan," she said, and fussed out the door. Which left me and Mister Red and Papa all alone in the store, and I was pretty sure Papa had just as well forgot about me.

"Don't come as much of a surprise, Jon, I know. But it can't be easy."

Papa shook his head left and right, shook it slow. "He's lived a sorry life, Red. That's the truth of it. Rufus has been working on this death sentence since we was six years old."

It got mighty quiet in the Mercantile. Papa picked up an old rag and wrung it, and Mister Red had his hat, which he rubbed all along the edge like Mrs. Thorpe and the blue velvet. A good long time passed.

"When's it planned for?" Papa asked.

"Friday week," Mister Red said. "Here at the fort."

Papa commenced to rubbing at the counter before him, and Mister Red waited. After a while, the wiping stopped. They both stood quiet, the air around us filled now with a lifetime of trouble. Papa's look turned from sadness to anger, and his voice came bitter as a June apple. "Good riddance," he said.

They were the last words I heard my Papa speak over his brother, his twin brother, Rufus Young—before my Uncle Ruck was set to be hanged for murder.

BY THE TIME I GOT TO THE FORT, WHO DID I SEE BUT Mister Red. He was just outside the jailhouse, and he was having what looked to be a mighty serious conversation with the sheriff. I stepped behind a post knowing was I to get caught he'd be obliged to tell Papa, who'd have a fit for more reasons than one. I gave them plenty of time to finish their business, then when Mister Red took his leave, I counted to a hundred, gathered up my courage, and walked the long planks to the jail's dark door.

"Elizabeth Young. I sure wasn't expecting you." It was the sheriff, which I couldn't see but I could tell by his gravelly voice. My eyes were working hard to switch from outside, to in.

"Yessir," I said. "Yessir, I expect not. But as Rufus Young is my uncle and my only living relative on my papa's side, I would hope you understand my desire to tell him goodbye before...well, before next Friday."

He thought on this a good long time. I did not move but stood stock still, the shadows melting and the jail filling in around me. "I will let you talk to Ruck for five minutes, no more. And neither of us will ever breathe a word of this to your daddy. Ever, under any circumstances. Do we have an agreement, young lady?"

"Yessir," I said.

He nodded for me to go on back.

AND THERE HE WAS, UNCLE RUCK, SITTING ON A RICK-ety old bed that had seen better days. His head was down and his shoulders were hunched and this came at me hard, it being so out of character. Just that fast all my feelings drained out making room for a whole big load of sad. I walked over to the bars and said, braver than I felt, "It's me, Uncle Ruck. It's Elizabeth." His head raised up, and I made my voice go on before my nerves could stop it. "I know you are sentenced to hang. I do not know what that feels like. But if I was the one in here waiting, I sure would want to know there is somebody out there thinking about me, remembering the good times and not just looking at the bad. So I came to tell you, Uncle Ruck. I remember. I remember them all."

"Elizabeth," he said.

There was a lantern hanging against the gray stone wall and even its light looked sorrowful. Uncle Ruck didn't get up, and I felt relief as this tiny distance helped keep me standing. His eyes reached mine and I realized they were eyes I knew—so like Papa's, but for being deep blue. How similar they are as brothers, I thought. How different they are as men.

"Like I remember that time you and Papa took me and Will and Lucy on that long ride across Stone Mountain. We were looking to cut down a Christmas tree and nothing would do but I find the very most perfect one. Papa kept saying, 'Now girl, this one here is a fine tree. Why it's a pretty pine, and a six-footer at that!' And I would say, 'No Papa, that ain't the tree I'm a-looking for.' And we kept riding until we got to the crest of High Knob, and by then Papa was getting frustrated and it was starting to snow. He took Will and Lucy and headed for home, but you stayed with me, Uncle Ruck. You said we'd look all night if that's what it took to find me that tree. And that's just what we did."

I stopped for a breath, wondered could he recollect, knew my uncle had a great deal taking up his mind.

"We rode and rode hardly talking. Snow was falling, and it was quiet—that peaceful kind of quiet that sits around you and goes all the way through. Then just beyond the trail to Bark Camp, up toward the lake there she was—a tall Red Cedar with berries made of shimmery blue. We cut her down and you tied one end of a long rope around her trunk and the other around your waist and we rode down that mountain together in the cold, getting to the farm about daybreak. It was a night that had magic, don't you remember? 'Look up girl,' is what you told me—"

"'—even in the snow, you can see the stars.'"

I nodded. I smiled. I pushed on.

"There's other things, too, like that time when Ray Dale Cooper got shot in the leg."

Uncle Ruck showed surprise although he did not speak.

"You remember what he did, that old buzzard. He put the blame for it right on Mister Red."

Uncle Ruck got up now, and he moved toward the bars, so I stepped back to keep the nearness from stopping me.

"It was quite an unexpected accusation, as Mister Red is known to be a decent and honorable man. But Salley Belle Cooper was sweet on him, and her papa, Ray Cooper? He didn't like that one bit. He held a strange, fitful jealous a father shouldn't have over a daughter, if you know what I mean."

"Elizabeth, I—"

"You took the blame. You did, Uncle Ruck, and you went straight to jail. And Mister Red, he went straight to the Coopers' and took Salley Belle right out of there. And then he married her."

The tiniest smile got surrendered by Uncle Ruck, and I gave it a moment, liking the feel of him and me and a little sweetness surrounding us. Then I cleared my throat.

"But that ain't the whole story. Because you nor Mister Red neither one was nowhere near the Coopers' at the time of the shooting. You two was hunting together up on Buckner's Ridge. Which means it was Salley Belle herself, or Mrs. Cooper, is my guess—who actually pulled that trigger."

It was mighty still in the jailhouse.

"The point is, Uncle Ruck, you may've done some things in this life people think of as bad. But me and the Lord? We know there's a lot more to most of it than meets the eye."

Uncle Ruck reached through the bars and I stepped close, taking hold of his hands. They were strong and rough and warm, and I could feel thick calluses that put to mind the way of a good man's life. Then a voice came down the hall. "Okay, Elizabeth." It was Sheriff Counts.

It's just as well, I thought, as my heart was starting to break.

Uncle Ruck's fingers tightened. "Thank you, Tess," he said, "for coming." He was seeing me so deep my eyes couldn't hold on, and I let them loose and they looked to my muddy boots and at the light laying flat across the cold stone floor. "I want you to know something," he said. I felt him tug and this brought my face back to his. "I'm gonna stay close. I'm gonna be there, keeping my eye on you." I did not know what he meant, all things considered, and still that promise wrapped itself around and around me.

Then there was Sheriff Counts, with his own soft words. "Better head out, girl. I've let you stay too long as it is."

I held on tight, but I could feel my uncle slipping away.

"Sheriff's right. Can't have you in those woods after dark." There was a deeper squeeze, and then my hands fell free.

I stood without moving, trying to think of the right last thing to say, words beautiful and perfect and everlasting. But it was tears that came instead, so I turned my body away not wanting his last look to be of me broke-hearted. I willed my feet to carry me toward the door. And even if I can't explain it—even if I don't know how—I could feel Uncle Ruck behind me, and he was covering me up with love.

AS IT TURNED OUT THE HANGING DID NOT TAKE PLACE at Blackmore's Fort like they planned, but it got moved to Estilville instead, on account of so many coming to town to witness it. I don't understand this, really, except to say for most folks a hanging is a curiosity. There was hundreds showed up from miles around, old men hunched over canes, women dressed fancy and some in rags, children running wild with excitement. I found a spot a proper distance from the gallows and tucked myself between a stranger stretched on tiptoe and a boy hoisted high, his father doing his best to give the child a better view.

A man up on the platform moved about, checking and rechecking the ropes. I was focused on this, trying to keep low and stay out of sight when a hand grabbed my arm from behind. I whipped quick to see it was my brother, Will—two years older and still believing he was meant to be my keeper.

"What are you doing here?" I whispered.

Papa would be furious, that was for sure, him having laid down law wasn't none of us to get anywhere near this "spectacle." Then Will pointed, and I turned back around to see it was Sheriff Counts coming 'round the far side of the gallows. His face looked stern but his walk was slow, like a man with a terrible job to do. Then there was Uncle Ruck, his hands bound together in front.

At first the crowd hushed. There came a cheer, and then a mass of hollering and clapping which turned to jeering when the two men climbed the five steps to the platform. They crossed to the middle and that's when I saw the sheriff kept his hand on Ruck's back, which I took to be a kindness. It would be worse, far worse you'd have to think, to have your sentence carried out by a lawman with a cold heart. The sheriff got Uncle Ruck positioned so he was just under the crossbar, right at the hanging noose, and he turned him to face the crowd. People yelled louder, and this made the sheriff madder, and so he stepped toward the front and raised his hands to wait for decency and quiet.

EVERYTHING GOING ON AROUND ME WAS HATEFUL AND cruel and still I could not look away. I wanted to understand how something like this happens, how a person kind and good and loving ends up with a fate such as this. These were strangers nearly all, people who knew nothing of Rufus Young but who traveled here with their families like this was entertainment, like this hanging was a show put on for their enjoyment. It made me sick in my stomach; it filled me with disgust for these people and this place and whatever it is that makes such a horrible act acceptable, that makes something so sad and awful in these mountains seem okay.

And what of Papa? What of his dismissal and hate?

There were things between them two, of this I was certain, hurt that probably started way back when they were just boys and also little lost orphans. Or maybe that didn't have nothing to do with it but there was something else entirely, a load of bad feelings built hard over time regarding family perhaps, or circumstance. Whatever the case, there were secrets, old devil secrets that had done the terrible work of breaking these brothers apart, then hiding; of crouching deep in the dark while year over year, carrying on still, with their damage.

I would stop it. That's what came to me then, I'd get the bottom. I'd uncover truth. I'd bring those secrets to light and they would release, give up their hold. The hurt would be over, and Papa could forgive, and Uncle Ruck could lie in peace, and I could—I would—

Go.

I would leave. I would kiss these mountains goodbye, what with their hills and hollers and coves, their nooks and crannies and caves with all those secret spots for all that secret keeping. I'd find me a place where the land is flat, where life is in the open, where a secret can't root because soon as it appears, a soft wind comes and just blows it away. It just tumbles and rolls right away.

I'd leave this place forever, and I'd do it for Uncle Ruck.

I'd leave this place for me.

THE CROWD CARRIED ON, SO SHERIFF COUNTS SPOKE and his voice was not loud but it was commanding. "I'm saying this only the one time. If you people can't be respectful of the law and this process, I'll clear ever' last one of you out. You hear me?" There was some shushing and mumbling and grumbling, then after a short time even that stopped. "All right then." He turned toward Ruck. This time, in a normal voice he said, "Rufus Young, you have been sentenced to death for the murder of Johnny James Martin. Was there anything you wanted to confess."

"Hell yes," said Ruck.

Then Sheriff Counts said, and this was sort of private, which was fine as the people were on pins and needles, "Well go on then, I reckon."

There wasn't a sound, everyone holding their breath, and Uncle Ruck stood there his mouth not moving nor coming forth with any words at all. Instead, he looked all around as if trying to find somebody in particular or maybe considering everyone in general. Will took my hand, which was good because I wanted to wave and shout, *I'm here, Uncle Ruck. Me and Will are here.* That's when I saw his eyes settle across the way, my uncle's face coming to rest on something at the edge of the mass of people opposite us.

"Judge not," is what he said.

I turned to see what'd caught his eye; I was curious to know what had got his attention. There was a young man up a tree with his long legs dangling; a pair of towheaded boys was pushing and whining and fussing;

a lady in a fine feathered hat—was that Miss Mary Lenore Kitchens, my new teacher? (It wasn't.) Then I saw Papa. He was under the elm, dressed in his Sunday best, his head held high as he faced straight on to Uncle Ruck and the platform. I didn't know what I should do, or what he would do, then real slow Papa dipped his head, removed his hat, and he took that hat and placed it square over his heart.

I took my eyes to the front, afraid now I might cry. Sheriff Counts was holding the black hood and with no fuss nor fanfare he raised it, put it over Uncle Ruck's head and with gentle motion pulled the bottom edge down. He said something into Ruck's ear, is how it looked to me, then he reached up and got the noose free. He slipped it over the hood and the fat, heavy loop came to settle around my uncle's neck, resting on his broad shoulders. The sheriff took his time with all of this, checking the rope, the knot, some detail or other of the trap door at their feet. Then he stood again and he arranged the noose so it pulled tighter. With that, Sheriff Counts turned toward the stairs and made his way down them.

Will shifted his weight.

"Papa's here," I whispered.

That's when Ruck said, it having a great deal more sound this time and coming through the hood loud and clear: "*Lest ye be judged.*"

The sheriff reached for the lever and in one sharp motion he pulled. The latch snapped and the trapdoor opened and in one quick jerk Uncle Ruck was hanging, his feet dangling below the floor.

The ground beneath my own feet moved.

Eye for an eye! Justice is done! That's how we treat murderers!

The crowd was in a frenzy, and Will tightened his hold, pulling me close until my face was buried in his coat. We rocked back and forth, the two of us together, I don't know how long or if Will even realized. After a time he whispered, "It's over, Tess. They're cutting him down." His hand let go of my head and that's when I remembered: *Papa.* I raised up and pulled away and looked across to find him. The towhead boys were wide-eyed; the space where Papa had been was empty.

There was noise from the platform; it was Mister Red, who was help-ing the sheriff, and also Dr. R. J. Peters who came to call time of death. They moved Ruck's body to a plain pine box that got loaded onto a farm cart waiting behind the gallows. Then with the crowd watching and the sheriff's own horse doing the pulling, Mister Red drove my uncle away.

CHAPTER TWO

Patrick Hagan

THE COMMOTION WAS LOUD AND DISTRACTING, SOME-
thing I should have expected but did not when planning my morning
of study for this third-floor alcove in the Scott County courthouse. My
spot sits high above the town of Estilville, and still wild outbursts rose to
meet me. I tried to concentrate, to block out the noise, but this proved
impossible. And so I gave in. I got up, I went to the tall window, and
just as I looked down, I saw the primitive hearse pass by. A single driver
sat on the transport's front bench; the flat top and wide brim of a well-
worn hat was my only view to this person. But there was no obscuring
the wagon's load. A crude wood box laid long on the flat bed that carried
it, and like the cart itself was plain, *simpli*, holding the body, I knew, of
convicted murderer Rufus Young.

I meant to look away but I did not. I watched as the farm cart
bumped down the street, as boys running alongside jumped and
shouted, jubilant in their cries of victory. I made an offering, the sign
of the cross, a prayer for this man who had come to such an unjust end.
For I believe execution by hanging is barbaric, no matter the crime.

There are those who say I should have been there. That as a man of
the court, or very nearly so, I should have considered it my responsibility, aye my duty, to stand in support. Then I say judge me as you will. For
it is my belief that capital punishment has no place in enlightened society. As did the great Frenchman, Baron Charles-Louis de Montesquieu,

I know it to be a brutal act that neither deters crime nor promotes public order. I will not be a party to it.

Except that I will, when in a fortnight I am admitted, God willing, to practice law in the commonwealth of Virginia. This is something I can scarcely believe, having become a naturalized citizen only a few months ago. It is a dream for which my uncle, Joseph P. Hagan, has been my champion and my patron. He sent for me in the midst of our country's darkest hours, and without his path for escape I would be dead or so despondent in the potato blight's aftermath as to be near to it. The great debt for which I owe him, I shall dedicate my life to repaying.

There came the creak of the stairs; someone was approaching. I turned from the window to first see a tall poof of white hair ascend. I smiled knowing what was to come, and then there they were: the jovial eyes and unbridled demeanor of the incomparable Abijah Alley.

"Patrick Hagan, there you are." Alley is a large man, and as he climbed, his breathing was labored; still, his boisterous voice echoed through the empty building. "You would be on the top floor." He stopped then, having reached the landing, and he leaned forward, a great exhale escaping. On intake he straightened. "One might've guessed a good Irish Catholic would be at that hanging. Montesquieu your excuse?"

I laughed in spite of the seriousness of the subject. "That and an assortment of other well considered convictions."

Alley boomed, his laugh round and full.

"To what do I owe the honor?" I asked.

"Seems I've been invited to preach at Copper Creek. I thought you might find that…intriguing."

"*Primitive Baptist* Copper Creek?"

He nodded, his bright blue eyes displaying a tickled glint.

This was big news. Alley was a bold and demonstrative character, who—among other things—had divined his own religion. He had garnered a respectable following with the peddling of his god of hope and forgiveness, but his joy-filled worship held no resemblance to that of the strict Bible literalists who had extended this invitation. Primitive

Baptists believe we spend our lives suffering Adam's condemnation, and that God's grace is extended only to the "chosen" of their denomination. I could not fathom their interest in Alley's jubilation.

"How did *that* come to be, pray tell?" I asked.

"Perhaps their souls are hungry for a faith built of love, not sin. Oh, wait," he winked. "That would be you Catholics, wouldn't it."

I shook my head in feigned disgust, but Alley knew better. He and I have spent many an hour in lively discussion regarding our theologies and their conflicts. It is something for which I should have little patience—I am of the one true holy and apostolic church, after all—and to say the least, Abijah Alley is a man of great unorthodoxy. For one, some years ago he wrote a book of prophecy that foretells of a great war in which the Southern states will secede from the Union. (Even with unrest building in this country, I can scarcely imagine such a thing. This is America, after all.) For another, Alley has fashioned a creed of his own that does not adhere to conventional doctrine. His faith focuses on a love unconstrained, and on favor given to all from God, through Jesus. Still, the man exhibits a vast and insightful knowledge of scripture, and he brings to our discussions a genuine, insatiable curiosity. I am one of few Roman Catholics in the area—Uncle Joseph and his wife, Aileen, making up the other two—and I suppose I find these discussions a welcome oasis in a rather barren land, theologically speaking.

"As you are not one predisposed to go to Baptist preaching, I came by specifically to invite you. Two weeks from Friday."

Was this worth considering? Given my preference for conformity and order, such an open clash of faiths felt unseemly. "Uncle is not due back until Saturday," I said, "and I'll have to see about his schedule. Aileen alone in that cabin for too long is not an ideal situation."

Alley raised an inquisitive eyebrow.

"She's suffered a setback or two, I'm sorry to say."

"Well, bring her with you!" He offered this with such aplomb and enthusiasm, it may well have been what opened my heart to the possibility. Then he leaned closer, speaking more intently. "She just might find my message of hope a respite from all that Catholic guilt. God's love is unconditional, after all."

"God loves good works," I said.

"God loves Eye-leen," he said. "Just as she is."

I hold Abijah Alley in high regard, but I do not understand this unwavering belief in a god of his own creation. I suppose my skepticism showed.

"He made us all different, Patrick. Everyone unique. And He loves us for that very thing, don't you see? For the soul He put on this Earth, not for the favors it earns. 'The Lord looketh down from heaven, and beholdeth all the children of men. From the habitation of his dwelling, he beholdeth all them that dwell in the earth. He fashioneth their hearts every one, and understandeth all their works.'"

This was a challenge I knew, and I accepted. "Psalm 33. Although— not King James."

"1599 Geneva."

There was that broad smile. I do enjoy our sparring.

"Anyway, I'd best be getting on." Alley slapped the banister with his palm and held on. "You'd have heard about Copper Creek soon enough, I suppose, as it's sure to draw a crowd. But I figured you'd never come. And I want you there. It promises to be a memorable evening."

The question came to me then regarding Alley's "Little Band" of musicians and singers, a significant part of his joy-filled worship. "What will you do about music? You know the Baptists don't allow instruments in their sanctuary."

"Aah, yes. A cappella only." He shrugged. "At least that's what they say!" He turned for the stairs, his spirit light as air. When he reached the landing, he stopped. "And Patrick." He tossed the words up, them coming not so much as ending commentary but more as heartfelt encouragement. "Do bring Aunt Eye-leen. It promises to be a fascinating change from your high Catholic mass, and you both may find you like that."

What a scoundrel he was, this Abijah Alley.

Perhaps, I thought. Perhaps.

CHAPTER THREE

MARY LENORE KITCHENS

APRIL 1854

I GAVE IT GREAT CONSIDERATION BEFORE SUGGESTING
Elizabeth Young accompany me to the gathering at Copper Creek
Church. I had my own motives, I must confess, in addition to my keen
and rather obvious interest in the girl's education. She is quite a good
student with a grand curiosity; I am a young woman with few friends
and little opportunity for social interaction.

There is no surprise in this, I suppose, as I am an outsider here. It was
something I did not expect and yet realized shortly after my arrival. For
I came to these mountains to build a life of purpose—one in which my
childhood of privilege might extend a world of possibility to the children of this remote and isolated land. They are born deserving even if
their geography, as well as their circumstance, harbors certain inherent
limits. I have been here three months and already I am confident that
my work among them matters. Thus I accept the reality of my own dis-
appointing situation. For I believe my position as schoolmistress to the
seventy-five students of the Saratoga School, here on this wild edge of
the far western reaches of Virginia, is a very fine use of both my liberal
upbringing and my exceptional education. It may also be my best hope
for redemption.

THE JOURNEY TO THE CHURCH WAS NOT A DIFFICULT
one. It did require a traverse of the county; then at the Clinch, we turned

north, riding along the river trail headed for Osborne's Ford and the bridge. Elizabeth's mother had made for us a picnic, and I'd suggested to the girl that she decide when, and where, we stop to enjoy it.

We'd rounded a bend covered with a thick canopy when ahead a clearing revealed a wide expanse of water. It was a scene worthy of painting by an Old Master: beeches stretched out long and languid, dangling over the river; hickories stood proud, their branches raised tall and wide. Sun danced across the water's surface, and a million tiny glimmers of light skipped and sparkled and drew the eye, their dance a masquerade to the thousand secrets harbored in the deep below. I may have gasped upon seeing the power and beauty, an involuntary reaction I hoped was inaudible to my young companion. I looked to realize she, too, held a deep gaze.

"Let's eat here!" Elizabeth said, breaking the moment, enough giddy in her voice to remind me of the girl's exuberant if unrefined nature. She was all rough and tumble, this one, her spirit propelling her forward faster than common sense could regulate. She caught me looking and slowed. "Shall we enjoy our dinner here?" she corrected.

I walked toward the water as Elizabeth handled the horses. It was a warm day, unusually warm for spring, and she led them to a cool spot in the shade. *Fair river...by what eternal...sorry for the lost...* Brief bits of his poetry floated through even as I tried to push them away. They were painful memories even if I had been hardly more than a girl myself, naïve in spite of my permissive upbringing. *She is not much younger now than I was then*, is what occurred to me, and I reminded myself that while but six or seven years separated us in age, our upbringings rendered our experiences vastly different.

I glanced back to see that Elizabeth was sitting now, arranging and rearranging our simple dinner, anticipating my return. *What does the future hold for a girl like her*, I wondered, *bright, eager, so determined?* I turned to rejoin her, and she clasped her hands in her lap and giggled.

WE TOOK OUR LEISURE, ENJOYING THE SUNNY AFTER-noon and savoring the bread and dried beef as if it were a king's feast.

I'd just reached for an egg hard-boiled when the inquiry, dreaded if not unexpected, came.

"What was it, Miss Kitchens, that made you come to these mountains in the first place?" The question had barely escaped her mouth before Elizabeth rushed with an apology. "I'm sorry. That's none of my business. Shouldn't be asking something so personal." I might have offered a response, but then she pushed on. "It's just that everybody's wanting to know. I mean, you have everything. You're young and pretty and also smart. You could go anywhere, do anything you want." She looked around as if trying to spot something she hadn't seen. "Why come *here*?"

I tapped the egg to crack it. "Were that true, Elizabeth, and I'm not saying it is, but if your assumptions were true, then what stands to reason?"

"You want to be here, I guess."

"Yes."

"But why? That's what I'm asking."

I was crafting an answer, carefully considered as it needed to be, when like a gift Elizabeth went on.

"Nothing ever happens. People are stuck in their ways. Like look at Papa. I had to beg him, I was on hands and knees practically, just to get to come with you today. It's not fair, it's ridiculous. He didn't want me to come just because he thinks you're—" She stopped, embarrassed suddenly, and unsure what to say next.

"Yes?" I meant this to sound encouraging, when in truth I was already offended.

"Sophisticated." Elizabeth smiled, relieved to have found a reframe. "But I'll just tell you I'm sick of him and everybody else thinking they can decide what's right for me. And all of it based on their old ways. You'd think there was laws written all over these hills declaring we can't change, we won't change, we're gonna do things the same old way forever and ever until the end of days." (Heavens, she was puffed up.) "Well, not me. I'll just tell you that. I'm taking my leave. I'm going where I can make my own life, my own decisions. I'm gonna do things *my own way*."

I did not respond—how could I, knowing the truth in her perspective? Then just like that, I watched her deflate, a bouncing ball losing its air. Two weeks had passed since the execution of her uncle, and while she and I had never discussed the situation (distasteful and public as it was), it was clearly a loss she felt deeply. She'd been teased a time or two by our more ruffian students, something I knew was quite hurtful.

"What is it?" I asked, reaching to touch her hand. It was an action that startled us both.

"It's just—nothing."

I nodded. I wasn't sure what to do, my attempt at providing comfort feeling now more an embarrassment. I looked to the egg I held and began to peel it.

"It's what you did, Miss Kitchens."

I scrambled, lost in our conversation. "Oh?"

"Of course you did. You know you did, I mean, look, you're *here*." The eager in her eyes was restored, her heart was filled with a wanting I certainly understood.

"It was different for me. When I was your age—" I stopped, and I set the egg atop the small pile of shell fragments in my lap. Should I share this? Any of this? "At your age, I, too, wanted to get away. My parents— my mother, really, although she used my father's position as influence— my mother saw to it that I was accepted for admission at Valley Union Seminary. I had not completed my secondary-school studies, and it was midterm, so it was a rather unusual request. But I was a good student, and she can be very persuasive."

"You got to go away for college at sixteen?"

"Seventeen, actually. Had just turned seventeen."

"And my papa don't even care if I finish out the school year." She took a final bite of an apple and threw it, the core covering impressive distance fueled by her disgust. With a raise of my eyebrows I corrected her grammar, and I felt some relief that the conversation had turned from me, to her.

"I understand your frustration. Really I do. But your father has allowed you more education than many girls get."

"Yeah, well, that don't make it right."

I did not respond. How could I? Instead I gathered the corners of the cloth covering my lap, I shook out the shells, and I suggested to my young charge that were we to get to the church on time, we'd best be moving along.

I'D NEVER BEFORE VISITED THE PRIMITIVE BAPTISTS, I should make this clear. The child of proper Episcopalians, I discovered that worship among my denomination was not an option here and so, instead, I spent my Sunday mornings reading or catching up on correspondence. But there had been so much talk about this gathering and its many peculiarities that I had become quite interested. Alley would be in the pulpit, and there was great speculation as to the response of the Hard Shell Baptists once Alley introduced his free-spirited god in their sanctuary.

The contrast was evident from the moment we arrived. Set against the spectacular new-leaf greens of Moccasin Ridge, the church was plain, simple, so unadorned as to not even offer a cross. Its members were dressed in somber black and gray, while visitors and the curious roamed the grounds in more colorful wear. Horses and buggies and children were everywhere, and without so much as a word Elizabeth took my hand and headed for the door, worming our way through the mass of people.

—*Beulah says he fancies hisself a prophet, have you ever heard such a thing,* said a woman in a large bonnet.

—*Well I never,* said another, stretching for a better view.

—*Some people,* said a third. *Look. There he is!*

In no time we'd reached the front of the church where Elizabeth turned sideways and managed, somehow, to squeeze us onto a long, full bench. People fanned like it was July; men wiped their brows, women chattered or looked dour, sour frowns demonstrating their displeasure.

"Wonder where's the Little Band," Elizabeth said, twisting to look around. She leaned toward me and whispered. "You know Alley's got him a whole group made up of banjos and fiddles and singers and what all, and they play as part of his worship. It's real happy and joyful, not like boring old hymns but more like King David did in the Bible. That's why Alley's built that temple over in Long Holler, is what I say, which is just like King Solomon's."

A temple? Here in these mountains? The idea was preposterous.

"It's got olive trees and everything! At least that's what they say." She pointed. "Look!"

A man had just come forward, stepping to an altar so crudely built, it may well have been added just for this occasion. There was a lectern to the left, but he did not go to it. Instead he raised his arms (which revealed broad, dark stains on his dull shirt and vest) and said, "Let us PRAY." His hands punctuated the words. "We thank you, Lord, for this gathering and this day. We ask your blessings over our congregation and these guests. In particular, we ask for your guidance over Brother Alley's words, for may he remember he is your MESSENGER delivering the gospel as wrote, fearful, obedient, and with respect for the ELECTED, broke by SIN and made whole in TRUTH."

(He went on like this a while.)

"And last we just ask you this, Lord, be with us today, those of the Old Church and not, chosen and not, that your words first and foremost be heard AS WRITTEN in the Bible. Because punishment of the wicked is everlasting, and the joy of the righteous is eternal. Amen. Amen. AMEN."

With no invitation, a large man in a striking robe stepped forward, singing, "How firm a foundation, ye saints of the Lord, is laid for your faith in his excellent word!" This was Alley, there could be no mistaking, for in every way he provided stark contrast to the monochrome of his host. He traversed the altar, his long garment trailing, its bright greens and golds celebrated with broad swaths of purple that swirled throughout. On his head he wore a flat, funny hat from which wild poofs of hair escaped—the same curly white as the long, thick beard that like an avalanche tumbled mouth to belly. One might think the entire getup comic, but it was not so. There was something captivating about the man, magnetic and warm, his smile was so genuine, his presence, pure joy.

He gestured that the congregation was to stand and join in, and so we did. His rich, deep base underpinned the tune, and by the end of the hymn, Abijah Alley had complete control of that room, every eye upon him and every ear tuned.

"I thank Brother McConnell and all the elders of Copper Creek Church for inviting me to be here with you tonight. It is my great privilege to bring the good news that you are loved—each and every one of you—deeply loved and treasured."

I glanced left to see Elizabeth was equally enthralled.

"Yes!" he said with so much enthusiasm that my eyes shot back. "Yes, as Elder McConnell said, the Bible is the word of our Lord and He expects us to study it, to revere it, and most importantly, to live it. Yes! So let's begin with a reading of the scripture upon which I shall speak tonight." He held a Bible that he kissed, then he turned and offered it, hands outstretched, to an astonished McConnell. "You choose it, my friend. Any verse at all."

Now this was quite an offer. Even renowned scholars agree the most familiar scripture requires review and contemplation. And yet Abijah Alley stood before this packed sanctuary confident he could preach on any verse put before him, with neither notes nor prior consideration.

McConnell took the Bible. He stepped toward the lectern, where he laid it down. He opened the cover, flipped front to back, back to front. The crowd leaned closer, and he ran a forefinger down a page's inner edge. He turned the page again, and inches from the text, he smiled a sly smile.

Alley wasn't remotely interested in what McConnell was doing. Instead, he stood before the crowd with his back to the lectern and his eyes locked squarely on the church's east window. I noticed he was looking at a woman of about forty, her face dim, her demeanor shy. She was accompanied, or appeared to be, by a younger man who stood close beside her. He was dressed in a finely cut suit.

"The book of Matthew!" announced McConnell. "Chapter 24, verses 11 through 13! 'And many false prophets shall rise and shall deceive many! Wickedness shall abound. The love of many shall wax cold.'"

Alley picked up where his host had left off. "'But he that shall endure unto the end, the same shall be saved.'" He smiled at the woman in the window, then he turned to face McConnell. "It seems we have reverence for the same passage. For I feel as did the Apostle Paul in Athens when his spirit was provoked by the city full of idols and fools....'"

McConnell turned ghostlike, and I looked to the ground as if to see if his color had drained there. He closed the Bible and stepped away while Alley launched into an extemporaneous lesson on Matthew 24 that was so learned, so insightful, it held my attention for nearly an hour. During its delivery he moved here and there, stepping up, stepping down; he moved through the people like Jesus at Capernaum. Not once did he refer to sin, but he spoke, instead, of Christ as our way and heaven as our end.

In closing, he stepped for the first time to the pulpit, where the open Bible still lay. "Stand your guard against false teachers, for as history has taught us and as the future will surely bear witness, false teachers deceive many." The room was silent. "When we lose our way, it is wickedness that intervenes." Then Alley's face broke into a broad smile, and he began to sing:

Blest be the tie that binds
Our hearts in Christian love.

That's when the back of the church started to empty, men tapping each other on shoulders and groups rushing through the door and into the evening light. Shouting came from beyond the wood walls, and Elizabeth jumped to her feet so fast I grabbed at her, intending to pull her back to the bench where she might be corralled until I could determine the nature of the happenings. But she slipped from my grasp and joined the early throng exiting the building, tension escalating as wives and mothers shouted *Stop!* then jumped up to follow. In no time the sanctuary was empty, and worshipers were locked in a fierce battle that spread across the church grounds and beyond.

I kept my distance, something I am not ashamed to say, for I did not understand the nature of the tumult, nor did I even belong here. Arms and legs were flailing, and curse words were flying at a rate most unexpected in a crowd of Christians. I scanned, looking for Elizabeth when here she came flying, her excitement high and her face flushed. "It started over the Little Band. I knew it!" Before I could grab her, she'd run back into the ruckus. *What to do, what to do,* I wondered. *What in heaven's name do I do?*

The fighting continued, and it escalated. Men were down, and others were standing over them. Women grabbed at coattails and then threw strong punches. I'd never seen such behavior—churlish and ill-bred as it was—when there at the center appeared Abijah Alley, who raised his arms, clapped three times, and said, his voice booming, "In the name of Jesus Christ!" And silence descended, I embellish not, for whatever they were doing, people simply stopped. Wrestling on the ground or standing with fists raised; face shouting, hair pulling, gut punching—they relented. Calm reigned. And Alley said, "A new commandment I give unto you, that you love one another as I have loved you." He glanced around. There were people everywhere, and they all looked dazed. And he said, "Shake the hand of the beloved before you, and we'll pray together."

That's what happened. Two by two that's just what happened, I exaggerate not: A wave came over the crowd, and Alley said, "The Honorable Patrick Hagan will now lead us in the Lord's Prayer."

The crowd divided, and a man stepped through. It was evident he had not been in on the fighting. He carried himself like a gentleman, one would say, and that's when I realized it was the fellow from the window. He bowed his head and began to speak.

Our Father, who art in heaven, hallowed be thy...

His voice rode the mountain air, and it rendered the prayer music.

...on earth, as 'tis in heaven.

Irish. Good heavens, this man was Irish.

...not into temptation, but deliver us from evil.

He stopped there, not for effect or emphasis but because this was the proper ending of his Catholic Lord's Prayer. I looked up just as Alley carried on: "For thine is the kingdom, and the power, and the glory forever! Amen!"

Amen, yelled the people. Amen! Spirits soared, hearts were overcome in a communion of love and brotherhood and goodness. Alley raised his arms and with a sweeping glance over the crowd, smiled. "Go now, in peace," he said.

I was near tears—it was a powerful moment. My eyes searched for Elizabeth when again I saw the Irishman. Hagan, did he say? It would certainly be improper for me to approach him—how my mother would disapprove! But surely he would welcome the introduction. Surely among these folk, it would be his delight to have found an equal.

I brushed at my dress, straightened my shoulders, and walked in his direction. I found him in conversation with another woman (she some years older than I, I noticed, although this was neither here nor there), and I studied him as I awaited the completion of their business. He was younger than I expected, twenty-three or twenty-four perhaps, and handsome in a refined way. He was also charming, leaning in as she made some point or another, then glancing my direction ever so quickly before turning his attention back to her. At long last the feckless monologue was ended when a running child slammed heedlessly into her skirts, at which point Mr. Hagan bade the poor woman adieu and turned toward me.

"Oh, hello, I'm Mary Lenore Kitchens," I said, extending my hand, something I did far too soon as I was still some distance from the gentleman. "I'm the teacher at the Saratoga School."

"Miss Kitchens," he said, taking my hand. "Patrick Hagan. 'Tis indeed a pleasure."

"If I may be so bold." I could feel myself blushing, so I looked to the ground, then back at him. Goodness, but his eyes were blue. "One would assume you are not from around here, given the lovely accent. Ireland, I would suppose. Northern Ireland, I might guess?"

"Aye," he said, pleased. "Dungannon, in County Tyrone. Do you know of it?"

"Not specifically. But my father is professor of languages at the University of Virginia. In Charlottesville. And he saw to it that my education was unconfined by geography." I gave a glance around, to further my point, but this he did not acknowledge. He did not, in fact, take his eyes from me.

"And did you study at the University?"

"Well, no. I mean, I was meant to, and then circumstances changed, and so I attended Valley Union. Perhaps you know it by its more recent name, Roanoke Female Seminary. In Roanoke." I was making rather a mess of this, and so I forged quickly on. "Anyway, I am recently arrived as the new teacher at the Saratoga School, and I wondered if I might call on you to visit our classes. Our older students are to begin a study of Europe soon, and I'm quite certain your observations of Irish life would be quite fascinating to these mountain children. They are not accustomed to such broad horizons."

A familiar voice came barreling from behind with such enthusiasm that I was nearly knocked over. "You're from Ireland?" it said.

"Elizabeth!" I twisted toward her, my voice more stern than I meant. She took a step back.

"I come from Ireland, yes," said the gentleman. "My name's Patrick Hagan, and it's my guess you're called Elizabeth. 'Twould be *Eilís* in my native tongue."

"Eye-lish," she tried to repeat; you could see the word as it rolled around in her head. "That sounds nice."

"As I was saying, Mr. Hagan. I believe our students would find great benefit if you could make time in your busy schedule for a visit."

"'Twould be an honor, of course," he said. "I am opening a law office in Estilville within the month, and you can get a message to me there when you determine the day you'd like me to come."

I could feel the questions rising in Elizabeth's mind, questions such as *How did you learn to talk like that?* and *What's it like to go across the ocean?* I knew it best to move along before she could launch into them, and so I stated the obvious again, that I would be in touch. That's when Elizabeth extended *her* hand, offering, "'Tis indeed a pleasure, Mr. Hagan. I do hope our paths get crossed again."

How his eyes sparkled. Then he looked in my direction, tipped his hat, and turned to go.

I should take this impetuous girl and march her straight to our horses, came my reaction. But by the time the thought had formed, Elizabeth was off and gone, skipping across the churchyard.

CHAPTER FOUR

ELIZABETH

APRIL 1854

IT WAS JUST BEFORE ME AND MISS KITCHENS TOOK OUR leave from the Copper Creek Church that a dark-haired boy came wandering up acting like he knew me, which he didn't. I was standing alone, looking things over and trying to work out how the events of the evening had come to be. People were milling about here and there, it seeming the place had a hold, children and grown-ups alike feeling like something unusual had took place even if it was hard to say just what that was.

"Just goes to show," he said. He'd got right beside me, us both looking out, and I could tell he wanted me to ask, so I didn't. "I mean, grab a person's fiddle and throw it in the fire and"—I looked at him now, how could I help it—"that's what started it. We were over in that clearing where we'd laid a bed of wood but not lit it, and we were holding instruments but not playing them, and a chill came on so we—"

"You're in the Little Band," I said.

Yes, he nodded, but he kept up with the story like this wasn't the interesting part. "—we got the fire going. We were sitting around, just sitting and waiting, and a good long time passed. Then somebody started up humming 'There's a Light Upon the Mountains.' It was just real quiet, you know, and then somebody joined in. And then somebody else. And before you know it there was five-part harmony and also a mandolin. Then a bass, and a fiddle, and the pace picked up. And hell if that song didn't—"

"Ride up the path and right into the church."

He was looking at me and he grinned, and I saw his big dark eyes had shiny flecks like the kind that draws you to fool's gold.

"It was your fiddle, I'm to reckon."

"Naw. I'm on banjo mostly. Name's Ben Grubb."

Right then is when I saw Miss Kitchens, and she was stomping up the hill, looking fit to be tied. "I could not find you anywhere!" she said. Her voice was short and breathy.

"Been right here." I said this and it came out sassy, which I really didn't mean for it to.

"It's time we go." She gave Ben a look, then she turned on her heel and started right back down like she just expected me to follow.

Ben winked, and I shrugged my shoulders and stepped away like none of this even mattered. I'd got a good distance when I realized I'd never said my name. "Elizabeth. My name's Elizabeth."

He grinned and spoke soft. "I know who you are."

"My papa calls me Tess." I added this, hollering a bit, then wondered why I'd even tell him.

"Well then," Ben Grubb said. "I reckon Tess it is."

IT WAS MR. HORACE MANN WHO ACCOMPANIED US ON our ride back across the mountain, the hour having got late and us being women traveling alone. This meant I couldn't ask Miss Kitchens any of the questions I had regarding the surprising things that had happened that day, of which Ben Grubb was one. And so I followed along silent in the dark, my stomach filled with a thousand tiny butterflies that were flapping their wings and making a dance of light.

CHAPTER FIVE

PATRICK

April 1854

"'TIS M'DEEPEST PRAYER, JUDGE EVANS, THAT YOU FIND me a fit and capable man, for I am eager to serve the fine people of this county in matters of the law. I stand before you humbly, knowing it is law that marks a society as civilized, and it is justice—and the relentless pursuit thereto—that is the promise of great nations. 'Tis also the promise of our Lord, is it not?"

I delivered it from my heart, though not my head, for who knows better than I the accepted practice for petitioning the court? Colonel Stras had spent much of the previous week counseling me on this appearance before the judge, and not once did he suggest I offer my own closing argument following the bar examination.

Judge Evans looked over his spectacles and down his nose at me. "Mr. Hagan. While I...*admire*...the passion with which you made your 'statement,' let me assure you it is the word of your esteemed sponsor, Col. Stras, that most carries weight in this decision."

"Your honor, of course. *Cinnte.*"

I had been overcome by the magnitude of it all, standing before the bench in this Estilville courthouse. The windows were tall and the wood dark, and the morning sun streamed through, illuminating every airborne particle. It was light made manifest, as if from heaven.

I have worked so hard to get here, I thought. *I have come so far.*

"With this motion, Patrick M. Hagan is hereby licensed to practice law in the Commonwealth of Virginia, and in this Scott County court."

The judge rapped the gavel once, and its ring was glorious as it echoed throughout the courtroom. "Congratulations, my boy. There's no more noble calling than protecting the rights of your fellow citizens." He leaned closer. "See that you remember that when the case is difficult and the man you're representing is not so noble."

"*Sea, ar ndóigh.* I will, sir."

He straightened, collected his papers. "By the way, where's your uncle today? I thought he would be here."

"Philadelphia, sir. A deal involving mineral rights, I believe."

"Jesus turned water to wine. And Joseph Hagan? That man turns land into gold."

"'Tis true enough," I said.

Judge Evans stood, picked up the leather binder. "Well, he's a good friend, and a fine man who invests where he sees opportunity. He certainly believes in you, son. See that you don't let him down."

I WAS IN THAT COURTROOM AT MY UNCLE'S BEHEST, IT was an undeniable fact. He had sent for me seven years earlier and had done everything required to bring me to America, and to educate me, in spite of my father's fervid protests. For my dad, Conor Seamus O'Hagan, was a laborer long on sons and short on temper. It was my mother who petitioned Uncle for interference, and to this day I worry over the repercussions she suffered in the wake of my departure. Still, once engaged, Uncle would not be denied. I left home, boarded a boat, and came to Boston to inhabit a new life filled with travel, studies, and greater exposure to finance and commerce than a lad of my upbringing should ever dare dream.

My uncle had already amassed a fortune by then, it should be said. He is a shrewd businessman who seems also to benefit from a wee bit of fabled good luck. The acreage here, for instance, he bought for a pittance when he came upon a land auction in Richmond. He heard the auctioneer hawk 50,000 acres on the wild, western edge of Virginia. "Mountains reaching to the sky! Rivers running with trout! Land so undiscovered, a description can't do it justice!" Uncle had neither visited this region nor given a moment's consideration to investing in it; still he presented an opening bid of twenty-five dollars.

"Twenty-five dollars," echoed the auctioneer. "Do I hear a more respectable twenty-five *hundred*?"

A fevered discourse followed, with boisterous comments from the crowd regarding bands of roving Indians, dangerous wild mountain beasts, the lawlessness of the area's uncivilized population. Another bidder could not be engaged, and so passerby Joseph Hagan—astute businessman evermore—walked away 50,000 acres richer.

THIS WAS THE LAND I CROSSED IN REACHING HUNTER'S Valley, the final leg of my journey from the Estilville courthouse to Joseph and Aileen's modest mountain home. The ride is an impressive one, crossing fifteen miles south to north over a series of angling ridges and valleys. The stoic peaks were formed millions of years ago from a violent collision beneath the sea, earth-against-earth in a force so great that the land jetted sideways and up toward the sky. High mountains formed out of rock and stone; it was an angry, fierce terrain that challenged Mother Nature for eons. Still, over time, her patient and insistent will won out. Great rivers and tiny streams, wild storms, rockslides, floods, long freezing and thawing spells—all have worked to dull the sharp edges and leave long ancient ridges that angle across the landscape for hundreds of miles. They stand in rows, gapless, thick, and virtually impassable. *We've been doing fine for ages*, these mountains say, *and there's nothing we ask of you now*. Even the valleys, caged in as they are by the Appalachians, seem fully confident and complete.

Nothing meanders here.

And still there is a kinship I feel with this land, a connection that binds my gentle Irish heart to these foreign hills. Perhaps it is the passion born of their very defiance. Every sense feels heightened. There is so much to gain, and there is so much to lose.

I am an attorney at law, I marveled, *in the United States of America*.

WE TURNED TO FOLLOW THE CREEK, DANNY AND I. A red-tailed hawk circled overhead. I knew the carefree flight belied the reality of its intention, and so I, too, looked to the ground, where last year's leaves provided a slick but deceiving cover. Danny adjusted his rhythm; he is an intuitive horse. We moved along, water gurgling beside us as it passed over the creek's rocky bottom. Then we reached a latent pool formed by a massive beaver dam that, in time, we will need to address. For now, though, Uncle has chosen to leave it. Their work has created a spot Aileen enjoys, for with some regularity he finds her here, sitting among the rocks, her hands deep in cool mud or her fingers making trails in the pond's still surface. She has gathered quite an ephemeral collection that she arranges and rearranges in a bright south-facing window—twigs and leaves and feathers, smooth flat stones of differing colors, butterfly wings and beetle shells and any other miscellanea that happen to strike her fancy.

We reached the clearing, and I pulled Danny to a stop. Aileen was on the porch and in conversation with someone I could see only from the back. Still there was no mistaking: It was Abijah Alley. For a moment I waited and watched. He was talking; she was listening, and her head cocked with a familiarity between them that I would not have expected. She stepped from the porch and he turned, as together they moved in my direction.

I tapped Danny and he walked forward, bringing us out of shadow. Aileen must have seen us, for her body shrank. Not so the visitor.

"Say, ho there, Patrick! How does it go this fine afternoon?" He raised a hand in greeting, looking for all the world as if I were the one come to call. "It is one of our Lord's more glorious days. Wouldn't you say?"

"Aye, if it isn't the one and only Abijah Alley, right here in our valley." I rode toward them, dismounted, extended my hand. He took it, smiled, then pulled me in for a full-contact embrace.

"What is it that brings you here today?" I asked.

"Oh, just taking a glory ride up these hills, seeing what the Lord would have me do."

He looked to Aileen and then back to me, rubbing his long beard chin to stomach. "I do believe I am looking at Scott County's newest lawyer, am I not? Well, that's just fine. Very fine, indeed."

I noticed Aileen start to comment, but she reconsidered.

"Well, then," Alley said, a spell broken. "I'll be getting on." His arm came 'round my shoulder again, which he pounded with good nature. He looked to Aileen. "You remember what I said, now."

A hint of a smile came to her lips, but she didn't respond, and he turned to walk toward the road and the outer post where he'd tied his horse. His stride was long, his step confident as he made his way around the front meadow. At the curve, I heard him sing, "Just as I am thou wilt receive, wilt welcome, pardon, cleanse, relieve." Aileen watched him, too, then without a word she turned and disappeared through the cabin's front door.

CHAPTER SIX

MARILEE

MAY 1854

PATRICK HAGAN WAS TRUE TO HIS WORD AND VISITED Saratoga three times in the weeks after I first extended the invitation at the church. I am pleased to say that for the most part our students were attentive and well mannered, as Mr. Hagan is quite the good speaker. He demonstrates a deep understanding of the history of Ireland and ties those stories to life here in a way that makes the lessons colorful and relevant. (No doubt this is a skill that will serve him well in his work as a defense attorney.) He did pay particular attention to Elizabeth, something she neither acknowledged nor realized, as for her it is never enough. One question answered leads to two more asked. And thus my energies were largely focused on maintaining a sliver of space for other students to engage.

For his part, Patrick proved amenable to both her interrogation and her fiery challenges. "They should have just planted a different crop!" was her response to his detailed description of the potato blight and its devastating impact on the people of Ireland. He outlined the country's feudalistic society, describing his own life as the son of a poor tenant farmer beholden to the acreage-owning lord and to the British crown. "But why is England over Ireland?" she asked.

Patrick offered a well-considered response, then he told of leaving his family, boarding a steamer bound for America, and arriving here to find the land plentiful and the opportunity boundless. "'Tis the owning of acreage that affords independence," he said, his tone one of significant conclusion, a point to be remembered. "Land represents freedom."

"But wasn't your brothers mad you got to leave? Are they still mad?"

That was enough, and I stepped in to end the lesson, tasking the students with drawing maps of Ireland.

IT WAS VISIT NUMBER THREE WHEN THE MODICUM OF peace I'd found in these hills was set to flame. I'd known poetry would eventually have to be part of my curriculum here; still, to have it roll in like a storm on the breath of a student—Elizabeth Young, of course— was unnerving. Plus, her choice of verse was embarrassing and insensitive to the generous man standing before the class having fled his homeland. Still, she read:

And, as a bird each fond endearment tries,
To tempt its new-fledged offspring to the skies;
He tried each art, reproved each dull delay,
Allured to brighter worlds, and led the way.

They were lines from the pastoral "The Deserted Village" by the Irish poet Oliver Goldsmith. To my shock, Patrick did not appear to share my consternation. Instead, he seemed to delight in both her choice of poet and stanza.

"He was a rather odd fellow, Goldsmith, but I do hold him in high regard. For he was certainly not afraid to call out damage wrought by excessive wealth. When it is in the wrong hands, of course."

Elizabeth looked confused. "But it's a poem about leaving a dull place. Going somewhere else to make a better life."

"Aye, but is it?" he said.

The classroom erupted in snickers. I did not have time to address this before Patrick did.

"'Tis the beauty of poetry, Eilís. The poet writes knowing a reader will bring his or her own experiences to the work. So no matter how intentional, no matter how finely crafted, there will always be variations in interpretation." (How I hated poetry. How I hated poets.) "But as this is Miss Kitchens's area of expertise, I shall leave it there. Unless there are other questions about Ireland, or the famine—"

Elizabeth looked bewildered, and I took the opportunity to step forward. "Well, class, I do believe we have had our poetry lesson for the day. So once we have properly thanked Mr. Hagan, you may take your afternoon recess."

Six or seven boys jumped to go. I would have stopped them, but I was eager for the room to empty. I looked to Patrick, who was standing near my desk, his arms crossed, his demeanor suggesting that he was satisfied.

"I so appreciate how you—" I had gotten just that far when an arm shot from behind me, and in it was a pamphlet containing Goldsmith's work. Patrick reached to take it.

"I don't think he is the poet for me." It was Elizabeth.

"Then you must keep searching," he said.

She bounced from the room, and I raised an eyebrow at my guest.

"My uncle has an extensive library. I knew he would be pleased that there is a student who has taken such an interest." We walked together toward the door. "Speaking of. I expect him to return from his travels in the next day or two, and that will offer some freedom. Might you care to join me for dinner?"

"Oh?" I said, feeling my inflection skip like silly Elizabeth.

"I was thinking of the dining room at the Nickelsville Hotel. Saturday night? The food is quite good."

I hesitated as if my social calendar were full.

"But if—"

"Saturday will be fine."

He nodded. "Then I shall come to *fetch* you, as one would say around here."

There was a sweet glimmer in his eye, I am certain I saw it, and I felt a blush rise from my chest to my cheeks. *He plans to call for me. At the boarding house.* I looked away to conceal my high color. This would never be done in Charlottesville, not among proper families—but as he'd already pointed out, we were in a different world now.

"I shall let them know to expect us at six. If that suits."

"Yes, yes," I said, casting my own nonchalance. I reminded myself that I am, after all, a grown woman and not a schoolgirl.

"Very well, *go dtí sin*," he said. "Until then."

I watched him go and thought how remarkable it was that we had both found ourselves here, in this primitive land, disparate among the locals. Fate, could it be?

No, no, Marilee. No.

I went back to the classroom, and while I wiped the chalkboard clean, I pictured the handful of gowns I'd brought along to this wild place—daffodil yellow, spring green, robin's-egg blue. One by one I flipped through. Patrick Hagan, Esquire, had invited me for dinner.

CHAPTER SEVEN

ELIZABETH

IT WAS JUST THREE WEEKS LATER WHEN I LEARNED Ben's father, Stoley Grubb, had passed on. As he was known to be a fine and respected man, I knew Papa would likely go for the service. I told him I'd like to come along, to keep him company in paying respects. Which was true, mostly. But also I wanted to see Ben. I'd been thinking of him since our meeting at Alley's service, and I wanted him to know I was out here, willing to help carry part of his heavy sorrow.

The day of the burial came dreary and gray, and I was glad of it. I held on to Papa as we climbed the steep hill, the clouds closing in around us. I thought how this felt right, the world seeming small. Once you got up at the top, you could tell on a clear day the view would be pretty, it being high on Clinch Mountain, a real nice place to spend eternity. There were chairs for the family and the elderly up at the front, and Papa led us to join the mourners standing behind. I put my hand in the crook of his elbow, and he reached out and pulled me close, a bird tucking a baby under its broad wing. All of a sudden I wanted to memorize everything about that moment: the pull of his arm across my shoulder; the musty smell of his old wool coat; the sound of his breath as it hit the cool mountain air. I bent my neck so my head rested up against him. He leaned to kiss the top of my head, and I nestled in closer.

And then I saw the Freemasons. They were coming up the hill two by two, the long pine box between them. Right away I saw it was Mister Red Hopkins holding the right front. He is a big man and still you could tell that coffin was heavy. There was a line of people that followed behind and when they got closer I knew it was family first, with other Masons following, I'd say thirty or more.

There was a crooked old apple tree just at the edge of the burying yard and the whole group of them had to go around it to get to the grave. It felt strange to watch this, but what was you supposed to do? It was like a parade, I thought, a sad parade, and for a minute I bowed my head just to give them some privacy. When I looked back up the family was close and I saw Ben was walking with his mother, Jenny Mae, just behind the coffin. He had a good grip, and her own arms were crossed in front like she was using them to hold herself together. Behind them came a boy of about ten and another of about seven, and then an older boy my age who carried a young girl on his hip. They all walked with their heads held high, even the littlest ones.

The Masons brought the casket to the spot just this side of the empty grave and sat it down gentle on the ground. The family moved into the chairs, and soon as they were settled Red and another man draped the casket with a black cloth and on top of that they spread Stoley's white Mason apron. Mister Red motioned for us to step in around the family and we did, forming a wall between that sacred place and the sinful world outside.

T. O. Rollins came forward. He started by saying a thing or two about the customs of the Fraternity of the Ancient, Free and Accepted Masons, time immortal, last tributes. I could hardly take it in as I'd never been to a funeral like this, and I wondered if Ben's father would make it to heaven without a real preacher doing the service.

"Brother Stoley Bartholomew Grubb, Master Mason. Member of Catlett Lodge Number 35. Entered into rest this 10 October 1854, age forty-nine years, two months, and seventeen days. Almighty Father, into Thy hands we commend the soul of our beloved Brother."

Jenny Mae let out a small cry, and Ben's arm went around her and he whispered something in her ear. She shook her head yes with the slightest motion, and he turned his eyes back to T. O., who was continuing with some bit about shadows and death and dust. Then he got to a part about life being uncertain and we should embrace the present moment while we're afforded time and opportunity.

I was giving this powerful consideration when T. O. finished and looked to Ben. Ben got up and walked over to the side where somebody handed him a banjo. He put the strap over his shoulder and turned to give his mama a sweet smile. Then he started up picking "Amazing Grace."

He played the tune simple at first, one slow note at a time. It was beautiful played that way, sorrowful, as if the song was saying all it needed to, like the banjo itself couldn't bear anything more. But then he added just the tiniest bit of harmony, some chords here and there on the longest notes. And the hymn became something more.

It's the song of his heart, I thought. *He's playing what his heart feels.*

His head was bowed, his eyes were down, but then he raised up and lifted his face to the heavens. The music turned, too, becoming round and full and filling the forest with sound and life. His fingers moved across those strings, picking up speed and turning "Amazing Grace" into something else entirely—a cry against the woes of life, the pain that comes with loss, the price of loving somebody so much.

Ben stood there a minute when the song was finished, his eyes still closed. Papa squeezed my hand and I looked to him, his face in profile but showing a peace I hadn't seen on him in a long, long time. I turned back to Ben who by then was sitting, leaning forward, his hands clasped in front and every little Grubb turned up the row to see him. He was giving them that smile and that wink, I knew.

T. O. commenced with some other readings, then he said it was Mrs. Grubb's wish that anybody who wanted to offer words about Stoley Grubb was invited to do so. Three or four of the Freemasons spoke, referencing in particular Brother Stoley's fine morals and outstanding character. Then Mister Red stepped forward.

"When I'm standing at the Pearly Gates of Heaven," he said, then he stopped and laughed a little, "assuming I *get* to the Pearly Gates of Heaven—I'll say to St. Peter: 'I am a man of little consequence. But I was once considered a friend by two of your great Archangels. One was Rufus

Young. The other, Stoley Bartholomew Grubb.' I think that might just get me in."

Some people laughed, some shook their heads, but Papa, he grew stiff.

T. O. produced a branch of evergreen and started in on its significance as a sign of immortality. Papa took my elbow and pulled me to leave.

"No, Papa," I whispered, "the service isn't over yet."

"Time for us to go," he said.

I prayed hard Ben would see me as we left, catch sight before Papa and me both disappeared over the hill. But his eyes were on the Freemasons as they stepped forward one by one to place their sprigs of greenery in the grave. He never once turned around, and I left Stoley's funeral with his son Ben Grubb never even knowing I was there.

CHAPTER EIGHT

RED HOPKINS

JONATHAN YOUNG SLOWLY COME UNDONE AND I watched it all happen. He was right there under my nose, us close as brothers, and still there weren't a damn thing I could do about it.

That ain't to say I didn't try. But nothing ever made a difference, leastways not in the end.

How did it start? Why, most would reckon it was the day of Ruck's hanging, a sad and spectacular day here in these mountains where hundreds of people come to town to witness it. But in truth it started near to fifty years ago, when Jonathan and Ruck's family was killed in the last Indian raid in these parts. They was just little boys, twins not hardly six years old. Their older brother hid them in the woods and told them to STAY PUT, not to dare move. Then he run back toward the house and the mayhem and like the rest ended up dead, the babies and all, as well as their Mama and Daddy. Seven in total and the house burned to the ground.

I can't even say what that was like, can't hold the thought in my head how awful it must of been. And that ain't counting for the fact they was then lost in the woods for up on a week. Do you know what them little boys was in the midst of? Why that forest is wild, filled with bear and razorback and wolf. And panther, which I have seen with my own eyes. They's deadly snakes all over the place, plentiful enough that the long hunters who know these trails blind step real careful, watching every minute. They's tales a plenty of coming up on a hundred or more of them all denned up together, sometimes rattlers, sometimes coppers, sometimes a mix a both.

Good lord this is fierce country, even today.

Years ago I asked Jonathan about those days, what they ate, how him and Rufus stayed alive. He got a faraway stare like he was looking it all over and remembering some terrible awful things. He didn't say anything, so after a minute I reached over and touched his arm. "Jonathan, my friend," I said.

He looked to me, his eyes flat and full. "Can't do it, Red. Can't talk about it."

"Course not," I said. "I won't be asking again."

THE YEARS THAT FOLLOWED WAS JUST AS BAD, MAYBE worse, for now they was orphans and also separated. Ruck got took in by the Barneses, the people who found him and Jon in the woods. You might think this was a blessing but they happen to be the sorriest lot on Clinch Mountain—why, they ain't nothing but a bunch of thieves and liars, the whole mess of them. Ruck would take all he could, then he'd run off trying to get to Jonathan, to a better kind of life. But Jon, too, was in a hard place. He lived with the Reverend and Mrs. Bishop, which sounds good but weren't, something I learned much later from Ruck.

A lot of things I know from Ruck. That's the truth. Like what happened with Tilly, who was Jonathan's wife although Ruck is the one who loved her first. Like what happened to Audley Anderson that night on the Trace.

They're private things, things a man keeps to hisself for good reason. Still he had occasion to tell me, had little choice in the matter, really, as it was a requirement of the situation. And I'm glad of it, I'll say that. The truth can be a heavy cross when it's one man carries it for so many years.

It's mine to carry now. My conscience nags like a bitter ol' wife: Tell him. Tell Jonathan. Tell it all. It would release them memories tearing him apart, it would give Jonathan Young some peace.

But of course I cannot. I am bound by the Brotherhood, by a code I cannot break.

So mote it be.

CHAPTER NINE

PATRICK

MAY 1854

MISS KITCHENS TOPPED THE STAIRS RESPLENDENT IN blue, and for the first time I noticed she is beautiful, quite beautiful really, her cheeks high and flushed, her hair expertly tucked into a bonnet of silk and pearls. She stood rather in contrast to the bare wood walls of her surroundings, and it occurred to me then we are immigrants here, she and I, me having crossed the sea and her having arrived with an unmatched style and elegance. It showed there amidst the boarding house, the room clean but sparse, the upholstered sofa threadbare with an old broom that rested against its worn and weathered arm. A woman I assumed to be the proprietor stood nearly out of view, her arms crossed and resting above a broad belly, her dress and hair the same dull shade of gray. She closely surveyed us both.

Marilee descended; her hand traced the spine of the banister. It was a gentle touch that offered aplomb, not support. She smiled and I smiled back.

"And what time should I look for you to return, Miss?"

Marilee had just taken my arm, and thus came the landlady's response, her voice pitched and falsely formal.

"Mrs. Vicars!" my companion snapped. "I do not expect it will be late. And there is *certainly* no need for you to wait up."

I MADE A MENTAL NOTE TO INQUIRE AS TO THE WOMAN, to ask Marilee about life as a boarder. It is something with which I have some familiarity, my Aunt Aileen having suffered so as a young lass newly arrived in Boston. She was a servant in a hateful Brahman household when, one December evening, she was let go and turned out into the snow. Uncle happened to be among the invited dinner guests that night, and upon witnessing the girl's constant berating and then her ultimate dismissal he excused himself, left the mansion, and looked to find Aileen shivering on a street corner in the cold. She had neither destination nor coat, so he wrapped her as best he could and walked with her toward the waterfront and an establishment he knew that was meant to board the Irish. He rapped on the door and eventually it was opened; the conditions were abhorrent, the smell noxious and there was no heat to speak of. Families were packed on families, and babies' cries came weak from hunger. Aileen insisted she could stay but Joseph would not hear of it. She was shivering and her thin boots were soaked through, and he was certain she had already suffered frostbite. So he took her to his Broad Street residence, where, for a week, a nurse he hired cared for her. He then bought the boarding house and spent much of the next year petitioning for tenement standards and their enforcement.

A romantic would believe he fell for her then, beautiful and needy as she was. But Uncle said something different the only time he spoke of it to me. She suffered typhus some time later, and upon her release from the pauper's hospital he again insisted she come to Broad Street for recovery. She had no money, no family, and due to the hateful nature of her former mistress, no options for employment. And the illness had left her changed. Wild hallucinations carried on, and when she spoke it was often in a strange combination of Gaelic and English that left the meaning indecipherable. Morphine calmed her, but over time even this became less effective. Her fits escalated and pushed her to a terrifying hysteria. Joseph ordered it withheld.

Those were dark days. He stopped traveling altogether, and over time Aileen's body did what it needed to, to—in part—tame the demons. She began to show signs of recovery, and as she made each tiny step back into the light, Joseph was at her side. Within the year they were married, and within two she had put flame to drape, burning Uncle Joseph's fine Boston mansion to the ground.

I LOOKED AT MISS KITCHENS ACROSS THE TABLE, NOTing her poise and elegance. There was a quality about her I could not name, something proper but also distant. When I'd suggested she consider the Beef Tongue—a dish I'd enjoyed and knew to be quite good— she simply smiled, then looked around as if to assess the other patrons. "Oh," she said, seeing my reaction. "You're serious." In the end she ordered Roast Pork and Apples, and I chose Veal. I asked that a small sample of the chilled Tongue be brought to our table for tasting, but she would not be persuaded. For all her education, I realized *adventurous* was not an adjective to describe Marilee Kitchens.

She was, however, a fine sparring partner. This I found encouraging and delightful—for there is nothing I love more than hearty discourse, and with the growing unrest in our country there was much to be considered and decided. I was quite interested in her political leanings, her position on the expansion of slavery, her take on developments with the Nebraska Territory. I felt these to be the most pressing issues in our country, and so I asked.

"The Act has already passed in the Senate, has it not, with rather a wide margin. So I expect it will also survive the House." She said this dismissively, as if there were other topics more interesting.

"But sentiments are strong," I countered. "Arguments are growing more heated: violent, even. It points out the great divide between North and South, Industrial and Agrarian, strong federal government or strong states' rights. I fear what is to come."

"We won't lose our slaves, if that's what you're worried about," she said. "Slavery is protected in the Constitution."

This was not a pressing issue for most in this poor rural area, something I might have expected her to acknowledge though she did not. "Perhaps one might call the Constitution deliberately ambiguous on the matter," I said.

"Hmmm," she pretended to consider. "I could argue. At a minimum we can agree it is *operationally* proslavery."

"Still, there is expressly no recognition of 'property in men.'"

"You are a Democrat, are you not, Mr. Hagan? I do believe those politics lend themselves to the support of slavery as an institution."

"I am a Democrat, yes."

"And so—?"

"My position—which is in full alignment with the party—is that we not allow the federal government to crush the spirit upon which our country was founded. Liberty, which does not impose arbitrary restraints; which takes into account the rights of all involved; which fights the tyranny of the majority in the oppression of the minority."

"Which means you do *not* stand in support of slavery." She feigned a look of confusion. "Or you do? I am not clear."

"All men are equal. The Negro is the same as the white man, just as the poor man is the same as the rich. It is God's law, and it is not open to interpretation. Oppression, suppression, aggression—all of these are acts against God's very will. So yes, as an institution, slavery must end. But I also believe we must find a peaceable means to it."

"And what of the Kansas–Nebraska Act?" she asked.

"I believe in sovereignty, as I've already said."

"So you stand in support. You believe the territories themselves should choose, even though that overturns slavery's outlawing via the Missouri Compromise."

"I believe we cannot allow the federal government to dictate how we live."

"Even if the particular dictate stands in direct opposition to a belief you hold true. To what God commands, in your eyes." Hers held a delighted twinkle, I noticed.

"'Tis a complicated circumstance. I will admit this. But good men are capable of good decisions. Good men make virtuous citizens, strong defenders of liberty who challenge greed and corruption wherever it exists."

"In government. Primarily. You would say." Miss Kitchens was smiling then, clearly pleased with her understated argument.

"Wherever it resides."

She shook her head yes, not in agreement but in acknowledgment.

That's when I realized I had gained very little insight as to what *she* believes. I then baited, I cajoled, but it amounted to little. No matter how I tried to engage her, she did not share much.

"And what of your family?" I asked eventually, pointedly changing the tenor of our conversation. I already knew a bit about Mary Lenore Kitchens, as I had been consulted last year when Uncle made the final teacher selection on behalf of the Saratoga School. He is the benefactor who pays her salary, something she does not know as his requirement is that the fact be kept secret.

"What *of* my family?" It was terse, defensive. She sensed my surprise, and her expression softened. "I believe I've mentioned. My father is a professor of modern languages at the University of Virginia. My mother...well, my mother is a socialite, I suppose one would say."

She looked as if she might take a sip of her wine, but she did not. Instead she rubbed her forefinger around the rim of the goblet and did not say more.

"'Twould seem to me—" I nudged, but her eyes blinked up with a dare that made me stop.

"What?" she said.

"'Twould stand to reason, I was going to say, that your house would be filled with interesting people. Learned men of strong conviction and of varying ideals. I expect this is why you can deftly hold your own in any discussion." My observation pleased her, and I was emboldened to go on. "Colorful characters, one would think—writers, philosophers. Explorers of the word and world." She liked the turn of phrase; a tiny smile emerged. "I can imagine being a child, hiding behind curtains, peeking from the top of the stairs, as such goings-on must have been impossible to resist."

"Oh, there was no hiding, Patrick; about that you are mistaken. I am an only child, and while my mother would have preferred I be elsewhere when they entertained, my father was most insistent I be exposed to it all."

I could see this.

"I never needed to hide *under* the table because I was seated *at it*."

I found this fascinating, this premise of a child surrounded by a rotating cast, immersed in their language, their opinions, their discourse. What an opportunity for a young mind to grow and to be influenced by the day's most forward-thinking intellectuals. We could not be more different in terms of upbringing, to myself I acknowledged, the gulf between our childhood experiences far wider than the ocean and cultures that separated us. "Do give me an example, won't you?" I said.

"I don't know," she resisted.

"Tell me who was there. Tell me how an evening changed you."

She cocked her head, calculating. "I will make a deal with you, Patrick Hagan. I'll tell you that story if, on the other end, you are equally generous."

I had not expected this, would never have agreed to it but for the of-my-own-making corner I found myself in. I nodded in agreement, and thus she began.

"AS YOU GUESSED, OUR HOME—ALBEMARLE PLACE—WAS invariably filled with guests who, via rather coveted invitation, attended my parents' salons and dinner parties. When I was in my third year at Valley Union, and all of fifteen—"

I leaned forward.

"—I was summoned home. I was told to abandon my classes, temporary though it may have been, for the 'superior opportunity' about to present itself in Charlottesville. Edgar Allan Poe was coming for dinner and a reading."

"Poe," I said. "And you were fifteen. This must have been near the time—"

"Yes. Two months before he died."

I caught something in her breath, her voice, her demeanor. Was it sorrow? Remorse? Regret?

"He was traveling about, trying to drum up financial support for a new endeavor, a literary journal called *The Stylus*. My father was quite enthusiastic."

She paused to take a sip, and perhaps to collect her thoughts, and it gave me time to do the same. Poe had been a brilliant writer but also a scoundrel. Even details of his death remained sketchy.

She smiled and returned to me. "I did as I was told, of course. I arrived home the afternoon of the gathering and was immediately sent to my room. I sat in the high window seat and watched as Mother barked orders at Abram and another colored man I didn't recognize, both of whom were doing their best to keep up with her demands. The lawn and grounds were perfect, but she would not be satisfied.

"I snuck down the back stairs to the kitchen where I found Hannah and Gemm, both with dripping brows, both fretting. How Mother could work Hannah over. She was the best cook in Albemarle, still she would not get a moment's peace nor a word of praise no matter how delicious the meal. She saw me, though, and stopped everything she was doing to reach and pull me tight. It was warm and familiar, even if rather wet. 'There you are, girl chile, now dis house feel better.' She chuckled and it was like the rumble of distant thunder, a sound that came from somewhere deep. She handed me a chocolate truffle and slipped another into my pocket. 'Now shoo!' she said, and I did, leaving the two of them to attend to every prescribed detail of the dinner.

"I was still at the window when, some hours later, guests began to arrive. I remember thinking how peaceful it must all look, the tree-lined drive leading to a broad front porch; our elegant home set against summer-green hills that rolled forever to the horizon. Carriages delivered professors, ladies of fashion, even a politician or two, and my mother was fully in her element greeting every guest, kissing every cheek, remembering every name. *How is that darling Sophie? Is Charles enjoying school? Why, Arthur, you look more handsome every time I see you!*

"My father executed with equal fervor. His wild gray hair topped a ruffled suit that moments earlier, had been perfectly pressed. He dispensed with the niceties and, upon seeing Dean Richards Childers, went straight for him—the two always had unfinished business in the discussion of this matter or that, this publication or that. Twice Mother retrieved him, slipping her hand through his arm and guiding him back to stand with her at the top of the porch's stairs. But then Senator Cummings appeared, and Father was gone again."

I smiled, thought what a wonderful storyteller Marilee Kitchens was.

"And that's how it was that when Edgar Allan Poe arrived, my mother descended the broad brick steps alone. I watched from above as in a most dramatic fashion, she swept her arm wide in greeting. 'Why, Mr. Poe, what an honor it is to welcome you to our little corner of the Commonwealth,' she said, the folds in her proper accent particularly prim and pressed. 'I am Mrs. Elsworth Kitchens. But please, do call me Amelia.'

"Poe showed absolutely no emotion. But he did step toward her. 'Well, you certainly are handsome,' Mother said, and I wondered to whom she was speaking. The man I saw was dark and disheveled in a manner oddly unnerving. He wore a broad black cape that floated behind him, and tucked beneath his arm was a leather pouch wrapped several times with a leather cord. His hand gripped a carved wood walking stick, and as he was not using it, I could see the bit of brass that encircled the shaft at the top. 'I do trust that your journey was a pleasant one.' He didn't respond; then just before they passed under the portico and out of my view, I saw my mother's hand slip into deep gray wool bunched at his elbow. *I am making my entrance on the arm of Edgar Allan Poe,* I knew her to be thinking. *'Dear god, let there be someone in the foyer to see it.'*"

I laughed, and Marilee laughed too.

"Not long after, Hannah rushed to get me. I was not yet dressed, as I wasn't expected to join the gathering so soon. There was to have been a leisurely time of cocktails during which the guests and Poe were to mingle, but instead the writer downed two Sazeracs, fixed himself a third, and commenced to reading. Folks scrambled for seats, and from below I heard strains of 'Ulalume, Ulalume'—as in one motion Hannah pulled the silk over my head, tied a bow at my back, and sent me out, muttering *Hannah do this no Hannah do that* and *has to do it all.* She was on to a *ruint-dinner* tirade when I kissed her cheek and headed for the stairs.

"He was deep into a poem I did not know. I stood in the doorway and waited for him to finish, but Poe looked up, saw me there and quit reading. Mid-line he simply stopped. The moment stretched long like pulled taffy, and everyone turned—my mother looking especially appalled—and my father stood to speak. 'Mr. Poe, I do hope you will pardon this unorthodox interruption of your most impressive reading. It is my great privilege to introduce to you my daughter, Mary Lenore Kitchens.' Father motioned, and I thought he meant for me to come but I wasn't sure, and everyone was watching, and heaven help me I think I may have curtsied."

I laughed again, and so did she, and from nowhere Mr. Jake James, the hotel's proprietor, delivered two small glasses of bourbon. "It's a pleasure to have you both this evening." It was a near whisper. "Do enjoy."

Jake backed away, then I raised my glass to Marilee. "To a very fine raconteur, *scéalaí*, and to her willingness to carry forth to the end." We clinked glasses, we sipped, and to my delight, she did.

"So Poe dropped the page and as it fell to the floor, he said my name. 'Mary Lenore. Mary Lenore. Mary Lenore.' Mother clapped her hands—just the once, but that's all it took—and she patted a six-inch space on the upholstered bench beside her.

"I was mortified in the way only a fifteen-year-old girl can be. Still, I crossed the room, stepping around chairs and passing between senators just as my mother had demanded. Poe took the opportunity to request another drink, then he looked straight to me and said, 'It would be my honor to read for you, dear, if there is something you'd like to hear.'

"Of course I hesitated; this was Edgar Allan Poe. So Father stepped in with his own attempt to keep the evening on track. 'You know the great writer's work, darling, and he has made a request of you.'

"'I suppose...a bit of 'The Raven,' if you please.'

"'Aah,' said Poe, 'a wonderful selection. For it is the story of another rare and radiant maiden, whom the angels call Lenore.'"

This time Marilee raised her bourbon and there was a delicate but unmistakable gulp.

"Your mother must have been incensed," I said, knowing it was a comment too personal for our young friendship.

"Oh, yes," she said. "He read on for another hour. By the time we were seated for dinner the man was so drunk as to resemble an eel, slipping and sliding over muddy words, overrunning every conversation with his dark commentary, morbid and dreary as it was."

She stopped abruptly now, as if this were it. She straightened tableware, adjusted her napkin, moved her hand to her hair where a small curl had come loose and fallen free.

"And how did the evening end?"

She looked to the window but not at me. "Oh, I guess one would say it ended the next morning, when I found Mr. Poe passed out on the settee in the parlor."

I laughed aloud, which I recognized was not the most gentlemanly thing to do in the moment.

"Post-dinner, father had the task of corralling the overserved men in the drawing room. He did, in fact, make an effort to conduct the final business of pledging. But no one was paying him much heed, least of these Poe, and so Mother stepped in and that got their attention."

"Your mother did the asking?"

"She did." It was clear Marilee was neither delighted nor entertained by this turn of events, but it was obvious I was, and I was grateful she carried on. "They were gathered, voices loud and cigars in hand, when in she came. 'Gentlemen,' she said. She could not be heard, so she stepped on a footstool, rising above them. 'Gentlemen, please!' They looked, poked each other, then quieted. And so she stepped down, straightening her skirts. 'It would appear, gentlemen, you have enjoyed this evening immensely. And it is time for a show of support for our friend, Mr. Edgar Allan Poe. He is here not just for our good company but to seek financial backers for an exciting new venture. Please direct your attention to Mr. Poe, who will give you the particulars of his vision.'

"Poe looked as surprised as the others as Mother, silk layers swaying behind her, exited the room. He used his one free hand to steady himself, and he leaned heavy against the window frame. He tried to form a sentence, but as he did his legs gave way, and in rather slow, rather dramatic fashion the great writer slid, window to baseboard to floor, drunk as a fiddler."

I laughed aloud, delighted with the turn of the tale. "Didn't raise much capital, I'm assuming," I said.

"There was a promissory slip or two. But in the light of the morning sun, when I came downstairs to find Poe asleep and sprawled across the drawing-room settee with the notes around him, the penmanship was so illegible as to leave both the amount, and the contributor, indiscernible."

She retrieved her napkin, gathered it in her right hand, and rather deliberately placed it on the table. That meant she was finished with Poe, this I could tell, and so I shook my head in acquiescence. "Well, that sure surpassed all expectation. Thank you, Marilee, for the honor."

She gave a slow nod in satisfaction. "Your turn," she said.

"Goodness, no. Following that? I am quite certain you will find my storytelling to be woefully lacking."

"You forget, Mr. Hagan. I've already had the pleasure, when you came to Saratoga School."

"Aah, yes. Saratoga. Where there was much I omitted."

"As we all do," she said.

Her look was soft, and kind, and again I wondered what of the Poe experience she'd left out. Still, I was emboldened by her gentle understanding, and so I considered going on. What to tell a woman whose history is so different from mine? That the household I grew up in harbored violence? That when I left, my brothers and parents were already destitute? That eighteen months later, amidst the onslaught of the blight, all save one were dead—of starvation, of dysentery, of gunshot.

"I shall simply say this. Immigration to America was a grand opportunity, just as I presented to your class. But it was also escape. It was *all the more* escape, for while I studied economics and philosophy and literature in Philadelphia, my family scavenged for scraps in Dungannon. While I learned to speak well, dress well, dine well, my brothers—each of whom was resourceful enough and mean enough to do whatever it took to survive—were dying of starvation." I was the one, then, who looked away. "It was a great deal for a young man of sixteen to reckon with. It is a great deal, still." Marilee reached across the table and laid her hand over mine. "I pray every day that I prove worthy. I pray without ceasing that God will use me to His highest calling."

"But that would be the priesthood, would it not?" There was a lightness in her tone, a teasing, and she removed her hand. "I don't see you as a priest, Patrick Hagan."

"Highest *but for* the priesthood. For which I am far too opinionated, far too political, and far too sinful," I added.

"Thus one might say you have found your *perfect* calling."

"In law," I chuckled.

"In law," she smiled.

There was not more I cared to share in the moment, and the evening had grown late. "You have been a generous listener," I said.

"I am delighted to know you better. I treasure our friendship. I have so few equals in this desolate land; it is a relief to have someone with whom I can relate."

I did not respond, this being a comment that stung and surprised. I must have misheard her, that is what I decided, and I wiped the sentiment from my mind. We chatted about other things as we departed and made the short drive to the boarding house, much of my attention focused on guiding the horse and carriage. We were nearly there when she picked up a thread from earlier.

"I, too, feel a duty," she said. "A responsibility. To use my education, you know, in service to these children." I pulled right, but Danny pulled left, and I clicked to him, *tst, tst*. "I feel bad for them," she said. "I do, poor little unfortunates."

"Unfortunates," I said.

"I'm sure you understand, as you must experience the same in your practice. Dealing with people of such limited experience, stuck like they are in these hills. It stifles the imagination. Limits the mind. Good heavens, in your work you must see it all." A little laugh escaped, and she tucked her gloved hand into the crook of my arm.

"Surely, Marilee, you are not suggesting—"

"It's why I'm here, Patrick. To help. People deserve a path out of ignorance, and that's something I have to offer."

"But these are not ignorant people. They simply have a different way of life. Different priorities. Different values."

"That's certainly true."

"Values, I would argue, that are strong and noble. Values that put the land and family first."

She didn't respond, and I snapped the reins out of anger, not instruction. Danny raised his head and snorted.

"Do you remember when we first met at the church?" she asked. "Just after the melee? I was there seeking a better understanding of the culture here, of the backgrounds from which my students come. I want to do right by them, Patrick. I want to give them whatever it is they need to thrive. I believe education is the answer. I believe education is always the answer, no matter where one is, no matter what one's circumstance. That's all I mean. That's why I'm here."

We had reached the boarding house, and I pulled the carriage to a stop, conceding, at least in theory. I was not one to argue this matter; every advantage I have earned has come through the fine schooling my uncle financed. I got out to help Miss Kitchens down, and as she took my hand she looked into my eyes as if she were searching for something there. I did not look away, but I did not offer much. Her gaze held when she said, "Good evening, Mrs. Vicars," then she released my hand and stepped around. The woman was standing in the shadows, something Marilee had sensed that I had not.

"Come out for the stars," the voice said from the dark. Then the front door opened and shut as the woman made her passage through it. We were left alone.

"I am having an impact." Marilee turned back to me. "Just look at Elizabeth Young."

I nodded, unsure what I was to say.

"She is bright, as you know. She is inquisitive. She wants more than her circumstance will ever offer."

I had not considered this, knowing nothing of the girl's "circumstance." What I did understand is the pain that comes of a desire for more. The longing, the relentless reaching that becomes unbearable when there is no reciprocation, no hope. It's why I consider Uncle my savior, of a sort, and I could see how Marilee Kitchens with her privilege and position and exceptional mind could be of benefit to a girl like Elizabeth. Perhaps I had judged her comments too harshly.

"Well, anyway. Thank you for a lovely evening filled with stimulating conversation," she said. "And thank you for not insisting on the beef tongue. That may come in time, although I sincerely doubt it."

I took her hands and leaned in, lingered in her scent, for the first time in many months enticed by a beautiful woman. "I suppose we should give Mrs. Vicars at least a little of what she came for, don't you think?" I kissed her cheek, then I pulled back to see Marilee was smiling. I stepped away to wait by the carriage, and I watched until Miss Kitchens was safely in the door, and the light in the window went out.

CHAPTER TEN

___

RED

HOW DIFFERENT THINGS WOULD'VE BEEN IF JON AND Ruck both had come into the Freemasons. As it was, though, only Ruck ever showed interest. He come to the Lodge one day which surprised me, him not being one to go 'round looking for rules to follow, if you know what I mean. Still there he was, and the Junior Deacon won't let him in, and Ruck gets fighting mad. So I go to the door and say, "Him and me, we're gonna take a walk." I explain how things work. I tell Ruck I'd be proud to be his sponsor but he'll have to pass Examination. It was a fact he didn't like and over which, I have to say, I had my own worries. But there was no way around this requirement, so if Ruck Young wanted to join the Fraternity of the Ancient, Free and Accepted Masons, there was some things he was gonna have to come clean about.

It was a fight, believe you me. They was people involved who'd been knowing Ruck since he was a boy, most particular our Worshipful Master T. O. Rollins, who made it clear we had to get to the bottom of a matter I'd believed was buried in the grave with Tilly Perkins decades ago. They was also questions over Ruck's "judgment" and his jail time at the hands of the Barneses. This was something I knew enough about to believe we could get it resolved fine, but the thing with Tilly? All the years that'd passed, all the water that had flowed under that particular bridge, and still Ruck didn't want no one to know the truth of what happened.

You may be wondering why all this matters, if maybe this is just some people curious about other people's business. But I would say no, and for you to understand I will tell you a little about the Brotherhood.

I will not reveal secrets, as our trust in each other and in the Craft is the hold that binds us together. For it is a fact well known we believe in Truth above all, Truth of Pure Spirit, for it is Truth that keeps a man humble, serving God and his country. Also, we don't ask people if they want to join. This is something a man has to come to on his own and that is the rule no matter what. Like with Jon, over which I've spent many an hour asking the Lord for that particular door to be opened. But Jon showed no interest and no matter how hard I wished otherwise, I could not offer up the idea, even as a suggestion.

Ruck, though, was different. He inquired, he done the work, he passed. And even if that was touch and go at times, even if parts I had to handle on my own given the nature of some things, in 1846, Ruck Young became a member of Catlett Lodge No. 36. It was the year before I married Salley Belle Cooper, and it was twenty-one years since his love, Tilly Perkins Young, died in the arms of his brother.

CHAPTER ELEVEN

Elizabeth

November 1854

I HEARD TELL OF BEN GRUBB SEVERAL TIMES OVER THE next months, stories that wandered in here and there about what he was up to, what a sad state it was that the oldest boy of such a fine man had gone wild since his daddy died. Some of those stories I took to be a bit far-fetched, taking on a life of their own as they got released in the world and passed from one mouth to the next. But some of them rung true, including the one that involved a dare and Billy Ray Rucker and two weeks in the Russell County jail. I worried over him, I surely did. But after weeks and months had went by, I started opening up to what Miss Kitchens had said along and along, that perhaps she was making a good point after all. Maybe my mind would be better occupied if I was to be busy considering something other than Ben Grubb.

It didn't take long for that to happen.

We'd just finished supper when Papa got up to go out. It had been snowing all day—something more likely to happen later on in winter, not November—and he was worried about the roof on the barn. He was gone for the longest time, and Mama told Will to go see what was keeping him.

"I'll do it," I said. I saw Papa's footprints in the snow, and I tried my best to match them step for step, making a game of it, stretching to see if I could make the whole way without my boots getting wet. They took me right to the door of the barn and I pulled it open and went in.

I couldn't see much, it being mostly dark in there. "Papa?" I said.

He didn't answer, and when my eyes got used to the light I saw a shape on the ground and realized it was him. His body wasn't moving.

I ran to him, my knees hit the dirt, and my face got so close to his mouth I could feel it breathing. He was on his back, one leg stretched out and the other tucked under, his eyes closed shut. "Papa, can you hear me, Papa?"—but nothing came from him at all. His face was tilted to the side, so I turned it up straight where I saw there was a line of spittle running wet from his mouth to his ear. I took my hand and wiped it away, then I wiped at my eyes, then I ran my hands over him thinking there must be blood or a cut. I didn't find one, but his arm was bent odd next to his head, so I straightened it out. That's when I saw a little carved bird I reckoned he must have been holding. I reached for it and slipped it into my pocket.

After that some details feel blurry: Thomas and Will carrying him out; Papa laid flat on his bed, the wedding ring quilt tucked tight; Lucy taking charge, with Mama in a state.

Will took off after Doc Ramey. I knew he'd ride like the wind, still time stretched long as I pulled a chair up and told Mama to sit, hold his hand, and I thought what a funny thing it is when the child is the one telling the parent what to do. There was a blanket on the floor and for the first time in their lives the twins sat quiet, neither fussing nor fidgeting, just watching. "I'll read from the Bible," I said, opening the book to Psalms. I knew it to be a comfort, and so I started at verse one.

Mama pulled Papa's hand to her chest and she rocked back and forth. "Amen, amen, amen," she said over and over, and she shook her head caught up in the words like this was her prayer and it was on her to get this turned around, like if she prayed hard enough and petitioned fervent enough God might see fit to let Papa come to. I wasn't so sure. But I kept reading anyway, hoping Papa could hear, although if he did he never moved nor opened his eyes but just laid there, barely breathing.

"'For the Lord knoweth the way of the righteous: but the way of the ungodly shall perish.'"

Behind my words were thoughts I didn't want nobody to hear and that went double for God. I was thinking how ever since losing Uncle

Ruck, I could feel something was coming. Papa did what he had to, like running the store and keeping the farm going even if he leaned heavier on the boys. But it was other things I'm talking about, under-the-surface things where you know they're there but you can't quite get a clear picture. Like the trout that collect in the deep blue pool at Devil's Bathtub. From the time we were little, me and Will loved to go up there and lie on our bellies on the cool of the rocks of the outcropping. We'd scoot to the edge where our heads looked over and our arms hung loose over the ledge. You could smell the dirt and the moss and the leaves and the wet, and I'd breathe it in, letting the earth of it settle in my bones. Will was always trying to count the fish, making a game of it, and I would play along even knowing it was a silly and impossible thing to do. You'd see shadows pass here and there, gliding in deep water, but you could hardly ever make one out.

I had made it a good ways through the book of Psalms when Thomas got back with Doc Ramey. There wasn't much change in Papa, who was just laying there looking for all the world like he might already be dead. Doc asked us children to leave the room, and we did as he asked, even if I worried about Mama without me or Lucy to hold on to. She was fragile, was the thing. She'd already lost two children, and she wasn't sturdy mountain stock to begin with. She was ten years old when she came here from Pennsylvania and I guess by then a body knows what it's made of.

Lucy set about getting Aida and Amos ready for bed. They were ill-tempered so she tried being stern but that didn't do any good. We all felt a combination of tired and worried and worked up, and when that's the case it's awful hard to ask somebody to be patient and to wait. In time the door opened, and Doc Ramey stepped out. "It's very serious, I'm afraid," he said.

I reached for Lucy's hand.

"I want to explain what's happened, and your mother has asked me to discuss with you the decision that comes next."

Thomas pulled Aida in front of him and put his hands on her shoulders. Amos stepped closer to Will and stood there, a brave little soldier.

"The body is filled with tiny tubes that carry blood to and from the heart. Blood travels through these tubes to get to the tips of your fingers, and the ends of your toes, and even to the tip-top of your head." Aida nodded big, like this was something she had been knowing all her life. "This evening, there was a problem with one of the tubes in your father's brain. It got too full and started to leak, and his skull has filled with blood." He stopped here a minute, and when he did we could hear Mama praying in the room just behind. "There is something I can do that might help." He lifted a hand to his neck and rubbed up and down along the side. "I can make a cut into the big vein in his neck—the one right here—to let some of the blood drain out."

"Will it hurt?" asked Amos.

Doc Ramey smiled. "No, son. It's a miracle of the human body that when it has suffered a great trauma like this, it puts you in a very deep sleep. That's what's happened to your father. He won't feel anything that's going on."

The cabin was still, not a sound from the bedroom or Mama or any of us except for my beating heart.

"Is he gonna die?" I asked.

Doc Ramey looked at me with such kindness I thought I might cry. "I want to tell you everything will be fine, that we'll do this and Jonathan will wake up his old self again. But the truth is I don't know. Apoplexy of the brain is very serious. Bloodletting it is difficult business. There are lots of potential complications. And even if the venesection—that's what it's called, venesection—even if the procedure itself is successful, there's no guarantee your father hasn't suffered damage already. He could wake up paralyzed or with some loss of mental functioning."

He paused like something had just come to him. "Jon's not a young man. That makes it all the more risky."

I was fighting tears. "Then why do it? Why put him through something so terrible?"

"It's the best option we have for bringing your father out of the coma, and for minimizing any damage to his brain. But I can't do it without the family giving permission. And your mother is not up to the task."

All our lives she'd leaned on Papa, never willing to stand on her own two feet or take her own side on things. It was always "yes, Jonathan, of course, Jonathan, whatever you say, Jonathan." It'd never seemed right, not to me as a little girl, not to me then. And that's when I knew: I will never be like my mother.

"There is something else we must consider," Doc Ramey went on. "To have any chance of being effective, the bloodletting would have to begin immediately. I'd need at least one of you to help me. Two would be better."

"I'll do it," I said. "Me and Thomas. Lucy's too squeamish. And Will is better with Mama."

Doc looked around at each of us. "Are you children sure?"

Heads nodded "yes," one or two said it out loud.

Me and Thomas it was.

THERE WASN'T THAT MUCH TO DO TO BE READY FOR the bloodletting. We washed our hands to our elbows and Doc wiped down Papa's neck, then applied a tonic to it. Lucy got a bowl for collecting the blood.

Then Doc told Thomas to stand on the left and me on the right with him positioned in the middle, just above Papa's head.

"This is a very delicate procedure, but we need to move quickly. We don't want Jon to bleed out, and we don't want any air to get into the vein." He used his fingers to poke around on Papa's neck which I half expected him to open his eyes or cough or shift, but he didn't move at all. "We'll work together to make sure neither of those things happens." He was leaning over but raised his head to look stern at both of us. "Right?"

"Yes," I said.

"Yes," said Thomas.

"Now, Elizabeth. Reach across and place the fingers of your right hand at this point, here, on the vein. Feel that? You're going to press with enough pressure that you feel the vein, the circumference of it, but not so much that you cut off the flow." I nodded like I knew although I felt unsure. "Don't release the pressure at all until the moment I tell you to stop. It's very important that these actions be exact.

"Thomas, you hold this container just beneath the incision to catch the blood as it flows out. It should fill and be emptied two or three times, into the basin at your feet. Do this quickly; we don't want blood spilling. Both of you will need to watch what I'm doing and listen to me to be sure you do exactly as I instruct."

I looked at Thomas, trying to hide how scared I felt.

On the table next to Doc was a wood box holding three long, thin instruments. The plate across the top said STUDY NATURE NOT BOOKS and I have to say the thought in the moment did not bring comfort. But Doc Ramey moved with a flow that made me know he had done this many times before. He picked the one with the thickest wood handle and looked it over, holding the shiny blade so close to the lamplight, I saw it flash.

He found the spot again and I pressed like he had showed me. I could feel Papa's heartbeat in my fingers, every little thump as blood pushed through. A drawing in our school room showed a person without skin, just muscles and organs and veins running all around, a system. I tried to think of Papa's body like that, standing apart from it like a doctor would. But this was not easy. He was right there, his face so familiar and not two inches from my arm, so close I could feel his breath. I prayed he was dreaming sweet dreams that took him far away from this mountain, from whatever pain he was carrying, from this room and the awful thing we were doing to him.

Doc Ramey moved his hand lower, just above the collarbone. He brought the blade close, turned it face up and sliced into the skin. Red blood spurted into the air and my own heart jumped. Thomas moved quick to get the bowl beneath it. Doc Ramey reacted, too, and whatever he did got things to calm down, the stream not coming so fast. I don't know if I jerked at the surprise of it or not—I worried maybe I was pressing too hard, but Doc didn't give me any more directions. He wasn't talking at all, as a matter of fact—his attention was on what he was doing.

I looked over at Thomas, and his eyes were on the bowl in his hands which was now half full of Papa's blood. I wondered if he was thinking about how he was going to get it emptied and back to the bedside without making a mess. I was. That's when Doc Ramey said, "We've got the stream steady now. Good. Elizabeth, very slowly I want you to lift your fingers from Jon's neck. Slow and steady. There. Good. Now walk around behind Thomas and lift the basin until it is just below the bowl."

I did like he said, my arm now reaching between Thomas and Doc Ramey.

"Thomas, when I give you the word, dump the blood into the basin. Use one quick motion, then get the bowl back in place. Okay. Ready. Now."

Thomas did this like he'd been doing it all his life, a doctor's assistant by trade.

"Elizabeth, we'll need you to hold the basin there while we do this two more times. Can you do that?"

"Yes, sir," I said, although I wasn't sure. It wasn't an easy position to be in, my arm stuck straight out like it was, wedged between the two of them. I was afraid it might start to shake, especially if it got heavy. I couldn't let that happen. I had to prove to Doc and Thomas and even my own self that I was the kind of person you can count on. I had to do it for Papa.

"He's bleeding well," Doc said. "We're going to empty it a second time. Okay, Thomas, now."

I held my breath and he poured. It was quick and the bowl was back.

"This third will be enough. Elizabeth, put the basin on the table and come back around beside me."

Thomas had to step to the side for me to pull the container back between them, and he did this without me asking. There was a lot of blood when I looked down into the white metal bowl, the shocking red now turning a deeper hue as if it, too, was settling into this awful situation. I held to the bowl's broad lip with both hands as I set the container down on the pine table, the thick blood sloshing just a little.

I looked again at Papa as I came back to the right side of the bed. Was there a change? Did his face show relief?

"I'm going to stop the bleeding by tying off the vein. Elizabeth, put your fingers in the same position they were in when we started. Yes, there, good. This time I'd like you to apply a little more pressure than before. Press down hard, as if you are trying to stop the blood from flowing. All right. Now."

I pressed and the vein slipped as if it had had enough and wanted to get away from me.

"That's all right. Try again. Find the pressure point just before the vein wants to move; use the flat of your fingertips to feel. They will tell you. Yes. Right up to the edge of it. Good."

I closed my eyes, picturing the veins, trusting.

And then it was done. Doc Ramey had slipped a thin thread and tied a quick knot, doubling back for good measure, and the bleeding stopped. I pushed the skin together with my pointer fingers (this was more difficult than it sounds) and he put a bandage over it. Thomas poured the third bowl of blood into the basin.

"Wash up now. And take care to do it thoroughly, just as before."

I stood by Papa's bed not wanting to move. "What happens next?"

"We wait," said Doc. "I'll stay here through the morning to keep an eye on him. These next hours are critical."

I nodded my head yes, looking at Papa.

"There is the matter of disposing of the blood. Some people will simply throw it out, like a pail of old dishwater. But in respect to the body, I believe human blood should be buried, and right away."

"Yes," I said. "And we can pray over it, pray for Papa's return to us."

The words had hardly left my mouth when Papa's body twitched, the first time he had moved since I found him in the barn. There was one quick jerk, a tiny one, and then he was still again.

"He's likely to do that off and on as he adjusts to the new blood volume. It's not necessarily a good sign—but it's not a bad one either. So we'll just be patient and wait. We need to give his body time to do some work we can't influence."

"We can influence it by praying," I said. "I'll find something to hold the blood."

Thomas put his hand on Papa's arm and rubbed it, his eyes more serious than I had ever seen them.

"I want you to know something before you leave this room. You have done something remarkable tonight," said Doc Ramey. "Apoplexy of the brain is traumatic, and we don't know the extent of the damage. We don't know if Jonathan will or even can recover. But what you have done here has given him the very best chance." He tilted his head down and looked at us over his glasses. "Your father would be very proud of you both."

I FOUND A MILK JUG IN THE CUPBOARD AND TOOK IT without asking, figuring this to be one more thing Mama wouldn't be able to make her mind up over. Thomas cleared a spot for the burying which all of us agreed Papa would like, it being under the crab apple he planted just after Uncle Ruck died. It was something to see, Thomas's shadow digging in the dark. He'd brought a lantern that hung on a low limb, and I have to say it was quite beautiful the way the light hit the snow. My sister'd got the twins to sleep, and Mama wasn't leaving the bedside now that Doc had let her back in, so the blood-burying and the praying over it was up to the four of us.

Snow crunched under our boots as we made our way to the tree. Will was carrying the jug, and when we got there he handed it to Thomas, who leaned over and slipped it in. This seemed right, Thomas having done the collecting in the first place, and when he stood back up he took Lucy's hand and she took mine and that started us all making a circle.

"I'll do it," I said.

We bowed our heads.

"These have been some hard years, Lord," I prayed. "You know that, I reckon, it being your job to keep watch. But the thing is Papa's wore out from all the trouble he's had to deal with. He's hard on all of us, I won't say different. But he doesn't deserve all this. Papa doesn't deserve pain and suffering because at his heart he's a good man, a decent man who his whole life has only tried to do what was right. What he believed was right, anyway."

I could feel three sets of eyes staring at me.

"So what I'm asking, Lord, is this. Don't make Papa suffer. He's done a life of that already. Bring him back to us, if that is your will. But if not, please don't make him suffer anymore.

"Thank you," I said. "AMEN."

Amen, came the chorus, some of these with less enthusiasm than the others, in particular Lucy who was giving me the side-eye. We each got a cold handful of dirt and threw it in. Will covered the hole, and Thomas tamped it down and pressed it with his boot. There were four flat stones, and he laid them on top. "Sun'll be up soon," he said. "We'd best be getting back to check on Mama."

Now that this was done, I was starting to get a chill on, and I put my hands in the pockets of my coat to warm them. That's when I felt the carving. Had that only been last night? It seemed a lifetime ago, and I rubbed my thumb over the bird knowing its shape, feeling the surface and thinking how sanding and time both had worn the wood down smooth. Where had it come from, the little bird? Why was Papa carrying it?

I felt ridges along the flat bottom where something seemed etched. A name, was it? Or a date? I wanted to pull it out to see but I didn't, the path still being dark, and also there being others around and this felt secret. I liked having it secret, something between Papa and me even if he wasn't yet aware. I got to the house and I climbed into the loft and I held that little bird to what little light there was. Sure enough, there on the bottom in tiny carved letters it said M.R.Y. Around the letters was a heart.

I tucked the little thing under my mattress, then I crawled under the blanket, and after a time I slept.

THERE WAS NO CHANGE IN PAPA FOR THREE DAYS. THEN his skin started to swell and Doc Ramey came back with the leeches.

It was a nasty business. Those slimy creatures latched onto Papa's neck and temples and their bodies puffed up as they sucked out the blood and infection. Over four days Doc applied sixteen of the things,

letting them get their fill until they let go on their own. It was all I could
do to go into the bedroom to see him during that time. I found it disgusting; I gagged, and I choked it down. But I knew this was something I
had to do. It had become my practice to sit with Papa whenever I could,
telling him how everything was going fine, how Thomas was filling in
for him at the Mercantile with help from Mister Red; how Will and
me were taking care of the farm, which didn't require that much as it
was the dead of winter; how people of this community were stopping
by on a regular basis to check on Mama and to wish him well. He was
loved, I told him over and over, this was why people traveled here to see
what was needed, how they could be of help. All the while I hoped and
prayed. I hoped and prayed that this deep, deep sleep was fixing something that needed fixing, that Papa would come back to us and when he
did, he would be restored.

Then one day I was doing chores when I came back to find of all
people Ben Grubb standing on our porch. I didn't realize it was him at
first, seeing him only from the back, then Lucy motioned and he turned
around.

"Look what the cat drug in," I said. "If it ain't that boy from the
Little Band."

He laughed and it was like light dancing through the trees in summer. "If it ain't that pretty girl with all them big opinions," he said. "At
least I think it's that girl."

I was caked in winter mud having been with the hogs. I took the
back of my hand and tried to brush a big stiff chunk away from my face.
He sat back on his heels looking me over, looking tickled.

And then my sister invited him for dinner and good lord but he accepted. I stomped right past the both of them not even caring about the
trail of filth I was leaving behind. How dare she, I thought, how dare
he. Why months had passed, months and months since we'd met at the
Primitive Baptist Church and what had Ben Grubb done over all that
time but get himself quite a reputation.

The very idea.

I poured water into the washing bowl and splashed it on my face, rubbing in circles to loosen the dirt. It was ice cold of which I was glad, me needing to get my head in order, needing clear thoughts on what I was gonna say to Ben. I wiped down my neck and arms and hands, then I took to my hair with a wide-tooth comb. That was no use, the clumps were too thick, so I leaned over the bowl and let the ends swish until the water itself turned milky brown. I pulled it all back, gave it a twist, and pinned the dripping mess where it was at least up off my neck.

I got out of the muddy britches and put on my work frock and apron. I could have picked the good dress, I suppose—it is the prettiest shade of blue—but Ben would know I had thought of it like that and I was not about to give him the satisfaction.

HE WAS ADDING WOOD TO THE FIRE WHEN I WALKED IN and saw there was a neat, new stack by the hearth. Lucy had the table laid with such a spread of food, she must have pulled out every morsel anybody ever brought. I was about to offer this when she turned to me and said, "There you are, Elizabeth, don't you look pretty. I'll get the twins and we'll eat. Ben, you sit here." She was touching Thomas's chair, the one beside her and right across from me.

We hadn't been alone two seconds when Ben said, in a whisper, "I just learned your father is ill. I was worried. I had to see you."

"Who's that?" said Amos, Aida on his heels.

"Why, this is Mr. Ben Grubb," said Lucy before I could even speak.

"I'm a friend of Elizabeth's," Ben said. Then he stuck out his hand toward my little brother.

"I'm Amos Darnell Young, and this here's my sister Aida. Aida Marie."

"How do you do," said Aida, and I swear if she didn't curtsy.

"Where's Will?" I asked, not wanting to sit where I could not escape Ben's eyes.

"The supply coach came in this morning so Thomas asked him to help at the store. Mama's sleeping—she was up most of the night—so looks like it's just us for dinner. Shall we?"

Ben stepped behind Lucy's chair and made a grand gesture of pulling it out for her. The rest of us just sat.

"Elizabeth, perhaps you could offer grace," Lucy said.

I answered her with squinting eyes. "Let's pray," I said. "Heavenly Father. We thank you for watching over our daddy, Jonathan Young, and we thank you for the food we are about to receive." Lucy cleared her throat. "We are grateful for the love of family. We are grateful every day brings with it the opportunity to be surprised. Amen."

I COULDN'T SAY WHAT WE TALKED ABOUT OVER THAT meal, although we must have discussed something. Seems like much of it centered around Ben and his brothers, one of which is my age and then two younger. He has a sister they call Boo, who is slow, I was interested in that. But I didn't say much. Mostly I kept my attention on my food. Then when lunch was finished, Ben asked would I like to take a walk.

I couldn't possibly, is what I said, there was so much needed tending to.

"For heaven's sake, go with the boy," Lucy said, which I didn't even know she was listening.

"I won't be long," I said.

WE WALKED A GOOD WAYS WITHOUT TALKING AT ALL. The calendar had turned to December but still it was a beautiful day, bright and sunny, the air crisp and clean. The snow had melted but for the patches hanging on in shady spots, and the trees reached for the sky in that way I love, their limbs raised and bare.

"I was at your daddy's funeral," I pronounced, my patience pushed by the long silence. It came out brash, me having thought about this for so long the meaning had got sucked right out of it.

Ben didn't comment, didn't say anything at all.

"I wanted to be there. I wanted you to see me there."

A mockingbird flew past and landed on a branch just ahead. He whistled four times then trilled, hopping to face us as he spread his gray wings wide. There was a flash of white and he folded them back in.

"There were so many of us behind you, I was sorry you never did."

"I saw you," he said. "I saw you as I walked up. I saw you as I played. I saw you walk away." He stopped, reached for my elbow and turned me around, squaring my body to his. "It's why I've come." His hands were on my shoulders. "I needed you, Tess, and you were there. And now you need me."

Ben leaned in and put his lips to mine and we kissed. And I closed my eyes, and the world disappeared, and I was lost in time and space, without an anchor to hold me.

CALL TO ARMS

CHAPTER TWELVE

RED

IN TIME, JON YOUNG WOKE. IT WAS A MIRACLE AND A blessing but it was heartrending, too, him not regaining his speech nor his spirit. Doc said this happens sometimes when a body's been through a great suffering. Its brain will do odd things. I am sure this is true, but also I believe it's the case a person can decide his own darkness, he can draw a heavy curtain for partition when the light of life gets to be too much. I seen my friend do this. I visited him on the regular over those five or six years, and every time I found him right there on the porch, sitting back in that old rocker, his eyes laid up against Clinch Mountain like it was the only thing giving him breath, its color changing season to season and that rugged ridge line holding back the sky.

Year tumbled over year, and around Jon Young the world carried on. His children grew. Will left, and Thomas took over the Mercantile even if it wasn't what he had planned for his life. Lucy was running the household, watching over the twins and doing a good job at it—her looking to be an old maid, I reckoned then, plus her mother, Sara, never quite having the aptitude for it. And that Elizabeth. Lord, that Elizabeth, who stayed a handful even if you'd think as a woman of nineteen she might have grown out of it. She had not. She continued to do her own way in things, defying her daddy ever' chance she got, most specific being with Ben Grubb who she continued to see off and on even after she was strictly forbid to do so. Jon held quite a grudge against the boy, which he never did release, which made people wonder as to why this would be. I can tell you why. It was because Ben was so like Ruck is what

I think, striking in looks and also demeanor. Both tall and dark. Both wild at heart. Both good men at their core. Plus consider it—time Ruck was gone who come waltzing in but Ben, which right from the first and right out from under her daddy, what did he do but go about stealing Elizabeth's attention and her favor.

There was war coming, too, even if this was something it took us a while to realize. We knew of the issues and arguments, of course, politicians seeing to it of that. It just felt like those things didn't have nothing to do with us here, hid away like we was in the mountains. Why they're rugged, and hard to cross; they kept others out but also held us in. This made for ways of doing that was unto our own and carried generation to generation. We are of these mountains, is how it felt, our feet rooted to the earth like the oaks of the forest, standing strong, grounded deep, our will not bending to time nor circumstance. Neighbor fight neighbor? Brother turn on brother? In the early months of 1860, there wasn't many among us—save Pat Hagan, or maybe some of the lawmakers—who thought this was even a possibility. We was just going on with our days, our land and our families being what we valued most; our land and our families, it turning out, being what we was fierce to protect.

———

CHAPTER THIRTEEN

PATRICK

JUNE 1860

IT WAS WITH GREAT CONCERN THAT I READ THIS MORN-
ing's *Abingdon Virginian*. My interest in the approaching presidential
election is great, so confident am I its outcome will determine much
about the future of our country and our way of life in the South. I find
Senator Lincoln to be a thoughtful, brilliant man, but I do fear his election—if, in fact, he is successful in that effort—will lead to mayhem in
our country. South Carolina is already talking of secession from the
Union, and that bravado is sure to set the tone for much carryover sentiment among neighboring states.

I do understand the reasoning, may I just say that. Governor Gist has
notified other Southern governors of his belief in a state's sovereignty
and that because each freely joined the Union, each is free to leave if
the federal government fails to protect their rights and privileges. It is a
powerful argument.

And yet I stand in support of Stephen Douglas, a position not
shared by many Democrats in these Southern states. Some have gone so
far as to call Judge Douglas a traitor and are incensed he is traveling beyond his home state of Illinois spreading a message of compromise. He
goes on to point out that the South's favored candidate for president,
Breckinridge, has refused to even answer the question of secession but
has, instead, danced around it. He makes a strong case that support for
Major Breckinridge is, in a backward way, a real vote for the election of
Lincoln—creating the undeniable excuse to secede.

As to Marilee Kitchens, she stands with the majority of Virginians in backing Senator John Bell of Tennessee. He is popular largely due to his "neutral" stance on slavery, stating—as she has become vehement in arguing—secession is unnecessary since our constitution already protects the institution. I recognize it as the political play it is, made by a political operative, having little to do with ethics or values or good leadership in government. Instead, it is a campaign platform built to allow a presidential candidate to skirt the most pressing issue we have ever faced, all the while retaining his ability to maneuver wildly within it.

I said as much to Marilee yesterday, when we walked the valley road. It had been months since we'd talked politics; her father had passed unexpectedly in the year just prior, and the loss had left my friend distracted and distant. It was good to see her color return.

"This hatred you have of Bell," she said. "I do not understand it. He wants what you want: a country united under a constitution and system of laws already established."

"He is a federalist. He wants power and control."

"He wants unity," she repeated.

"He's a Whig."

"He's a *former* Whig."

"He's worse than a Whig. He's a Whig in sheep's clothing."

"Patrick," she chided.

"Whigs stand in opposition to everything I believe in. They are anti-individualism, anti-Catholic, anti-immigrant—"

"He is a *former* Whig who simply finds the options of Democrat or Republican too polarizing."

I was worked up, it was certainly true, the old Marilee in form with her ability to argue every position, to challenge any point, to jump sides on a whim. 'Tis the mark of a fine debater, yes, but as a trait it can be incensing.

(And it is the very reason, I suspect, she finds John Bell so appealing.)

Still the point is I do my best to stay apprised of political developments, and I take the opportunity as it comes to talk over these complicated matters with my fellow citizens. Some of the men here along the Commonwealth's western edge are informed, or at least passionate, while many are rather oblivious to the ominous beating of war drums, distant though they may be. This is understandable, the one thing upon which Marilee and I agree even if our paths to that conclusion are very different. She attributes the apathy to generational ignorance, understated though her actual accusation may be. I find this offensive and as much as told her so.

"I am an educator, Patrick. I am in the school, and day after day I see the challenges these children face. Very few of them have the encouragement and opportunities you and I have had. And you know why? Because their parents didn't. Because their grandparents didn't. And on, and on. It's not their fault, you understand, I am not casting blame. I'm simply stating fact."

"The *fact* is when it comes to the issue at the root of this presidential election, it is of little consequence here," I countered. "The *fact* is, in these mountains, the preservation of the institution of slavery is practically irrelevant."

"How can you say that? Virginia has the highest population of slaves in the country. Our entire economy depends on it. Surely you know that."

"Yes. And that population does not reside here, but is concentrated *east* of the Blue Ridge, where there are plantations and grand homes and money."

"Grand estates? That's the point you want to make? When you have just walked with me along the lines you have staked for an estate far grander than any this rural county has ever seen?" She stopped, put her hands on her hips, and turned to face me. "I have never before heard hypocrisy from you, Patrick Hagan. I find it rather shocking."

She looked beautiful in her rage, controlled though it was, and I smiled, lightening the mood. "You're changing the subject, Marilee, but I deserve that, I suppose."

"Then let's bring it back. How do you plan to build your grand estate, and run it, if not with slave labor?"

"I don't believe we were talking about my position on the matter." I did not care for her turning this discussion on me, even if it was a smart move defensively. "I believe what we were discussing is the lack of engagement in choosing our next president."

"And its impetus," she clarified.

"Yes."

"And what of the lack of foresight? There are significant ramifications. It's not just a matter of slavery."

"Yes," I said.

"Secession."

"Yes."

"War."

"Yes, potentially. Probably." I had read so much about this and still it felt shocking to hear the affirmation come from my own mouth. "And if war is the outcome, it will impact the western region of Virginia with the same vehemence as the rest of the Commonwealth."

"And yet your argument is people here are disengaged because they are unaffected, not because they are ill-informed."

Good heavens, but she could be infuriating.

"You have a right to your opinion, Marilee. I'm simply suggesting we would do well to talk about these issues, to raise the concerns as opportunities present themselves. 'Tis far better to be realistic than to skirt the issue, or worse—to go on believing these mountains provide some sort of protection or isolation. They don't. They won't."

She did not respond, and so I put a period on the end of our discussion.

"We *must* find a peaceable resolution. 'Tis the only way."

ALBEIT TO LITTLE AVAIL, I HAD FIRST TAKEN UP THIS cause the night of abolitionist John Brown's hanging, six months earlier. I was in my first year as Lee County's Commonwealth's Attorney, and I had taken a room in Mump's Fort, in the upstairs quarters of Coley's Tavern. At the end of a long day I would sometimes join the regulars for a pint or two, and on this particular evening there was debate concerning Brown, who had just been hanged for his role in the Harper's Ferry raid. Pleasant Kilgore vehemently supported Brown for every action, including Brown's inadvertent shooting of a freed Negro in the effort to engage and liberate slaves of the town. George Muncey took another view, saying Brown's actions were nothing more than the rantings of a crazy man intent on gaining fame of his own. I weighed in as I could, suggesting we take a moment to look at the situation from a broader perspective, consider the impact more nationally.

"To John Brown!" Kilgore trampled, raising his glass.

"Ain't toasting to that," responded Muncey.

I STAYED TOO LONG, AND I DRANK TOO MUCH. I MADE IT to bed around two in the morning and immediately I fell into a deep, dream-filled sleep anchored by a vision I could not shake. I was in a broad field where before me, in the distance, a grand mansion rose. It was stately and tall, with three pointed gables that stood in silhouette against the mountain that framed it. A high ridge ran long above, and rich mineral water flowed beneath, something I knew in the manner of dreams. The left third of the structure stepped forward from the rest, its lower brick featuring a curving bay window, and upstairs, a long single pane. The pointed roof was punctuated by a pretty round window, its details floral and feminine, while the house's right two-thirds were in a shadow created by broad double porches that wrapped the front, then the corner, then the side, all the way to the building's back edge.

A pathway lined in jonquils led to the house, and I began to walk it, their yellow blossoms swaying.

The front hall greeted me with wide wooden steps and a grand staircase. Large, steadying newels—mahogany, I believed—were carved in the detail of dogwood blossoms, while a smooth, polished banister curved up and away to a new landing on the second floor. A library was to the right, its walls lined with leather-bound books floor to ceiling, and on the massive desk lay open Montesquieu's *Law of the Land*. A stack of newsprint on the floor reached a foot high. To the left was a parlor, elegant but warm, and the portrait of a beautiful woman rested on the mantel above the fireplace. I studied her face and found it to be familiar and also not. She wore a long gown the color of wheat, the sash tied wide at her waist in...what? What color was that? Goldenrod, one might say? Her pose was formal, but her head was turned just toward the artist, a playfulness in her eyes, a mischievous smile on her lips. A breeze came through the open windows, and the drapes floated in, then out, the motion that of a summer day.

I journeyed upstairs, downstairs, through seventeen rooms. And then words came to me unvoiced but sure, something in context I found neither strange nor unsettling.

"What do you know of destiny, Patrick? What do you know of fate?"

I awoke and found myself so deeply moved, so struck by the dream's vivid detail that I arose and lit the lamp. I commenced to sketching what I had seen.

Three nights later the dream returned. This time I could see neither the house nor the land although I knew they were there, and I found myself kneeling in a mass of wet leaves and weeds, my palms cupped beneath the arc of a cool stream of water. My hands felt alive with the moisture and a great energy passed up my arms, into my shoulders, out to every part of my body. I did not move; I had no inclination to do so. Instead I stared as the water pooled and then danced along the edge of my fingers, a thousand tiny weightless droplets.

My beloved servant—I was on my knees—*I have blessed you.* My head was bowed, my hands outstretched. *There is work to be done. Go forth, son.*

Here I am.

Go with courage. Go in love.

There was a loud clap of thunder and I awoke. A storm was raging outside the window at my bed; lightning flashed and rain blew in sheets and I lay there until dawn, watching it all play out.

THREE MONTHS LATER I STAKED THE LINES FOR THE house, where Marilee and I yesterday walked. The land has been entrusted to me by Uncle, part of the Hunter's Valley acreage that holds the log cabin in which he and Aileen live. It is an offering of well-considered design, I know, as it anchors me here, our trio re-established with my return to the valley. It also gives me the distance I need for my own life to take root.

"So you're planning to return here full time?" she said. Marilee tossed the question in like it had little weight, like this was a topic we might simply bat about, lackadaisically.

"No," I said. "I will stay on as Lee County's Commonwealth's Attorney, in addition to maintaining my law practice here. I will continue to travel, doing both."

"Then why the need for such a house? Such an estate." She looked about. "I mean, is that prudent?"

For a single man, is what she meant. People were gossiping, I knew, just as Marilee's own hopes were rising.

"I believe land to be the most valuable of assets. I believe a man should honor his good fortune, should he be blessed. I believe it is appropriate and important that in service to my fellow man—"

"Good heavens, Patrick, this is neither a Sunday School lesson nor a citizenship test. I am merely curious as to your motivation. Just the other day, Elizabeth Young asked if you—"

"Eilís?"

"Yes. Eilís. She asked if you are content here. If you plan to stay. I wasn't sure how to answer, it being something you and I have never discussed. Although one would think"—she motioned about—"all this would indicate yes."

"Yes," I said.

"And so you have found your place."

"Yes."

She nodded.

"Why, do you suppose, did Eilís ask? 'Tis been months, maybe a year, since we've encountered each other."

"I don't know, Patrick. She can't settle herself, I suppose. She's in a predicament, living with that backwards father who went from strict and vociferous to strict and silent. And now her dreams are bridled to work at that farm. She admires you, I would say. She admires your journey. She's still carrying on with Ben Grubb, but awake in her is a need for more. For different. A person can't fault her for that. Certainly neither of us can."

"No." I considered Ben Grubb. "The banjo player."

She shook her head, her look one of pity. "Rich in talent, poor as a church mouse. Wild as a proverbial buck."

"Well, she always seemed a special one, Eilís. I hope she gets what she wants. I hope she's able to see through to what that is."

Marilee looked at me oddly, but she didn't offer more. Instead she turned the conversation back to where it had begun.

"Tell me again of the rooms. Walk me through one by one. I want to imagine them all; I want to hear every detail you can think a woman would love." She put her arm through mine, and then gently, surely, she guided us in the direction of my home's rising frame.

CHAPTER FOURTEEN

RED

I ALREADY HAD MORE THAN I COULD SAY GRACE OVER that day Ben come asking did I have time to talk. I remember being at the Livery early, there being a pack of politicians passing through and their horses requiring as much tending as they did, hanging about and stirring up trouble. There was a great deal of fussing over the election of our new president, which at that time was just a couple of months away. So I told him, "Grab you a pitchfork," and out we set to walking. Day was coming on in a layer of thick fog, and the field around us was flat and gray in that way that never suited me, how you can't see what is there and already familiar. It was the same feeling I was having with Ben, who now we'd got to the barn and I still didn't know what he was wanting. I had him climb to the loft and pitch down hay, which I piled high in the bed. It was good work, hard work, and with both of us at it, it didn't take long.

We loaded in. The wheels on the cart was just starting to roll when, "Ben," I said. "Son. You can help me all day but there ain't no pay." He grinned, then tucked his head. He rubbed at his knees. "Go on, now. Tell me what's got you so twisted up." His grin turned sheepish but praise the lord, he started.

"Well, Red—I'd say my question is—what I was wondering is— well, this." He took him a big breath, which in my experience is not what you want when you're sitting in my position. "As you know, me and Elizabeth Young have been courting for quite some time. And the thing is, well, I'm wanting to marry her." He said this like it was news, which it wasn't, the whole world was aware. "I need her to say yes is the problem. What I mean is, I need you to get her to say yes."

The path was bumpy, we jostled up and down, and I pulled gentle on the reins to get the gelding to slow. "Ben Grubb. You know well as I do that girl's got a mind of her own. Ain't me nor nobody else ever gonna get Elizabeth Young to do something she ain't inclined to do."

"Yessir, I know. I also know you love her like a daughter. And she's got this idea which is not serving her well. She thinks she's gonna leave here one day, and get a life far away that will be—I don't know, filled with poetry and palaces and primroses and such. But it's not real. For one, that place don't exist. And for another, she's not going anywhere. She won't leave her daddy. She won't leave her brothers, and she won't leave Lucy. She won't leave that farm, her believing now she's the only one can keep it going. Hell, she won't even leave Marilee Kitchens, which I believe that is the reason Elizabeth dreamed all this up in the first place. Naw. What that girl wants is a life of her own making. The problem is—time is passing on. Life is going by."

I should have considered. I meant to consider, but instead my mouth said, "You ain't helped things."

It came out hard, the way I said it, but Ben'd made some decisions over time that was bad and plenty that was questionable. He'd been reeling from the loss of his daddy, plus he'd had opportunity and gracious plenty of it. He'd left the Little Band by then, and he was playing with Donnie Taylor and that bunch night after night at one roadhouse and another. People came from miles around just to hear him play. There wasn't nobody better on a five-string banjo, and he was good on the mandolin, and the fiddle, and the harmonica, too. He had him a gift, which I'd say means the Almighty's up there watching over things and his intentions for Ben Grubb was mighty clear.

"There's parts of my past I am not proud of."

You don't say, is what I knew, there being many examples which included the one widow woman called Becky or Betsy or something along those lines who'd took to showing up ever' time they played. She had a nice voice and sometimes Donnie'd have her join in on the harmony, "Wayfaring Stranger" being one I particularly liked with her on them upper notes. Anyway, some things happened between her and Ben, some

I seen and some I heard about, and as a situation it did not end well.

"I mean it, Red. I want to do better. I want to be better. I want to become a man my daddy would be proud of."

"That'll take you some work, son."

"Yessir. Exactly. I know. It's why I've come to you. It's what I'm here to ask. I'm wanting to join up with the Masons, and I was hoping you'd be my sponsor."

If ever there was a bad idea, this was it, bad for so many reasons. For one, the Fraternity of the Ancient, Free and Accepted Masons don't exist for people to prove a point. Second, you don't "join the Masons," you approach the organization as a man already possessed of high morals and strong character and you are or are not accepted into the Brotherhood upon Examination. Third, and most significant in the case of whippsnapping Ben Grubb, apprenticeship takes time and commitment and attention—none of which this boy had in large supply.

"I'm wanting to join the Masons, Red, and I'm willing to give up my music to do it."

I pulled the cart to a stop even if it left the politicians waiting.

"Look, Red, my daddy told me was I ever to need anything, I was to go to you. You were the one he trusted. I was hoping you'd find your way to honoring that." Ben rubbed at his britches, knowing what he was asking. "Also, if you don't mind, I was hoping you might see fit to speak on my behalf to Mr. Young. Because, well, as you know, he's never taken to me, even if to this day I can't say why."

I give Ben Grubb a good long look. Then I *tsk-tsked* to get the horse moving again. We rode a while, me not responding while on some level I reckoned we both knew it was already done. There was no sense trying to change Jon Young's mind, but Ben as a Freemason apprentice? The boy was right, Stoley would want it, and I owed my old friend that. Plus there was something of which I just then considered. Ben of the Brotherhood would allow me to tell some things, unburden some things in a way that might matter, that might make for some good.

"I'll think it over," I said. I glanced quick at Ben to see he'd accepted my answer as the yes we both knew it was.

IT WASN'T TWO WEEKS LATER WHEN HERE COME ELIZA-beth. She didn't mention Ben but held out a fat wood bird, which she asked did I know anything about it. I stepped from the porch where I could get a better look, holding the carving in the sunlight and rubbing my fingers along the curve of its back. I couldn't help but smile to feel the little thing in my hands.

"You recognize it then," she said.

I could smell the cedar, the pine, I could see my daddy whittling, little shavings dropping as a block of scrap turned into something new. "It's a Worry Bird. Mama'd give these out as comfort to people she come across who had bad troubles. You're meant to hold it like this—see? You hold it in your hand, then you rub your thumb along the belly, where it's smooth and round. You rub your worries away."

"Look under its tail," Elizabeth said.

I did, and I was surprised to see there was something carved there, tiny letters my old eyes couldn't make out.

"M.R.Y. And there's a little heart."

I think I may have nodded but I'm certain I did not speak.

"Who is that, Red?"

"Where'd you get this?"

She reached and jerked the bird away, she stuffed it in her pocket and braced. "Papa had it that day I found him in the barn." She stared, testing me. "Look. I've been working on some things. Trying to figure some things. And come to find out—my daddy was married before." She was looking for me to react.

Lord oh lord oh lord.

"What I'm wondering, Red, is if there was a baby. I've come to think maybe yes, and I was hoping you would tell me."

"Tess, honey. You know it ain't my place to—"

"Urgh," she said, and shook balled fists, my response not even finished. She took a moment to collect. "Tell me this, then. You can confirm this, because I already found it out. Papa's wife was named Matilda. Matilda Jane Perkins."

"How did you—"

"So that part's true. Which means the MRY on this bird ain't carved for Matilda Jane...."

I had to stop this questioning, now. "I'm surprised at you. The very idea you asking me about your daddy's personal business."

She stepped back, the stern in my voice having done its work. Then just as fast she picked up and went on, the young woman before me holding familiar resemblance to a determined ten-year-old Elizabeth I remembered.

"If you won't tell me," she said, "if you *can't* tell me—which I suppose I expected—I have thought of another way. I am going to talk to Hester. There must be records—you might even have them here. I'd like to see them, that's all. Doesn't seem a lot to ask. Just a review of the facts, it regarding my family and all."

"There's no records here, honey."

"Then I'm going to Hoot Owl. She lives up there, right? I'll go alone, or perhaps you might take me, it being a bit of a journey."

"That ride ain't one for you to make on your own."

"I understand that. Really, I do. But I need answers, and I believe your mama has them. So I'm going, Mister Red. I'd be pleased to have your company, but either way, when I leave here I'm headed for Hoot Owl Holler."

Lord, but this girl was dogged.

"I'll get my coat," I said.

CHAPTER FIFTEEN

Marilee

September 1860

WEEKS PASSED AND I DID NOT HEAR FROM PATRICK. I waited, I wrote off the silence to his work, to my work, to our grand preoccupation with complex issues of national consequence. When weeks turned to months, I swallowed my pride and composed a note.

Patrick,

Forty days and forty nights until we elect a new president. Fortuitous? I think not. As the landscape has evolved since we've had the opportunity to discuss, I feel it is my duty as a conscientious Virginian to influence your position before you are set loose with a vote. I would also love to hear of the progress on your grand mansion, should you care to share.

Dinner, perhaps? At the Nickelsville Hotel?

I hear the Beef Tongue is excellent.

Affectionately,
Marilee

Two days later I received a response saying he would, in fact, be in Hunter's Valley on Saturday and he would send his man Isaac in the carriage to collect me. I could see the house in progress, then he and

I would return to Nickelsville for dining and discussion. Patrick was going to seek my opinion on things, is what I believed, whether as to Douglas's politics or the proper wall coverings for a formal parlor, it did not matter to me. He wanted my perspective, my input, and this was a very good sign indeed.

CHAPTER SIXTEEN

ELIZABETH

AS MUCH AS I'VE STOMPED OVER THESE MOUNTAINS, I'D never been to Hoot Owl, and despite my bluster I was glad when Red agreed to go with me. We took right out and as he'd said, the journey was not an easy one. Beyond the road the trail grew steep and narrow, and when we got to the dogleg, the rhododendron made into a laurel hell so thick I could not have found my way alone. A quarter mile on, we encountered another batch of branches so low both of us had to lie flat across our horses to pass.

"How long since you been up here?"

I asked him this because Mister Red is one I'd think of as doting, being kind in general and having a mother I figured to be elderly. He didn't answer. Whether he didn't hear or didn't care to, I still don't know.

On and on we rode, up and up, until against Clinch Mountain, and looking to be built into it, stood an old house of timber and stone, a waft of gray smoke winding from the chimney. In front was a woman with a mass of messy hair growing wild as a raspberry bramble. She was neither stout nor thin; young nor old; fazed nor unfazed. "Took you's a while," she said. I wondered how she could possibly have known we were coming, but Red didn't comment, and we simply followed her in.

The room was dark but warm, the rafters alive with herbs of every shape and kind hanging to dry: mugwort, cohosh, vervain, bittersweet, wormwood, hyssop, dandelion. At the hearth a fire burned, and a dance of shadows moved across the walls. Mister Red stopped just inside and removed his hat, which he hung on a peg by the door. "Hello, Hester," he said, and he crossed the rug to lean and kiss her cheek. It was an offering that struck me as more than the sum of its parts. She'd been a tall woman, Mrs. Hopkins, you could tell. She was stooped some now, but was still formidable. The gesture softened her.

"Go on now, sit. Both of you," she shooed.

She brought to the table three steaming mugs. I was anxious to get going, but before I could start it was Red who spoke.

"This here's Elizabeth Young. She's the daughter to Jonathan Young, who I believe you know."

Mrs. Hopkins nodded.

"She has some questions regarding Jon and—"

"She can talk, can't she, Red?" The scolding surprised and tickled me, and I would have laughed but for the woman's attention being full on me. "What is it you're looking for, child?"

I searched for how to start; I wanted to get this right. "My father, Jonathan Young, like Red said—well, of late some information's come to light that makes me think he might have been married some years ago, before he met my mother. There was a baby, at least I think there was a baby, and I was hoping you might could tell me something about it. About the birth. If there was a birth."

She did not react to this but looked at me like there was more I was needing to say.

"I suppose you're thinking I should ask him, which seems reasonable, but he has lost his speech and even if he could, he would not be willing to talk about it, at least to me. I know the name of his wife. I don't know what became of her or the baby, if there was a baby. Of late there's reasons I have become quite interested."

"Because you're with child yourself."

She said this matter-of-fact, like it was a normal comment to make.

"Oh, no ma'am. I'm not. I couldn't, that would be...." A little laugh escaped me.

Red sat back, his big body causing the chair he sat in to creak and moan.

"No ma'am. I am not."

Her eyes closed in on me like she still had things to consider. "Drink that tea, there," she said.

And so I did, and it tasted like wood smoke and green moss and licorice. I could feel something running through my bones, something unexpected, and it went up and down and all over, and I took another sip and the liquid soothed me.

"Maybe you don't remember," I said. "You must have delivered a hundred babies, Mrs. Hopkins, over all the years, more than a hundred. Perhaps there is a record we could look at together." An ember in the fireplace popped and it landed on an old rag rug where it settled and burned. I watched this and worried.

"Hester," she said.

"Ma'am?" I said.

"Hester." This time it was Red. "She never did like going by my daddy's name."

Hester got up now and walked to the hearth. "I remember," she said. "What I'm wondering is if it's worth revisiting. It was a long time ago." She turned to us, then stepped on the smolder to smother it.

"Yes, ma'am. Yes it was. The thing is, over those many years my father and his brother, Rufus Young—my Uncle Ruck, who...died—well, they seemed to have had quite a falling out. I don't understand it, really, I don't know why it happened. And now Papa is in a very bad way and I'm looking to help him. I believe it's his anger at Uncle Ruck that's at the root of it, and since it's too late for them to get things straightened out, to *reconcile* I would say, I thought maybe I could help. I hoped maybe I could find something—anything—from the past that might let Papa live his last years in peace."

I took another drink of the tea, and this time it tasted of snakeroot and honey. I set the cup back on the table and waited.

A *cluck cluck* came from Hester, an odd sound I heard though I didn't see her make it. "You was with me that night, wasn't you, son."

"I was," Red said, a fact that surprised me.

"You was a boy. What, twelve? Thirteen?"

"Something like that."

"And you remember."

"Yes'm. I do."

She nodded and then walked to us, taking up the seat at the other end of the long table and directly opposite Red. There was a great distance between them, and Hester closed her eyes and a long finger tapped the table, tap-tap-tapped until I couldn't wait any longer.

"Maybe we could start with his wife," I said.

Hester's lids flew open, and she put her gaze square on Red, and all three of us recognized it as the command it was. I turned to look at him, and when he caught my eye what he saw was a jumble of desperation and begging. He didn't start right away, but he did consider, and so I sat there, and I waited.

RED

IT WAS LIKE PICKING BONES, THE WAY OF MY TELLING, the choosing of what to pull loose and what to leave be. *A little shine might make this go easier.* I'd hardly had the thought when Mother set before me a big glug of her home-batch hooch. She was a woman who always believed a stiff drink held glory. I respected that about her.

I cleared my throat, the spirits having burned a path.

"Her name was Tilly Perkins. Matilda Jane Perkins, from over at Rye Cove. Her daddy was an old-time preacher from off somewhere else, I don't recall where. I don't believe there's any of that family left here in Scott County."

Mother nodded, closed her eyes, let me know her intent was for me to go on.

"Her and Jon was married, just as you found, and they was expecting a baby, just as you thought. But when time came for delivering, Miss Tilly's labor did not go good. Jon sent for Mama to help, and she had me come, too, and when we got there Tilly was in awful shape. Mama knew what to do, though, and she got right to it. She had me running here and there, fetching this and that while she said for Jon to get some air and some rest. He wouldn't budge, though, so she said hold Tilly's hand and offer comfort, which he did, rubbing her brow and talking sweet. I was just a boy at the time, impressionable you know, and it has always stayed with me how tender he was, how reassuring. It's what come back to me when my sweet Salley, God rest her—"

Grief overtook me then, fast and unexpected, the way fog rolls in over a high mountain. I willed it to pass, I closed myself off hoping the feeling might lift and fade. Elizabeth's hand come and covered mine and I noticed how warm it was, and soft. Ten years had passed since I'd lost my wife and I'd forgot what it is to feel a woman's touch.

I opened my eyes, took a slow drink.

"The baby got born just after midnight. She was tiny and sickly, and Mama wiped her off and wrapped her in a blanket and put her in Tilly's arms which was weak as water. Jonathan took her and he held her and he kissed that little baby's face and said her name, 'Rose, Mary Rose,' over and over. That got to me, so I slipped out, and I went down the stairs and waited in the dark."

"Mary Rose," said Elizabeth. "M.R.Y."

I sat quiet. It was bewildering what these old memories held.

"The baby died." It was Hester, who'd took up the telling, matter of fact but going on. "Its mother went into a deep sleep herself. I told Red to ride for Rufus, to get him and bring him back to the farm so he could help in taking care. But Jon would not allow it, and so it was Red I sent out to dig the tiny grave."

"But why didn't Papa—" Elizabeth tried, which Mama did not acknowledge and instead, addressed me.

"Ain't had a garden since, have you, son?"

Can't stand a shovel in dirt to this day.

We was near to the end of what Mama would tell, of what she could tell, if I was honest, and I was working to decide what would happen next. You could hear it when she spoke, her sound tendered.

"Tilly come to the second day. There wasn't no life left in her, but when she remembered about that baby? Out of her come a wail so deep it's the kind only made from a heartsick mother. In spite of what Jon'd said, I knew to send Red to bring back his brother."

I considered Jon and Ruck, and also Tilly, and who'd had a view to what, when. I considered Elizabeth and her hell-bent determination to get this entire story. I thought how Hester'd opened wide the door, and even so, there was plenty she'd never been privy to.

"I did like Mama said," I sighed. "I went after Ruck."

Elizabeth listened, now, her whole body leaning.

"Time I got to him he didn't ask no questions. He just jumped on his horse and rode. When we reached the farm gate he stopped. 'It's the baby,' he said. 'There's something wrong with the baby.' 'Yes,' I told him, 'the baby didn't make it. And Miss Tilly's not doing good either. Mama don't think she'll make it through the night.'

"Ruck took off, and when I got to the house he was already inside, and Mama was waiting for me on the porch. We stayed out there a good long time. It was just us two, there was a couple of chairs, and we sat and rocked not really talking just watching day turn to night. Lightning bugs had just started up—it's funny how I remember that—when Ruck come to the door saying Jon'd asked him to go home and to send the reverend. All things considered, he thought it was best if he did like his brother'd asked.

"Mama lit a candle for each of us and we went up the stairs. The bedroom was dark, but I could see Jonathan and Tilly both laying there, her head on his chest. Mama took my hand and we backed out the door, leaving them like that. She checked in through the night, then when the sun come up in the morning, Tilly was dead."

Hoot Owl was still, the air around us loosened in the sadness.

Hmm was what Elizabeth said.

I took me a drink.

Mama got up, and I knew just why. She was going to fetch the book.

Elizabeth

NOW THERE WERE THREE GLASSES FULL.

"To family," Red toasted, and all of us drank. The ancient ledger sat right there; it was hard to be patient and impossible, I noticed, to tell the last time the old thing had been opened. So many births recorded there, I expected, the histories of so many families. I wanted to get at it, to dig in. But I waited. Then later—two or three shots later, and with no prelude at all—Hester reached and slow, with such careful motion, cracked open the spine. Red held a light and page by yellowed page she looked through. Eternity passed. "Here we are," she said, finally. "1825. August."

She turned the heavy volume so it was between her and me. I could not understand what I saw, the pages filled with symbols and notations, the records, I guessed, of a woman who could neither read nor write. But here and there I did see words crudely spelled, words I supposed to have been written in a young Red's hand. "Jonathan Young," I read out loud. "Matilda Jane Perkins Young." Beside Tilly's I saw a notation and pointed.

"Child bed fever," Hester said.

Then words that looked to be *Rufus Young*. "Uncle Ruck? That's odd."

"That mark there," she pointed. "Father."

"But Uncle Ruck wasn't the—"

But yes, Hester nodded.

Uncle Ruck and Tilly? "No wonder Papa was so mad."

Hester rested her hands, her fingers spread wide over the pages. Her look turned peaceful, like all I'd wanted, she'd given. "I don't believe Jonathan knew," she said.

Red sat silent; I was more confused than ever. "Then Uncle Ruck claimed it."

"I don't believe Rufus knew," said Hester. "It was Tilly told me. Her and I was alone, and she said she wanted it wrote somewhere, she wanted a record of the truth."

"But if Papa didn't know, and Uncle Ruck didn't know, I don't see how—"

"Let me give you some advice, child," Hester said. Her voice had regained its edge, and it was thick with wisdom, and age, and experience. "You come here seeking truth, believing there's only one way of it. But the fact is truth comes with many sides. Your daddy was married before, yes. Your daddy had a baby and she died. Ruck may of been the baby's father, but it's just as true your daddy was the one its mama chose to marry. Jon and Ruck may never've saw eye to eye, but it's also true it was the deep love of brothers that went between them. The point is two things can both be the case at the same time. And accepting this is something might serve you well, Miss Elizabeth Young, was you to choose to remember it."

"But it doesn't explain anything," I said.

"Then I will add this. I been a midwife over sixty years, and in that time there's a great deal I've had a view to. What I can say is ain't no family nowhere ever gets it all worked out. Big feelings grow from hardly nothing at all, and your uncle and your daddy loving the same woman is gracious plenty to be worked up over. That's enough to build on for a lifetime compared to others I've seen. So let it be enough. Let the fact you got what you came for be enough. Your daddy's a good man, and your uncle was a good man, and they both done the best they could, that's what's the truth. And beyond that? It ain't yours nor Red's nor mine to figure."

I was working this over, trying to think how this could sound like enough and be not nearly enough all at the same time. That's when Red stood and announced it was time to get going, lest we'd find ourselves riding in the dark.

"You go on out, son," Hester said. "She'll just be a minute."

Red collected his hat and his coat, and he gave his mother a kiss and stepped to the porch to wait. He was hardly out of earshot when Hester's fingers took my chin and turned it so my face faced hers. "You, my dear, are expecting," she said.

"It can't be," I said.

Her fingers held tight, her eyes unrelenting. "I know what I see."

"But I can't be."

"You've had your courses, then."

The sting of tears surprised me.

"Your bleeding. When was the last time it came?"

I gathered. I tried to count. "June. Early July maybe."

"And it was as usual."

There had been more discomfort, less to show. I did not know how to talk about this.

"It often happens that a woman newly conceived will still find such evidence. Was that the case with you?"

"Yes," I said.

"And since. In the months since."

August, September, nothing. Hester read this like it was written in the air between us.

"Let's talk about what you're gonna do. You know who's the father?"

"But I'm not—"

"Elizabeth."

"Yes," I said. Yes.

"You plan on telling him?"

I've got no plan, is what I thought, but for one to get out of here, to live in a place where people don't lie and hide and cover, where your beloved hasn't already done business with god knows who and where everybody but you seems to know about it. Where you don't live out your days under your papa's roof with a mama who frets like it's her earthly calling to look after his every need; who makes space for his ridiculous silence, which by the way gets to hold sway over everything and everybody in every moment. Where your whole family's history ain't based on things that apparently were never true in the first place. Plan? My plan is to get the hell away, to get the hell out of these mountains.

"There are options," Hester said. It made me shiver. "Which I am not suggesting. I'm just saying you should know. Sometimes women, sometimes girls, decide it might be better if—" She stopped there, clasped her hands, glanced to her lap then back at me. "Well. I ain't meaning to convince you of anything. I just want you to understand your choices. Because it is a decision to be made now, Elizabeth, before I can't help you. The line you're straddling is already a fine one."

I stood and was relieved to find my legs held. "Thank you, Mrs. Hopkins, *Hester*, for this afternoon. I remain perplexed over Uncle Ruck and Papa, but at least parts of the story have come into the clear for me. I will try to be grateful for that."

There came a knock and there was Red, his head slipping through the door's opening. "Sorry, ladies, but night'll be coming on soon."

Hester rose. "I'll get it for you, child," she said. Red was waiting in the door it half opened and half closed, and by the time I'd readied to go she'd returned with a small sack, tied with a piece of brown twine. "This'll take away the lady pains. Boil it into one strong cup of tea." She reached the sack toward me and I took it; there was nothing else to do. Then she came closer, her voice at my ear. "Before the Harvest Moon. See to it." I nodded, I understood. "Now get on," she said, *cluck cluck cluck*. "Both of you."

IT TOOK ME UNTIL THE IVY HELL TO WORK MYSELF UP to asking. "Might you know, Red, when the Harvest Moon is?"

"That's Sunday, I believe," he said. "Yes, the Harvest Moon is Sunday."

Sunday. The day after tomorrow.

CHAPTER SEVENTEEN

MARILEE

SEPTEMBER 1860

WE ROUNDED THE BEND AND THERE IT WAS—THE FRAME of Patrick's home rising toward the heavens, its rafters touching like fingertips stretched in prayer. I could hardly take it in, grand in scale as the house was and set here, in these impoverished Appalachians. The size would be far more appropriate for Virginia's northern counties, which was not a surprise, of course; Patrick had talked in detail of the design and scope in all the conversations we'd had, and on the afternoon those months ago when we'd walked this valley and imagined it. He was so animated then, so filled with joy at the prospect. I'd felt it as well, listening to him talk of destiny and dreams, of blessings and responsibility.

Now, seeing the mansion literally take shape, a new realization formed. Patrick's establishment of this magnificent home was equally his *chef d'oeuvre*, his crowning achievement in the demonstration of all he had accomplished, of what he had overcome, of that which he had manifested through the opportunities presented to him in this country. *I did not squander it*, I felt the structure say, and I offered a prayer that Patrick's magnum opus would go a long way in silencing whatever voices he hears that demand such proof. I was reared in such a home myself, but it's equally true over my years here I have grown accustomed to life in a simpler space. My room in the boarding house is small, and over time I've considered leaving it, finding a suitable place that would allow me to spread out, to establish here a more proper residence. But every time the appeal fades. In the light of day (or dark of night), a single woman living alone in this wilderness is simply not practical.

And also, what would Patrick make of it, my taking such a bold move?

I looked around for my host as Isaac pulled the carriage to a stop. He secured things, then stepped down and came around to assist me, taking my hand as I disembarked. A great deal of mud greeted me, something of which I had been warned and for which he now supplied a large pair of men's boots. I was grateful even if the size made it difficult to walk. I was not accustomed to traipsing around on a work site like this, and of course I had dressed for dinner. I looked a sight with the silk of my skirts lifted and gathered, the boots laced high. Several times I nearly fell as I made my way toward the house, the mud deep and insistent, making known its preference to hold with every step whether my foot stayed in or not. Nevertheless I carried on, holding my head high and knowing others were watching.

"There you are, there you are," came Patrick's voice as he rounded the side of the house, his arms loaded with a short stack of bricks. "I'll just get these delivered." He walked away and I felt an inconvenience, an interruption, as if he had been assigned an important task and my arrival had delayed its completion. I did my best to shake off his lack of a warm reception and for the moment I simply waited. I was positioned so I could see the home's long east edge, and the depth was surely impressive. There were to be seventeen rooms; I could understand this now, with double porches that crossed the front, then wrapped, running this side the full distance front to back. I allowed myself the indulgent imagining of an early morning, the sun on my face as I stood on the upper level. I would stroll lazily down the line, past this bedroom and that, a fingertip trailing the porch's railing.

Then suddenly there he was, Patrick again, his shirt changed, his hair combed back. "Shall we?" he said and smiled.

I took his arm and we walked to the front. There he described the house's exterior, its seven gables, his plans for the wonder of *indoor* privies and modern steam heat. He'd had Stephen Gold design the system himself, and Patrick provided me with a very detailed description of boilers and low-pressure piping and radiators. I didn't care a thing about how it all worked, but I found the thought of a warm house without endless trips to a woodpile—not to mention an outhouse—very appealing. Who could imagine such luxury? We climbed the makeshift stairs, and he followed me as I stepped across the threshold to the interior of the framed-in structure.

Here was the front hall that would anchor an elegant staircase and carved banister (a girl could picture herself descending such stairs), a large library, a parlor and adjoining music room with a grand piano, a dining room and large kitchen, two bedrooms, and two separate privies. He held to my arm as we ventured up: four more bedrooms, these of note due to their number as well as their extraordinary views. I stood at the window facing west, and while it wasn't discussed, I knew Patrick owned every acre of land in every direction we could see and for miles beyond. He told me of his plans to plant the various fields, pointing them out; of adding a small dairy; of building a corral for sheep.

"It is certainly ambitious," I said. "Do you expect to continue your practice of law? Or will you devote your energies to all of this?" I swept my hand in a broad, very dramatic gesture, overemphasizing my point.

"Both," he said. "Which reminds me: We must take a walk to the springs. Blue Sulphur. An elixir, a holy gift that flows right through this property. I will drink of it every morning, and that will do much to keep me strong and healthy." I remembered this from his dream, still I was surprised at his declaration. "There is so much God has for me to do."

I walked with him through the muck and mud, further soiling the hem of my dress. I did not care for the smell as we got closer—eggs left to rot in hot sun—still, Patrick insisted I "take the waters," cupping my hands under the flow and bringing them to my lips. The taste was foul, and I spit it out. Then hastily I reminded Patrick of our plans for dinner. He eyed me as if deciding whether to push. He did not but acquiesced. "Yes, then," he said. "Let's be on our way."

THE RIDE TO NICKELSVILLE WAS A PLEASANT ONE, THE afternoon pretty and our conversation filled with stories from our lives in recent weeks. I loved it most when he'd get going with tales of the people he served and their trials and tribulations, which often involved copious amounts of alcohol and the most absurd resulting situations. I told him of school, of life at the boarding house, of letters from home. It was conversation that came easily, for we were a companionable pair. "Your finest table!" he said, once we reached the hotel, and his voice was jubilant even if his request was unnecessary. For everyone in Scott County knew Mr. Patrick Hagan, Esquire, and we were quickly shown to the most intimate spot in the dining room. I looked across at him, and my pulse quickened. My heart fluttered, I am not ashamed to say.

"Jake Johns, my good man," Patrick said as the familiar proprietor approached. They slapped backs good-naturedly, then Jake turned to me. It was a familiar scene, us three, even if it had been some time since we'd last dined here. "And you, Miss, as well," Johns nodded.

"Miss Kitchens and I are celebrating tonight, *an aontaíonn tú*? Bring us your finest brandy!" This surprised me a little, and excited me a lot, as I could only guess as to what he was referring. "Yessir," said Johns, and he winked at me as he walked away. *He's going...to propose*, the dream formed, *tonight. This will be the night.* I tried to push the thought away, but instead it hung there in my consciousness, brash as knickers on a clothesline.

Patrick talked on, about what, I've no idea. Then as soon as the drinks arrived, he raised high his glass. The moment stretched long and gorgeous as the amber liquid shone gold in evening's light. He looked deep into my eyes as he waited for me to reciprocate. I blushed, looked down, then raised my own brandy to toast.

"To the girl of my dreams," he said. "Hagan Hall. And to Sulphur Springs, the name I have given my estate."

His smile broadened, and he tipped his glass toward mine, to clink. *To both*, I may have said, or maybe not, for as I sipped, I tried not to choke and hoped he wouldn't notice.

DO YOU KNOW WHAT IT IS LIKE TO FULLY INFLATE YOUR lungs? To lift your chest, and expand your torso, to breathe air in, in, in, in, until you have reached maximum capacity? You can hold it there only a moment, confident and satisfied and satiated, until minutely— almost imperceptibly—you realize the only choice available to you is *let go*. Release. And so you do. Slow, controlled, your body deflates until your muscles relax and there is simply no more. There is only empty. You have been emptied.

So it was with me in the afterward of those confusing brandy moments. Years of waiting, wishing, hoping. I let it all go slowly. I relaxed back into myself, and with the man of my dreams sitting right there across from me, I regained normal breathing.

It will not happen, I knew then, *not with Patrick Hagan. Not even if he asks.*

Which, of course, he never will.

———

CHAPTER EIGHTEEN

Elizabeth

RED AND I WERE JUST DOWN FROM HOOT OWL, NEAR TO the clearing, when who did we see but Ben Grubb. He was astride Buck, and him and the colt stood crossways over the trail. They looked to be one, all shadow and outline, a big round sun lowering behind them as the sky pushed a fire of orange through the trees. I pulled my horse to a stop.

Red rode up beside me.

"I need to talk to you, Tess." Ben's voice traveled sure and strong over the rocky path, flood waters clearing an overgrown ravine. "There's things to discuss. Things I need you to know."

My hand moved absent to my belly, which Red gave it a glance and I blushed.

"I'll ride on," he said, "that being what you want."

"Yes, Red. Thank you. For everything."

SUDDENLY RED WAS GONE AND WE WERE ALONE, BEN Grubb and me. Forty feet laid between us and we regarded each other at this distance, sitting stock-still. His eyes stayed trained until I couldn't take it anymore. Like always, I was the one who broke up the silence.

"What was it, then?"

Buck scratched at the ground, his head bobbing, him and Ben looking quite majestic profiled together in the light. "There's something I want to show you."

Now it was my horse acting impatient, a great gust of air blowing loud out her nose. "I need to be getting on," I said, leaning to rub her broad neck. "My family'll be looking for me."

"They won't, though. Lucy knows. We have time."

I should have been angry. I should have bucked up, a filly not willing to bridle in a situation she wasn't expecting. Instead my heels tapped and we walked toward them, and Ben click-turned his horse and so we followed.

Oh, Lucy, I thought. *Sweet Lucy, who always believes in love.*

WE RODE A WAYS, THEN WE CAME OUT OF THE FOREST and crossed a broad clearing to a grove fronting a stream. We wound along its path and, after a quarter mile or so, we turned again and I saw we'd reached a wide, rolling field. Tucked back was a tiny old cabin, a stocky stone chimney climbing up its side.

Ben dismounted, then he came and held up a hand for me.

"I can get myself off a daggone horse," I said.

"It's a nice spot, don't you think?"

I gave it a glance, not really noticing. Then over Ben's shoulder I spotted a big wide Buckeye tree. I happened to like that. "What was it you wanted to talk about, anyway?"

He smiled a satisfied smile. "It's ours, Tess. Yours and mine."

I had no idea what he was talking about. I thought maybe he'd got kicked in the head, or was trying to make a joke.

"It's land my daddy owned, and he's left it to me."

"But surely your Mama—" I said this, but he broke in.

"Nobody knew about it. Not even Mama, as the papers was just recently found. It took time to get it all verified, down at the courthouse you know, which Patrick Hagan was the one who discovered it in the first place. And now he's got things all worked out. It's done and it's mine, all of it. The land, the house, all of it. Which means it's ours, Tess."

He reached for my hand and this time he took it, pulling me forward with so much excitement I couldn't have stopped him if I'd tried.

"The old cabin is in bad shape, but we can fix it up. Me and Aaron and Levi already started. You'll see."

It was all I could do to keep Ben from running despite spent summer stalks nipping at his knees. My skirt caught everything an overgrown meadow holds: briars, grasses, tall weeds gone to seed. Plus the closer we got, the worse it looked, the house abandoned, the porch viney and rotting. There were big gaps in the rock foundation but the wide front stone step was swept, Ben's attempt at a picture of homekeeping, I could tell. On the right was a clutch of blooming mums somebody'd planted in a just-dug shallow hole.

"Don't say a word. Just come inside." The ancient front door creaked. "Wait. Hold on," and he lit an oil lamp that set off a nice glow. The place formed full around us.

It was good to have something to see by. We stood in a room framed by stacked split logs, the chinking between them old and crumbling. The left short wall had a stone fireplace and a slight hearth extending to a dirt floor. There was a long table pushed up against a back wall—the only furnishing in the room—and I could tell Ben had spent some time clearing the place out. He was still holding the small lamp as he walked toward me.

"Look behind you," he said.

I turned, and to the left of the door was...what was that? Three horizontal boards hung from a low ceiling beam, held by knots tied in three long ropes. I walked over, put my hand to the middle plank, and I rubbed it to find the finish smooth. It was something that must have taken great care and time. "What is this?"

"Shelves. For your books. Which I pledge right now over time we'll fill every one."

A library of my own, I'd never dreamed anything so grand, and I felt the wonder of his promise as my heart began to bend toward him with a wave of surprising affection.

"I want us to marry, Tess. We've talked about that. You know that. I'm not asking you to decide right now, but I want you to consider it.

Really consider it. Imagine us here. Together, in this home of our very own. Building the life we want, the life *you* want, whatever that looks like. We can do it, Tess. We can, right here. Because having this land and this cabin—that changes things."

"I don't know, Ben."

"But that's the point, don't you see? This makes for a new situation, and all I'm asking is for your consideration. You don't have to decide right now."

Oh, but I do, I knew.

"Look, Tess." Ben said this, and he stepped toward me, and he put his hands on either side of my face. "I'd marry you tonight. Right this very moment. I would have us move into this cabin and it just like this, dirt floor and all. But you deserve better, and I'm going to give it to you. I'm going to prove some things, regain your trust. I am determined to *earn* it. I've already started."

I turned and stepped away, I did not know what else to do. I was glad when Ben held his distance to give me some space. A fat tear formed and I wiped it away, my back to this man who with his whole heart believed every promise he'd made. If only things were as simple as Ben Grubb thought.

"I'll need to be getting on," I said. Whether he heard or not, I do not know; he did not move or speak. The front door stood open and through it I saw that night had overtaken day. I walked out into the dark.

Ben dimmed the lamp and came behind. "I'll see you home," he said. "I won't go beyond the gate, but I want to be sure you get there okay." And he did, us talking very little as we wound through the mountains making our way to the farm. A bright moon rose above the trees, seeming like it had come just to light our way. "Be full soon," Ben said, looking up.

"Yes," I replied, yes, as with every step, Hester's bottle knocked against my thigh. It was a disquieting reminder that be it for now, or be it forever, Elizabeth Young had a secret of her own to keep.

IT WAS SUNDAY AFTERNOON WHEN MARILEE KITCHENS came to say goodbye. I was shucking corn on the back stoop when Mama came 'round to say my teacher was here and requested a word with me. "My teacher," I said and laughed. How true that statement was, though, even if it'd been a long time since I'd thought of Marilee that way. What could she possibly want? Coming all the way here to Papa's? I got up, brushed the silks from my dress, and put the basket of cleaned cobs to the side. I went in to find she was waiting by the front door alone, and I was embarrassed my mother hadn't invited her to sit, or offered her a cup of tea. Marilee seemed all right, though, making me think there was something more important on her mind.

"I'm sorry I've come unannounced," she said. "But I've been called back to Charlottesville. Mother's had an incident, and I'm to leave to-morrow. Henry's coming to get me."

I rushed to her, put my arms around her, and felt my friend's stiff spine. It had been less than a year since her father had passed on, and I knew what a loss that had been. My nature was to pull Marilee in closer, hold her tighter, but as she had not relaxed, I stepped back and let my hands slide to her arms, where they held. "You okay?"

She nodded, but her look was unconvincing. "I won't be coming back. Mother needs me there, so I'm going home for good."

I pulled her back in tight; I did not know what else to do. Marilee consented this time, putting her arms around me even though they held slight. In short order, she patted and pulled away.

"I hoped you might have time for a walk. I've so little time left here in these mountains, and I'd like to spend it with you."

I was touched and also surprised. "Yes. Yes, of course. I'll pack us a picnic. There'll be no rush." I moved toward the cupboard and grabbed some things, hardly thinking, I was shaken and trying hard not to let it show. "A blanket. Let me get a blanket. It'll be like that day at the Clinch, all those years ago. Remember? You and me, headed for Alley's preaching."

"The night you first met Ben."

"The night you first met Patrick. Where is he today, by the way?"

"Oh, building his grand mansion, I am quite certain." There was a note of sarcasm I hadn't expected, and I made note to ask her about this again, once we were out of earshot. "Here, I've brought this satchel. Give me the quilt." She opened the satchel wide, and I saw at the bottom a pretty package she removed before stuffing the blanket in. "A little something for you. A parting gift, if you will. We'll save it to open later."

I gathered the handles, and we headed out the door. It was sunny and warm, and we took our time, walking and talking like the old friends we'd become, like we had all the time there is. The day was pretty around us, the sky its most perfect clear blue, and all this together caused me to look at things and see things in a way Marilee might, like you were figuring it could be for the last time.

So much of Scott County is fierce, all stark ridges and deep hardwood forests. But around here the land is gentle—friendly, even—with hills that rise and fall like the chest of a man laying in peaceful sleep. The fields spread out broad and easy, the colors of early fall starting to wash over like it'd been worked up by an artist with a wide, soft brush. This time can be tricky, though, late September, when it's both headed for winter and hanging on to summer. There were layers of the ripest mountain greens deepening still, while here and there a smattering of dry, crisp leaves rolled along our path. They seemed to have come from nowhere, their colors already burnt: dark scarlet reds; earthy browns in fawn and mushroom and dirt; waves of orange, gold, and crimson. The wind held tight, still it carried a slim chill and the quiet hint that change was afoot. Change, I knew, was coming.

We passed Papa's corn field, spent now, its long leaf stalks beginning to fade. The crop had been good this year, the rain sufficient in spite of Thomas's worries. We turned toward the valley where just ahead I knew of a giant old oak been there two hundred years. Before us rolled field after field, one after the other, until they reached the end-of-summer green of Clinch Mountain.

"I've done all the talking," Marilee said, the quilt now lofted and spread. We both were sitting, the basket beside me and her pretty package waiting, its lavender ribbon looped in a lazy, perfect bow. "Tell me about you. How is life at home? With your daddy."

There was so much to say and so little I could share. Ben, the baby, the herbs. Tonight was the Harvest Moon, and still I had not decided.

"Oh, you know. Papa is Papa—silent, disapproving. Still somehow his is the voice I hear."

Marilee nodded, and I knew it was in solidarity. We'd talked of her mother over the years, distant though they may have been, and while I didn't know the exact nature, I knew their relationship to be one of great complication.

"It must be hard for her, your mother. She must be very lonely since your father died. I know you being there will be a comfort to her."

"I suppose. But the two of us together, without him?" She shook her head. "He was always our buffer."

I wasn't sure what to say.

"My mother is...has always been...has created in me...oh, I don't know. I have come to realize I am damaged in some ways, and it's due to her hand."

"Her hand?"

"Her way, is what I mean. Her pressing. Her...insistence." Marilee looked to the quilt, picking at a loose thread. "I have always lived within her lines, I have always done exactly what she expected."

"I don't think that's—"

"Oh, it's true, Elizabeth. It's sadly true. And here I am now about to be not only an old maid but a *nurse* maid to a very bitter mother."

"You left home and came here. Surely that was not according to her plan."

"Hmmm," Marilee said, and a shadow crossed her face that chilled me. "I came because she demanded it."

"She demanded it? I don't understand."

"She banished me, Elizabeth. She believed I had embarrassed her, and so she saw to it I would never do that again."

"I can't imagine you doing anything of the sort. Why, you're so reasonable. So responsible!"

"Yes, well, I made the mistake of rebuking one very lecherous Edgar Allan Poe. And that, shall we say, infuriated her."

"Wait. I'm confused. You were a girl when you met Poe. That's what you told us in school."

"Yes. And he was a louse, and a drunk, and with me he was most inappropriate."

"Your mother condoned this?"

"She ignored it, at the very least. And all because she fancied her own status rising."

"Oh, Marilee."

"And then he came to Union to call on me—several times, actually, I cannot possibly understand why. But I refused to see him. They found him in the gutter dead not long after. Mother blamed me with it, some-how, Poe's sad, pitiful demise. And she demanded I admit as much to my father. I would not. And so she sent me away."

It was a new thought for me, and an unsettling one, to realize my friend had held this all these years while I'd babbled on about my own parents. It was a burdensome secret she'd harbored.

"Have you been happy here, Marilee?"

"Oh, I have been happy enough, I suppose." Her shoulders relaxed, her smile returned. "I've loved teaching. For some children, I think I have made a difference."

"You did with me. You made me believe I can go anywhere, do any-thing. And I am so grateful for that, even if—at the moment—I don't seem to have gone very far." The reality of this admission sat in my gut hard and heavy. Marilee regarded me in her most-Marilee way, and sud-denly I felt a child again, a schoolgirl who'd blurted out an answer her classmates knew was wrong.

"You don't have to go anywhere, Elizabeth. You can live a life of great fulfillment right here. You know that, don't you?"

"But I can't. There's so much to see. So much to do. You showed me that. You taught us that! Remember the day you had our class lie in the grass? You told us to look up at the clouds, that it's a big sky over a big world, and it extends far beyond what we could see. You said to remember that our view within these mountains—however lovely—is still a limited one."

She was uncomfortable. She didn't squirm, but she adjusted, then readjusted, then put both palms flat on the blanket we'd spread across the ground. "I have been the one with the limited view, I'm afraid."

"Whatever do you mean?" I asked.

Marilee smiled at my use of the fancy phrase, and so did I, knowing I was not a lady sipping from a porcelain cup but a girl with lemonade in a jar. "Just that I will be taking far more with me than I have contributed. I have learned a great deal in my time in Western Virginia, and much of it has been from you."

"Well that's just silly."

"It's not silly. Far from it."

"But you're everything I want to be. You're who I aspire to be. Why, you're Miss Kitchens!"

"I am, yes, and as it turns out, you already have what I so desperately want," she said.

"And what that would be, pray tell."

"Passion. Honesty. The courage of your convictions." She was being serious even if I found this hard to take in. "A willingness to do what you believe is right, even if it disappoints."

"Yeah, well, all that ain't worked out too well for me."

"Oh, but it has. Don't you see?" Marilee leaned forward, so close it made me itch. What would she come out with next? "You know who you are and you don't shy from letting people see it." She leaned back and regarded me from a distance. It was more than I could take in, given my predicament. I needed to think, I needed to work through some things but there was no time, there was the coming moon and Marilee leaving; tomorrow my dearest friend would be gone.

Tears came to my eyes. "I will miss you. More than you know."

"We'll write letters."

"You'll be back to visit. On the regular, I would think, what with Patrick and all."

Her look became wistful, but she didn't respond. She didn't need to.

"Anyway," she said. "This is for you." She reached for the pretty package, and I took it knowing full well it was a book. I untied the bow and the paper fell away. *Walden; or, Life in the Woods.* "Henry David Thoreau. He seeks to find meaning in simplicity. In communing with nature, and in self-reliance."

"Sounds like my life stuck in these mountains." I pulled the book close. "I will treasure it. Thank you."

We talked on until the afternoon got late, then we packed up the basket and started our walk back to the farm. "I won't come to the house," she said as we got near. "I've a ways to travel, and I'd best keep moving." We turned to each other and embraced, and this time it was full and warm.

"You have made a difference, Marilee. I want you to know that. Your work here has mattered. Your *life* here has mattered. It may not have ended the way you wanted, but good things are going to come. You'll see."

We hugged a final time, and I watched as she untied her horse. "If you think this place hasn't changed me, just look at this." She mounted, gathering her skirts and settling onto the saddle. "I couldn't do that when I arrived here. I *wouldn't* do that when I arrived here." She smiled, arranged the reins, and clicked to go. She turned back ever so briefly, allowing for a final word. "Don't give up on love, my friend."

"Don't give up on love," I repeated.

I WENT THROUGH THE GATE AND ON UP THE HILL, BUT I did not go inside. I circled around to the back, getting to Papa's crab apple where we'd prayed and also buried the blood. Hester's herbs were in my pocket, and I wondered how it could be that dried leaves and stems, common as pennyroyal and rue and bloodroot, could do what she'd suggested. Boil them up and my life would be my own; drink them down and this would be done, the quickening stopped before it could ever flutter in promise. And no one would know, that was the thing. No one would ever know but for me and Hester Hopkins, a wise old woman hid long up a holler, a woman who'd took one look and handed me a way out.

Except that I wasn't certain. I wasn't certain of anything; two days had passed and the whole world had turned upside down. Marilee was leaving, and her with only the choice to bend her life around a mother who was hateful and also demanding; Patrick Hagan, what of him, what of her and him, what of them? I had questions, so many questions and also a knowing it hadn't been right to ask them. They make a nice pair though, don't they? Him and her? And him building that mansion she would be perfect for?

And there was Ben, Ben and the cabin, Ben and the surprise of the cabin. Ben intent on us marrying. Ben, and me supposedly with child. How had *that* happened? All those years and we'd not laid together— me keeping up my guard. I'd not be like the others; I'd not be one of *those* girls. Then there being only the once. Once, and not even three months past. We'd kissed and he'd promised: *I was his girl, his only girl*—and the kisses were sweet, and then they were strong, and then stronger still. There was his touch, there were his hands, there was his love, and it felt protective. Sheltering. My body'd let go and my heart had believed; my heart had let go and said *yes*.

I reached in my pocket for the sack. I loosened the twine, and I pulled the bottle free.

I lifted it to the light.

There was not much to see, just shadows trapped in amber glass. So I twisted it—this way then that, upside-down then over. I put the container on its side and rolled it. I tossed the bottle high, it came back, I tossed it higher still.

I walked in circles. I kicked at the dirt. I considered all the things.

I pulled the stopper free.

The mouth was wide, the view inside was of bark and berries and stems. I brought the opening to my nose—earth, petals, moss, rain— and I lifted the bottle and in one hard motion I shook it. Brittle bits flew—a seed, a scrap of leaf, a stem—one shake, two shakes, three, and the wind picked up and pieces scattered, pieces swirled and parts twirled and dust fell over the ground; the decision lay around me. A lifetime had been decided.

—————

CHAPTER NINETEEN

MARILEE

OCTOBER 1860

HENRY ARRIVED TO COLLECT ME, JUST AS MOTHER HAD wired he would. He managed the heavy bags as together we boarded the train to Charlottesville. He rode in the back in the Negro car, and I took my place in front, in the luxury cabin. I ran my gloved hand over fine upholstery and polished wood trim, and it occurred to me for the very first time how odd this is, this separation of human beings based on class and status or money, this categorization based on allusion. These mountains have done their work in beginning to change me, I realized, and I considered how Elizabeth would delight in the revelation, how Patrick would nod, then grin.

At Lynchburg we stopped and disembarked for fresh air. I had hardly descended the steps when here came Henry; he is as protective as a mockingbird guarding against a circling hawk. "I'm fine, as you can see," I said, "but I do appreciate you worrying about me." Just then a man approached and, seeing my hands on Henry's shoulders, flew into a rage. I recognized him as a blustery bloke from my compartment who'd made repeated attempts to converse with me, and all to little avail. He spewed vile words that were directed toward Henry, and without so much as a thought I turned and slapped the man hard across the face. This stunned him but only for a moment, then he resumed his tirade. A second time, I slapped him.

A group was forming around us, men in tailored suits, women holding the hands of small children, many I expect wondering what offense the man had caused the lady. I stepped closer, my face inches from his. "I'd like you to apologize." He looked angry, trapped, surrounded, but he didn't speak. "Now, sir. Now."

It escaped gritted teeth, barely audible. "Apologies."

"To you both," I said.

He stared but did not speak.

I raised my eyebrows. "To you both."

His eyes burned with anger, but he acquiesced. "Both," he said, the sentiment incomplete. Still I felt moderate vindication, and I turned on my heels to find Henry standing by, looking equally shocked. "If you please, Mr. Noaks," I said. I reached for his arm, which he had not extended, and we walked through the gathered crowd together.

I WAS REBOARDING THE TRAIN WHEN A STRANGER, A woman in a black bonnet and cape, came and slipped a piece of paper into my satchel. "I saw what happened," she said quietly. "It is my hope you will join our effort." Then she disappeared.

I sat there a long while thinking about Henry and the awful man, about my impetuous reaction to his insults. I had surprised him, there was little question—but I had surprised myself as well, for where had my brash behavior come from? I know people like that boor exist; I have never been a stranger to divisive issues. In fact, it's the gift of my father's influence that I can hold such as separate: I can take a topic and, from afar, view it, a sphere in an outstretched hand. I can examine the curves and angles, seeing the pros and cons of them all. But it is cerebral, this sensitivity, an exercise one does in one's head. So a physical reaction— impulsive, passionate, committed—has never been part of my makeup.

It is why people find me to be stiff, I suppose, perhaps even rigid. I am tall to begin with, and I carry myself erect, my spine straight and long. I did not notice this until I arrived in Western Virginia and encountered the women here. They are not like my peers in Charlottesville, a plate of glass standing between them and the world. No. These mountain women are a different breed altogether, born of the earth with a strong, determined sense of right and wrong, tenacious women who fight their way through every day, fierce and proud. They pull food from the ground or wrestle it to butcher. They carry water and snap peas and churn butter. They chop wood and tend fires and nurse the sick; they lend a hand, caring for neighbors for miles around. They mind the children and suffer their husbands, who—without the tenacity of the female spirit—are often driven to excess in drink and self-indulgence. They bury their babies. They bury far too many babies, their wails echoing in cries that travel ridge to ridge, generation to generation. Life is a battle, a fact these women know and acknowledge freely, wearing its scars as armor. From this they draw their strength. Their very survival depends on it, I think, this determination and grit, their souls anchored like unwavering feet, their shoulders squared and sturdy. It is a posture I admire: one of loyalty, fierce and defiant. What it must be to feel something so sure.

There is a balance on the other side, I should say this too, something lovely and grace-filled. For these women hold hard to their faith. They love deep and wide, extending broad their arms with little reservation or judgment. They sweep you up and pull you close, rocking, singing, soothing whatever savage hold has you in its grips. And then they whisper: "There, now, baby. It's all right. Everything will be all right."

I have not found it elsewhere, the honesty in these women. There is a truth in their lives that makes you know even in the worst of times, even in the floods, the ground beneath their feet will hold.

I LEANED OVER AND REACHED INTO MY BAG, PULLING from it the slip of paper deposited there. It was small—not more than four inches in width—and folded in half. I looked around the car and, having determined that no one was paying me any mind, I opened it.

The top of the page read: UNITED IN FREEDOM.

It was underlined twice. Then:

CONDUCTORS, AGENTS, STOCKHOLDERS
INQUIRE:

Here the page was blank, but someone had handwritten just below:

Richmond, Norfolk, Petersburg

My face flushed, my palms sweating, I quickly folded the paper and shoved it deep in my bag. It was the Underground Railroad, I was sure, abolitionists who aid slaves in their journey to freedom in the North. It was dangerous work, *illegal*—why, it was my duty to turn this woman in. Where was she? I glanced around, my heart beating wild, my conscience willing my countenance to still. No one paid heed, and I pulled from my sleeve a thin handkerchief. I dabbed at my misting brow.

I considered. The Underground Railroad was serious business. The Fugitive Slave Act of 1850 had only served to make it more so. The legislation had backfired in many ways, for law based on such compromise serves no one well: not the Northerners who live in free states but are legally obligated to return runaway slaves to their owners; not the Southerners who have seen it create a great rise in the abolitionist movement; not the free Negroes who are endlessly harassed by bounty hunters. And certainly not the slaves who are taunted with dreams of freedom promised in the North but whose reality is oppression and terror. What was it like for them, the Negroes desperate for escape? Those who—unlike Henry and Hannah—suffered maltreatment at the hands of their owners? I mean, Mother could be demanding, even cruel, but she didn't have her servants whipped. Henry and Hannah were satisfied, grateful even, for their place in a lovely home.

Weren't they?

I looked to the window, where the West's rowdy mountains had given way to the Piedmont's gentle hills. I'd always loved this part of Virginia, fields spreading far and wide, swell after swell rolling as if nudged by the softest breeze. Here and there, dark dots of cattle dappled the landscape, like a painter just finished had taken one last look, then *flick flick flick* added a final, perfecting touch. It was Virginia at her most beautiful, or so I'd always thought, a genteel geography that suggests calm and peace; a terrain both restrained and mannerly. Now, though, in this speeding train with the West's fierce ridges and insistent valleys behind me, the view east looked...meek. Obedient, and complying.

I reached into my bag and felt for the paper. It was there, tucked, folded, hidden.

The aiding of fugitives, running for freedom.

I felt alive at the possibility.

CHAPTER TWENTY

ELIZABETH

OCTOBER 1860

TIME BEN LEARNED I WAS WILLING, WHAT DID HE DO but go straight to Papa to ask for blessings on our union. This seemed silly given my condition, but as my intended didn't know anything yet of the baby, and as I wasn't planning on telling him nor no one, ever, as shortly we would be properly married, I let Ben go on. Mama met him at the door and wouldn't you know it, this time she had her own opinion on things. It would be best, she said, for us to go on and do what we were gonna do anyway, Jonathan would never agree to our marrying and there was no sense upsetting him over it twice.

Ben did not think this was right, but what choice did we have. So the next day him and I, and a little gold band that came from his granny— we rode over the mountain to pretty Gladesville, and by nightfall, we were husband and wife.

This is how I thought it would feel to be married:
Like a part of you has been lost.

This is how it felt that first night:
Like a part of me had been found.

WE SPENT OUR WEDDING NIGHT JUST ACROSS FROM THE courthouse at the Virginia House Hotel. It took all the money Ben had, but he insisted we start our life together in a proper fashion. I was nervous as we stood together at the counter where the clerk addressed us as "Mr. and Mrs. Grubb." Then he leaned closer and said, "You will be in our Cumberland Room. It is very private, up at the end of the hall. Let me know if you need anything. Anything at all."

Blood rushed to my cheeks and I wondered if a person could die of embarrassment. But Ben acted like this was the most natural thing in the world. He stuck out his arm and I took it, and together we walked up the wide sweeping stairs to our room.

It was pretty, welcoming, with a bed and chest and a small table in front of a window. I put down the flowers I carried—a sweet lavender bouquet Jenny Mae had sent—and I pulled the curtain back to see that the view looked out over Main Street. It was around four and there were people everywhere, coming and going from the courthouse, the feed store, the druggist. I knew what Ben expected would happen next, and I jumped and dropped the drape when he came up behind and kissed my neck. He turned me so I faced him, and this time he leaned in to kiss my forehead, my cheeks, my lips.

Why did I agree to this? I thought. *It's all a big mistake.*

There was a ribbon at my neck and he untied it, removing the wrap from my shoulders. He walked to the corner where he laid it across the wide arm of a chair, handling that cloak like it was the most precious thing in the world. He came to me then, taking me in, sliding his hands up my back to my hair, where he pulled at a pin and smiled as he watched the broad bun release. "Turn for me," he said, and I did, facing away. He untied the sash. Then one by one he began to work the buttons, button after tiny button, there must have been a hundred; and as each released my head felt lighter, my heart beat faster like a flock of birds had got startled and, together, taken flight. Down, down, down Ben went, down my back, down to my waist, down below my waist to the lowest stays of my corset. By then the feeling was heat and the heat had settled low, and he slipped his hands in my dress and around my hips and there, just there—just at my bones—he put his hands flat and pulled me back tight against him. His lips were at my ear. *Let's get this dress off, why don't we.*

I considered. I wondered. Was I supposed to help? I'd hardly had the thought when his hands were again at my neck and he slipped them between collar and skin; he coaxed loose the silk, worn and woolen, and moved his palms slow, flat, across the long open space of my shoulders. Then just at the edges, just where they sloped and dropped, his fingers spread wide and he pushed the fabric forward. And off, his mouth coming quick to my skin. His hands moved over, and down; his wrists pulled the blue silk with them. *It's like peeling a potato*, I thought; then his palms reached my breasts which were small but lifted high and made round by the corset. He brushed ever so lightly over their tops. His touch was quick, slight—was he teasing? I didn't know; I wasn't certain, and I really can't say, but I think I may have trembled. His hands continued either way, over the puckers of the low-cut chemise; over the corset's stays which he traced down, down until at last, at long last, Ben's hands came to rest and the blue silk found itself held by the skirts at my hips and the unconsidered fasteners (plentiful as they were) that climbed each wrist.

I reached for a cuff and pulled. It did not come loose, there being the row of buttons, and Ben stepped around to take my imprisoned hand in his. He raised it to his lips. He kissed its back and palm. He held my arm to the side where all in all he could look, see, get a better view. Of a sudden I felt embarrassed, exposed; naked despite the corset and the chemise that hung low below my knees. My face flushed, my color rose, and I reminded myself I'd done this before, we'd done this before, and it not hardly three months ago. I was a girl then, that's how it was, I'd made an in-the-moment decision brought on by a mix of curiosity and frustration. There'd been no corset then, no drawers, which what would be the point? I was a farmer, a work horse, I spent my time hoeing and plowing and my wardrobe was comprised of a single pair of men's britches and a handful of day dresses long soiled by solid work. It was Lucy who'd seen that I was in this "finery" for my wedding; it was Lucy, as per usual, who tried to make of me a lady that I most certainly was not.

I closed my eyes. I opened them, and I blinked, and still there was Ben. He was staring at me tender, his eyes filled with something so deep I thought it might spill over and pour out. *You're just so beautiful.* He said this true, bare, honest. And I believed him. I believed him.

We got the dress free. Ben took it to the floor where the gown laid there in a stiff puddle. "Step out," he said, and I did, and he lifted the dress and rose. He winked at me and grinned. "About those petticoats," he said. I laughed, I had to laugh as he walked to the bureau to hang it. He took his time, giving me time, and I reached around to begin to unfasten. *My husband*, I thought, keeping an eye, and I watched as with his back to me he took off his waistcoat, his tie. He loosened the neck of his shirt, then he pulled the long tails from his trousers. He sat to remove his shoes. He stood then, turned, but didn't walk to me. "I only wore two," I said quick, too loud, as if he'd expected layer after petticoat layer, each finely embroidered and embellished. "And there's no crinoline. I don't *have* a crinoline." He crossed the room now, he crooked his forefinger and, reaching me, put it beneath my chin to lift my face to his. "You are perfect, Mrs. Grubb. Exactly as you are." He kissed me then, sweet, then sure, then very sure, and between us the heat rekindled. His arms went 'round and he found the corset's laces and in no time he had them untied. With my hands at his elbows and his eyes dead on mine, Ben clicked open clasp after clasp on the corset's front busk. "It's like picking a lock," I whispered. "Or a banjo," he said, and I giggled, and he finished the task, a sweet smile on his lips.

I drew back stiff arms and like a dancer, shimmied my shoulders until the split corset dropped. As it did, Ben reached. Ben touched. Ben rubbed, as all that remained between his hands and me was the thinnest barrier of a cotton chemise, of the cotton drawers beneath. It was titillating, too much, and fire shot through and I kissed him wild, I pulled him close. Our bodies were pressed together hard and still it was not enough. He lifted my leg and I wrapped it tight and of a sudden he was there, his fingers having found, my split drawers having parted.

I gasped, I could not breathe, I could not have imagined.

"I love you, Tess," he said, and my other leg wrapped and he lifted me, carried me, he laid me across the bed where I watched, breathless, as my husband undressed. He came to me then, he took his time, he kissed every part as moment by moment the full of my body was unveiled.

Then he loved me. Oh how Ben Grubb loved me—his wife, his life, the mother of his unknown child.

LATER, WE WALKED DOWNSTAIRS FOR SUPPER. WE WERE dressed again in our wedding clothes, and I knew we made a handsome pair. I held my head high as we walked through the dining room in spite of what we had been doing. Ben pulled out my chair and offered "Mrs. Grubb" as with great effect he swept his hand high above it. He looked then like he might giggle, or clap, and I paused, taking him in. *This was Ben. My Ben*. All dark curls and smiling eyes, so full of mischief. A boy become a man. Even when I was angry, I realized then, even when he'd deserved it—I never could make my heart turn away from Ben Grubb.

I looked about, just for a moment, and let myself pretend I was in a fine hotel in Boston, or New York City, or Atlanta. Then I took my seat in this dining room in Gladesville. I spread the napkin wide across my lap, and I put my hand to my belly, and I smiled.

CHAPTER TWENTY-ONE

RED

BEN WORKED HARD ONCE THEY WAS MARRIED, I FIGURE he had a lot to prove to Jonathan and he set about doing it. I'd have to say he was one of the finest young Apprentices ever admitted to the Freemasons, though it took a while for it to become known among the Brothers. We don't just take things on face value, is why. We expect a man to demonstrate his virtue through Good Works as well as study. And that's just what Ben done.

He worked hard on that old cabin, too, why in no time him and Elizabeth got the place right livable. Which was good, them finding out shortly she was expecting. Ben come and told me the news hisself and law' how he grinned. It didn't slow down Elizabeth none. Why she climbed on that roof and plowed her a winter garden and planted it so big she was forever taking baskets of greens to anybody who'd have them. And she helped out Ben's Mama, Jenny Mae, with many things and in particular with that little girl they call Boo. She's slow, you know, somebody who requires a whole lot of attention and patience and that's just what Elizabeth give her. Why she'd get that girl and bring her to town riding all the way together on a horse, and she'd always stop in to see me. First time they come I had a lollypop in my pocket and I give it to that child and you'd a thought I'd give her the moon. Now I keep one or two of them here at the Livery all the time, just in the event they might come by. That little Boo, she can't say my name but she likes to pull on my old red beard. I always smile when I see them coming.

I tell all this like across that winter, and over that spring, it's the part that matters. Like around us the country wasn't falling to pieces now that Abraham Lincoln was elected as president. States was seceding with South Carolina first who if nothing else you have to admire their gumption. And there was six more joined, calling theirselves the Confederate States. They named their own president, Jefferson Davis; I wasn't so sure about him. But it's all people talked about, you can see why, nobody knowing what would come next or if our home state of Virginia would go or stay. And there was Elizabeth and Ben, who like all of us was just trying to live by good measure and bring their baby into a peaceful and loving world. Which by the time she arrived—the thirteenth of April 1861—law', if it wasn't into a situation already carved out by war.

CHAPTER TWENTY-TWO

ELIZABETH

APRIL 1861

JENNY MAE WAS BESIDE ME, TRYING TO HELP COAX AND cajole the tiny newborn to feed. "Get it to latch on, honey. Pinch your nipple there between your fingers, like that; now rub it up against its mouth." I did not know how to do this, I felt shy and exposed and like I had no business being nobody's mama. Plus that baby was as confused as me, having popped out fast when for so long she didn't seem wont to come. That's when the door busted open. It was Ben, running like somebody was after him. The baby heard it too, and Jenny Mae, which she moved to the side where Ben could get to me, to us, and he did, leaning down, his lips covering my face with kisses.

"You're a filthy mess, Ben Grubb." Jenny said this, then she swatted him away. "Get yourself over to that basin where you can wash up. And don't touch that child until you're out of them nasty clothes. She's likely to catch her death from something on you."

His voice came quiet and pleased. "So it's a girl." His hand came to his heart, which then he put his other one over it and pressed. "We got ourselves a daughter."

He winked at me, then stepped away. I heard water pouring.

"Looks like she was excited to get here." I said this loud, like her coming was a surprise which of course to me it wasn't. My time was close and I'd known it and been nervous. Ben was gone so much, the Masons requiring of their apprentices an endless assignment of secret works and projects. But what could I say or do? Ben'd stepped full force into it all, thinking we still had some weeks to go.

There was pleasure in Jenny's voice as my husband came back to me. "I'll just take a little walk, get me a fill of some fresh spring air." The door opened and closed, and we were alone.

Ben sat on the bed, facing me. I handed over the baby and with no hesitation he took her. I remembered then all those siblings. He'd had practice.

"We'll be needing to give her a name," he said. He was looking at her little face, shaking her up and down. "Was there one you wanted?"

"Jane," I said. "I was thinking Jane. For Papa and for Uncle Ruck. Their mama was Ida Jane, and they were so young when they lost her. Plus as a name I like it."

He nodded.

"I'll pick Jane," I said, "you pick the other."

"Mary." He said this like it was something we'd already decided.

"Mary?"

"For Mary Lenore Kitchens."

Marilee?

"She brought us together, Tess. And her friendship has meant so much to you. Means so much, still."

"But that's giving me Mary *and* Jane."

"Well, I get Grubb, and that don't count for nothing."

Something happened in that moment, something I had not expected. Love overtook. My chest got hollow and it loosened and grew, and it swallowed the room and the cabin and the valley, and everything was wrapped in light and love. All there was was light and love and it was me and it was in me and it was all around me. I looked to Ben and he leaned and enfolded me and like I was floating above I saw we made a circle: Ben, and baby Jane, and me.

I SLEPT THEN, AND I WOKE TO DARK. BEN WAS TALKING. "Be over by June. July at the latest. And it won't have nothing to do with us here. Lord, Mama, why would it? There's nothing to come after. And even if there was, can you imagine a bunch of Yankees trying to move around in these mountains? It's ridiculous."

"I worry over it," his mama said. "And I worry over your brothers. Levi and Jonah's both already talking big about joining the Confederates."

"They can't mean it. Surely you see that. Levi can't do it without your permission. And Jonah—hell, he's just sixteen. He's not old enough either way."

"And what about you, son?"

"What about me?"

"You got a baby now. A wife. What happens if you get pulled in? Who'll take care of—?"

"What kind of question is that? You know I ain't going, Mama. I ain't fighting in a war I don't care about. I'm a musician, not a soldier. Plus I promised Tess I would never leave her, and that's a promise I'm meaning to keep."

The baby let out a cry, and in reaction I turned from the wall, tried to pull myself to sitting. This was not easy, and Jenny got up and to me by then, Jane in one arm and the other under mine. "Look who's hungry," she said. I got myself situated, and this time the baby latched easy. "You got to eat too, honey. I'll fix you a plate for when you're done there, then I'll be on my way."

I wasn't so sure about her leaving; there was still so much to learn. "Thank you, Jenny," I said. "For everything."

"Aww, you was easy, girl. Her, too, coming so fast. I'll be back around in the morning to check on you all."

"I'll ride you part of the way," Ben said.

"Don't be silly. It's fine. I'll be fine." Jenny turned some, took his chin in her hands, making her point even sharper. "You belong here now."

I took some comfort in Jenny's reminder, even as I held tight to Ben's promise. Still I couldn't help but pull our baby close, wondering and worrying over what might be forming out there, over what all might be coming.

CHAPTER TWENTY-THREE

PATRICK

JUNE 1861

THIS MORNING I STOOD IN WITNESS TO THE CALL TO Arms at Gladesville. It was a scene I hoped to never see and a day I shall never forget, as friends and neighbors, sons and fathers, brothers and cousins and uncles put on display their willingness to step up in service to the Confederacy. War comes ever closer to these remote mountains, and war is something for which we must diligently—if regrettably—prepare.

Still the mood was celebratory. Women flitted about, girls flirted, and from time to time a voice in the crowd erupted with a chant or a whoop or a holler. I stood with Abijah Alley, and both of us watched as on the lawn before us, and spilling to the street beyond, was the oddest collection of volunteers, many of whom were clients I had represented over the years. The courthouse and the jail rose behind me and this made of particular note one Mr. Beverly Dickenson. Just six weeks ago, Mr. Dickenson had been found guilty of murder and sentenced to one year in the penitentiary. This morning he was released, so as to join the Confederate Army.

The call was made: "Volunteers: Formation!" Last hugs were hugged, kisses were stolen, then men old and young—some of them boys hardly shaving—gathered up, lined up, and counted off. Someone yelled, "Yankee Catchers! Yankee Catchers!" and the volunteers joined in, arms raised and fists pumping. It stirred up the air with a nervousness they believed translated to thrill. But I knew better. Alley knew better, too, stepping up to offer a departing prayer that was both boisterous and solemn. He beseeched his god to offer strength and courage, righteousness and fortitude, protection and preservation.

He might have also asked for provisions. For the 101 men and boys who marched away behind their captain, young Logan Salyer, were in such disparate form it would have been comical but for the seriousness of the situation. No two were dressed alike; many didn't even have arms to carry. Judge Stump has called a meeting next week to determine how we can best support our soldiers, and I will attend. While I stand in opposition to this war on moral grounds, I believe it to be my duty as a man of the court to help see that, at a minimum, our volunteers are outfitted and trained as best we can, given our limited resources.

CHAPTER TWENTY-FOUR

MARILEE

I SUPPOSE IT IS A GOOD THING I WAS CALLED BACK TO be with Mother. For I wonder how she and Hannah and Henry would have managed, the fighting of this war nearly to our doorstep. Thousands of soldiers were killed or maimed most recently at Manassas, men from both sides, it being the bloodiest battle by far. All accounts report it was a horrific sight to behold, save for President Jefferson Davis, who seemed to see only honor and the potential for victory in the dead and stricken faces of those left lying there. The wounded are pouring into Richmond, where there is an appeal to residents to make room in their homes for them. Can you imagine? Mother cannot fully comprehend the news, which she still insists I read to her every day. I worried so with the report of the First Battle at Manassas, I feared she might be traumatized. But not so, as five minutes later she couldn't recall a single detail.

She was animated, I must say, as I read this commentary from the *Richmond Dispatch* dated July 26, 1861:

> *Our recent victories should only reinvigorate our exertions and redouble our preparations for an active prosecution of the war. Peace is our object, and we can obtain peace only by conquering it with force and arms.*

"Yes," Mother said. "Yes."

The dogged pertinacity of the Northern character will make them persist in this war as long as they can keep us on the defensive, and as long as danger does not actually threaten their own houses. So long as the battlefields are upon Southern soil, though we whip them in every engagement, yet we shall be little nearer peace than when the war began. We can obtain a cessation of war only by conquering it, and the conquest must be effected upon their own soil.

Mother raised a fist in solidarity; I raised an eyebrow.

The next paragraphs described how ill-equipped in horses the Northern forces are. Mother's eyes closed, her breathing became regular, and I stopped, put down the paper, and straightened my skirts to stand. Immediately she lifted a frail arm and, waving her bony fingers, ordered, "Read on, child, read on."

When engaged we should always threaten his flanks with our superior cavalry, shake his ranks with our superior artillery, and, advancing under this influence with our infantry, deliver our fire and charge with the bayonet.

The article continued for several more paragraphs suggesting, among other things, an unlimited supply of horses from Western Virginia and Tennessee to build an exceptional cavalry (taken from small family farms, no doubt) and a return to use of the medieval lance.

"Good god," Mother said, her eyes still closed.

The article finished, I scanned the notices and looked for any mention of a gathering that could be the Underground. There was none, of course, or at least none I could recognize. Still, their work was continuing. I was certain of this, even if the geography of the battles and of the marching and the posturing had most certainly disrupted it. Perhaps the reality of this war had bolstered their resolve. Maybe the confusion caused by Manassas had actually enhanced their ability to move slaves—undetected—toward freedom.

"I will be out tomorrow, Mother," I announced, surprised to hear the words come from my mouth. "I've an errand in Richmond."

There came no response. This time, she was sleeping.

CHAPTER TWENTY-FIVE

ELIZABETH

LEVI WAS GONE, AND NOT TWO WEEKS LATER JENNY MAE found a note written in Jonah's own hand saying he, too, had gone off to do his duty for his state and for the Confederacy: He was joining the volunteer army.

Ben was fit to be tied even if he was not surprised. There had been great excitement with people everywhere going on and on about Southern victories. President Jeff Davis talked biggest of all, high and mighty about the grand army of the North invading the sacred soil of Virginia and us "teaching them a lesson." That's all it took for Levi, who at least came to tell us goodbye.

"I have to go," he said to Ben, who hugged him so hard it about broke my heart. "I can't sit back and watch the Yankees come marching down believing they can take whatever they want. This is *our* state, *our* land, *our* property. We got a right to protect it."

"There's a better way, Levi," Ben said.

"It ain't up to us, Ben. We ain't marching *north*. We got an obligation to fight back when the enemy invades. We got a right to protect our families."

"Yeah, well, you'll be off doing that and leaving *your family* to survive without you. Who's gonna climb on the roof to repair it? Who will till and plant and harvest? Who'll load the goddamn rifle and point it at the goddamn bushwhacker come to steal whatever you got left? You're leaving all that to the women, you realize. The women and the old men."

"Come on now. It ain't like you've made your living hanging around here. I can't see as you've got a leg to stand on lecturing me about that."

I put my hand on my husband's back, knowing this was dangerous territory. "When are you leaving?" I asked.

"Tomorrow. Me and six others are meaning to join Floyd's Brigade up toward Hamilton." Levi looked at me, then back toward Ben. "Your time's gonna come, you know. It's a duty. You can't shirk it forever."

"Levi—" I said, scolding, a little angry, and he let go and held out his arms to me. I walked into them and held tight. "I'll pray for you," I said, "every day." I pulled away and looked him eye to eye, our arms still hugging. For the first time I noticed how much he looks like Ben, the shape of their faces, their sturdy chins. "You take care, Levi Grubb. We'll look forward to the day you come back home."

I wanted to give them some privacy: They needed to part on good terms. Neither said a word, and finally Ben stepped forward and slapped his brother on the back, and they moved apart. Levi put on his hat, and we followed him to the porch. He was ten or twelve steps away when Ben tossed, "I reckon we better hear that Rebel Yell, then."

Levi turned. He leaned back, then pushed from his gut and out through his mouth a sound that made my arm hairs stand.

"Yaaaaeehhooo!" he said. "*Yaaaaeeeehhoooooo*!!!"

His fists he raised above his head, he shook them twice, then he turned and walked away.

JONAH, HE DIDN'T TELL A SOUL GOODBYE BUT LEFT A note to "all" saying he was heading out, he was following Levi to the army. Ben wanted to set out after him, to find his little brother and bring him home. But Jenny wouldn't have it, saying Jonah, too, had something to prove and it wasn't right for Ben nor nobody to get in his way. This surprised me, following her talk with Ben, and her left behind with the younger ones and Boo being needy. It was that night when I brought it up, the idea we might want to move over to be with her.

Ben put down his fork and gave me a look like I'd never seen. "I thought you were happy here."

The baby was laying in her cradle kicking her little legs and cooing like she, too, wanted to be heard.

"I am. You know that. I'm just saying it might be good for us to be with Jenny for a while. Just until the worst of this is over. Maybe we'd all feel better, safer, if we were all together."

Ben pounded his fists, got up from the table, and gave me a look so hateful it scared me. "What do you want? What will it take? I am here all the time, Tess. I quit traveling. I gave up music. I've given up everything, just so I can be—"

"Ben, honey. I was thinking about Jenny and—"

"Didn't you hear her? Mama don't need us. She's fine with Levi going, she's fine with Jonah going, she's fine on her own. She made all that clear."

"That's not exactly what she—"

"Goddammit, Elizabeth." He walked away like he was trying to hold his temper. Then he came back. "I ain't having this conversation. I'm doing all I can, and if that's not enough, then maybe it would be best if I just marched off toward Hamilton or Harrisburg or wherever the hell it is my brothers have gone. With all the others from around here. It would be easier than trying to defend my decision to stay. But then, you don't know nothing about that, do you, since you're not the one facing it down." He took his hat and coat from the peg. He glared at me one more time. "You have no idea what it's like for me." And he walked out the door, and he slammed it hard behind him.

AFTER A WHILE IT GOT DARK AND BEN STILL WASN'T back. I put Jane down and lit the lamp, meaning to read a few pages of the Thoreau. I had been through the book cover to cover two times already, but I thought the words might calm me down, soothe my nerves a bit. Instead, I read the same passages over and over, my mind in other places. Eventually I gave up. I blew out the lamp, and I climbed into our bed alone.

CHAPTER TWENTY-SIX

RED

ME AND JAY JIM JONES HAD DONE BEEN AT THE TEMPLE a while the evening when Ben Grubb showed up. It's the damnedest thing, that temple, which Alley made to be the spitting image of King Solomon's from the Bible. You had to be a member in good standing of the Freemasons to even work on the thing, which there's a lot a person can read into that, our Order coming from the builders of that original temple which happened a thousand years before Christ. Alley holds his worship there and it's also where we have our meetings, and there's a place just for gathering which we call the Lodge. That day there was only me and Jay Jim when the door opened and here come Ben, looking like he was riding in on the afternoon's late light. It was good to see him. I asked after Elizabeth and also the baby, and Jay Jim inquired as to his mama.

"Doing all right," he said, and I was happy to hear it. I'd always liked Jenny Mae, liked her way of being in the world. Ben got him a whiskey and joined us. "Reckon you all heard my brothers are gone. Joined the Volunteers, Levi and Jonah both."

It was not the custom of gathered Freemasons to talk about such things, as we keep politics and religion and the like out of our midst, there being no reason to work over topics that bring up hard feelings and no answers. Still I could tell there was something weighing heavy on young Ben and I wanted to see what he needed to talk through. His hands was around his drink, which he was looking at hard, and Jay Jim pushed his chair out and stood.

"Won't be long until there ain't a man under forty left in these parts," he said.

Ben bristled, which is something I seen but Jay Jim did not.

"Anyway," Jay Jim went on, "I'll leave you gentlemen to it. The missus'll be wondering what I've got up to."

The door shut and I looked across at Ben. "What is it, son?"

He took a drink, set the glass down, looked me eye to eye. "A whole collection of things, Red. My wife, her discontent, her obvious disappointment in everything I say or do. Or *don't* do." He rubbed his hand through his hair, his curls stretching, then falling. "This war. This goddamn war nobody thought would last the summer and here we are. October, and them calling for more volunteers. People joining up right and left like it proves you're a man. I mean, Jonah ain't hardly sixteen! And I swear to you Aaron'd take off right now and go and him only twelve. I don't understand it. I really don't. It's a stupid war, and it's humiliating."

"Humiliating," I said.

"*Humiliating.* Folks judging me everywhere I go. Every glance. I am not a coward. I swear I am not. I just can't find nothing in the Confederate cause to believe in. I mean, our way of life ain't in question. We got no plantations."

But for Pat Hagan, I thought. *He just don't call it that.*

"And if it's a matter of principle, and I reckon it is, I'd land on the side of a man being free. As would ever' goddamn neighbor we've got, and that's the truth. Because if there's one thing we believe in these mountains, it's that a man ought to be able to live his life without somebody else lording over it." It was a good point, and he leaned back looking spent. His arms was gesturing but there wasn't much vim or vigor. "So. Here I am. Feeling like I ought to enlist but without a reason to fight. You tell me, what kind of soldier does that make?" He stared at the table, and I let the things he'd put in front of us lay there a minute. Then the question came I expected he was working up to. "What do you think, Red? What would you do?"

I wanted to give Ben room and sound counsel both. "It's a hard thing to answer. But I will tell you this. I've always believed if you don't know what to do, do what's right."

Ben considered this, and his look did not show as satisfied.

"It can be tricky," I said. "I'll give you that. Life has a way of complicating things, of requiring you to weigh them out again and again. So you just choose the first right thing, and then the next right thing, and so forth and so on, and when you go like that it seems to me things generally work out."

Ben still looked unsure.

"That's how your daddy lived, I'd say."

It was quiet, Ben holding these big thoughts, but then he broke the silence. "You ever been tested? Your resolve, I mean."

Have I been tested. I leaned back, crossed my arms, looked at the boy. So much of Stoley was there, the color, the shape, the intention. I sat up straighter, which then he did too. I leaned toward him. "There's a story I am going to tell you, Ben, I believe you ought to know. But it's a confidence. A *Freemason* confidence. Which means you're bound with it till death. Even if there's a good reason to share. Even if it happens to involve kin."

Ben looked wary, but he went ahead and nodded.

"You can't never tell a soul. You understand? Not even your wife. *Especially* your wife."

"I understand, Red. I do."

"Good," I said. "Because as secrets go, this here's a big one."

THE TELLING OF THIS PART COME AS A RELIEF, THE words pouring out and ever' one leaving me lighter. I told Ben of the shooting at the Compton Hotel, the card game, and Betty Sue Only. How Betty showed up, a swell in her belly, and right at the poker table her confronting Johnny James who had always been a sorry sort. "Tell your wife," she said, "or I will." How Johnny drew first, how Ruck took care of Johnny, how he was a man never could stand by and watch somebody done wrong. How Johnny'd had it coming, but how it was Rufus Young who'd paid the price.

"Elizabeth was there when he hanged," Ben said. "Did you ever know that? Defied her daddy and went. Witnessed the whole thing. She'll never get over it."

I had not known, and it made my telling of this next part far more difficult.

"Well, I was the one drove the cart after, it carrying Ruck and the coffin. I had to go along Main Street where people was hollering and cheering, and it made me sick to my stomach so I made the turn early to head up toward Copper Ridge. Things got quiet then, nothing but the sound of the horse and the wheels of the wagon as they beat against the path. I pulled the reins and we headed down the pass, toward Little Flat Lick and a hideaway spot where Abe Collins has him a hunting shanty built up against Clinch Mountain. It's tucked in where you ain't likely to find it if you don't know where to look. And Abe was waiting for us there, along with your pa, Stoley Grubb.

"First thing we done was open the top of that box where it had been nailed shut. It was no thing of beauty, like a proper coffin might be; this one was pine, and rough, like the outlaw it was meant to hold. There was a good bit of space between the long, splintered slats, and even closed you could see through to a body laying in there. It made the strangest sound, the way the wood cricked and cracked as we bent that lid back. Then soon as light hit the inside you could see sure enough it was Ruck, the hangman's black hood laid out flat over his broad chest and flat belly.

"I'll just tell you, for all my knowing it was gonna be Ruck in there, the sight of him still startled me. Then just like that he opened his eyes and looked up, and seeing his friends looking down, a sly smile come slow across his face. 'Goddamn it you need to learn to steer a horse cart, Red,' he said. 'My backside ain't never gonna be the same.'

"We laughed in relief, ever' one of us. Stoley stuck his hand down and Ruck grabbed on, taking the help getting pulled up. 'Sure is good to see you, my brother.'

Ben had him a look both confused and questioning. "Wait. Ruck was alive?"

I nodded.

"Brother?"

I sat back, and I watched as the smoke cleared from his eyes.

"Masons," Ben said. "You. Daddy. Sheriff Counts."

"Abe Collins. Doc Peters."

"And Ruck Young. Brothers."

I watched as Ben worked back through it all, sifting through details like he might find one that didn't work out.

"You got away with it."

I raised my eyebrows, I cinched my lips, and my head said yes, real slow.

"Nobody ever knew?"

I shook no.

"Unbelievable," Ben said.

We sat there a minute, Ben staring at the table and me staring at Ben, then he pushed hisself to stand and offered to the big empty room and me that he believe'd he'd have another whiskey, would I care to join?

I did not, wanting to keep my wits, but I watched as he downed a short one, then brought another to our table. I realized then that it was best I keep this moving.

"We'd planned it all, a'course, leastways the parts we could. We got Ruck outta those clothes and into some others first thing. Then he stretched his legs a bit—he really was awful sore from riding shut up in that casket. Him and Abe had it worked out that he had a horse and some money, a little food, Abe's gun. So after eating a bite and it getting on dark, Ruck headed out alone, bound for the great West. He was never to return to Virginia."

"But what about his family? And Jonathan? What about the burying? There was a funeral. Elizabeth has talked about it."

"There was a service down by the creek on the farm. That didn't require a body. The coffin I buried in an unmarked grave in the woods, according to the criminal laws of the day."

"Jesus Christ," Ben said. He put his hand to his head, which I reckoned was spinning. "So what happened to Ruck? You've heard from him, surely."

I considered should I tell more. "Not so much," I said. "It's not easy to get word, and like you can imagine, there's still danger. Or that's how Ruck sees it, anyway, which I expect his idea is more to look out for the rest of us." I smiled at the truth of this even if the fact of it was a lie. "Now." I slapped my hands to the table, making a point. "It's late, and I need to be getting home. And you, Ben—you need to be getting back to your wife."

The boy waited, like this was a sum that still needed figuring. But then he got up and I could see he was weak-legged, probably from the whiskey and the story both.

I reached for his shoulder. "Whoa there, brother."

"Just need me some air."

I closed up the place, and we walked out the door together. "Be glad to ride with you, son."

"Appreciate it. But I'll be okay."

I nodded. "Don't need a reminder, do you, Ben? You're bound with this confidence forever."

"Don't need a reminder."

I give him a hearty slap on the back, then I sent the boy off into the night. The air was cold, and the sky was dark, and for Ben, and for me, I was sure enough glad about both.

CHAPTER TWENTY-SEVEN

———

PATRICK

NOVEMBER 1861

THE STAKES CONTINUE TO RISE FOR US HERE IN THESE mountains, something that has come as a bit of a surprise to us all. Although it stands to reason, I suppose, when you consider our geography and geology.

To the north lies Pound Gap, the pathway through to the valuable mines at Saltville. Some say a loss there would cripple the entire Confederate Army, as the salt it provides is crucial for preserving provisions for troops far and near. There's also the railroad from Abingdon to Wytheville. It is deemed critical for a hundred reasons, not the least of which is the fact it connects the Eastern and Western theaters of this war. To the west is the Cumberland Gap, which for many years has served as the primary route to Kentucky and beyond. It's a trail first cut by Daniel Boone—a man I should like to have known, both for his daring and for his communion with the solitude of the wilderness.

Some years ago I read with interest Filson's *The Adventures of Colonel Daniel Boone*, and I have just begun Flint's *Biographical Memoir of Daniel Boone, the First Settler of Kentucky*. There is much I can learn from Col. Boone, not the least of which is a reminder that the mountain passes in our part of Virginia, rare as they are, serve as much more than soul-calming vistas. They are quite literally gateways that allow passage from one part of the country to the other.

There is also this. Kentucky is a state torn apart by this war as it lies in the virtual crossroads of all issues: north and south, east and west,

Democrat and Whig, etc. Vast populations are those of wealth, education, and privilege; many others live in poverty and squalor. But what they share, all of them, is a deep pride in being people of Kentucky even if, collectively, there is little unified allegiance to either cause. This renders the land of bluegrass deeply divided while still being one of great passion and commitment.

In contrast is our Commonwealth, for in Virginia today there is overwhelming support for the Confederacy. This is the case even on our western edge where there remain but a handful of Unionists—at least those willing to state it publicly. Despite my overarching belief that the issues of this war could have been resolved by more peaceable means, I have come to join the Rebel cause myself. At least I have done so in spirit, my primary work being that of helping organize and manage home guard units that will serve as protectors of our borders. It is important work filled with mounting pressure. There has been increased fighting on Kentucky soil in recent days—most notably the fierce battle at Camp Wildcat and then Ivy Mountain—both driven by Union desire to control our mountain passes. In their victories Northern troops march ever closer to us, to Pound Gap and Cumberland Gap, so close it's as if we can hear the beat of their regiment drums.

There is loss within the valley, too, a loss so great to me I find it difficult to acknowledge. For just this morning I shook the hand of my uncle and bade him farewell as he drove his carriage down the long drive that leads away from Hagan Hall. Behind him lay Aileen, so filled with laudanum as to cause intense, nearly comatose sleep. Judith Rawlings sat with her, Aileen's head in her lap, and in front on the bench with Uncle was his old friend Thomas Rawlings. They are bound for Staunton and the Central Insane Asylum. Aileen is to be admitted, and expectations are she will reside there for the rest of her days. I am to oversee the packing of their household, which I will deliver to Joseph myself once he establishes a residence there. He will stay in Staunton, to be near his wife.

To a great degree I feel responsible, may I just say that? For I cannot but wonder if the temporary peace we believed Aileen had found in these mountains might have continued had I not begun construction of such a mansion right in her line of sight. No one has offered this as a theory, at least not in my presence. But one can easily come to the conclusion that it offered a painful reminder of her difficult days in Brahmin Boston.

Abijah Alley was here last night, something Uncle tolerated if he did not approve. Aileen has found solace in his teaching and his strange, accepting church and I hoped—prayed, even—*that* might be her saving grace. Not so Joseph, who never came to understand the draw of an un-Catholic god. It was a matter on which I could not debate him, even if I wanted to, for I share his belief in doctrine and ritual. My soul is soothed by the solemnity and tradition of our Catholic faith as if it's the church's adherence to tradition that puts us in the presence of a mighty God. And is it not so? Do the teachings of the church need to swing and sway at the whims of a sinful population? Or is it the role of the church to remind us God is steadfast, the church *specifically* unchanging as it has been from the beginning of time? For when the winds of change are blowing, as in this damnable war, it is the pillars of the church upon which I lean for strength and consolation.

It is a debate I had with Mr. Alley, a lively one, when I visited his "temple" in concern over Aunt Aileen's growing involvement in his congregation. Neither of us ever spoke her name, and yet I believe it was clear to both what our theological discussion was really about.

"He is, above all, a loving God! Wouldn't you agree?" said Alley, his voice deep, a gleam in his eye.

"I would agree," I said.

"Then why would it be that a God of Love would withhold from any one of His beloved children the very thing he or she needs?" Alley talked bold of Redemption, how his god, "the God of All" he said, offers two things our Catholic Church does not: forgiveness without intercession, and forgiveness without judgment. "We are a sinful people doing our best to navigate a world filled with temptation. This our loving God knows. Absolution is His gift, His sacrifice. From Jesus on the cross, He has offered all sinners a direct path to Him, to righteousness."

I leaned back, crossed my arms over my chest.

"It is a road filled with grace, not bishops, my friend," he said.

You would think this comment offended me, but in fact it did not. I find it difficult to say just why. There is something about the man's good nature, his countenance. He radiates love, this Abijah Alley. Like the god he describes, he radiates love.

And so it came to be that however inconsequential, I withdrew my own quiet objections to Aileen and her connection to Alley's band of believers. She had stood in judgment every day of her life as a young Irish immigrant in Boston, and she was persecuted for it. She carries those scars to this day. If belief in a loving god that walks beside her gives her relief, quiets the voices in her head, who am I to question?

Of course it's not my place to have an opinion anyway. It is Uncle's. And needless to say, he did not share my view of the matter. He found Aileen's drifting from the Church disturbing, and, more importantly, believed it to be a major factor to her inability to find lasting peace. So he worked with the diocese to secure the services of a traveling priest who comes to Hunter's Valley once a month. We fashioned a temporary chapel adjacent to my new home where Father Lyons holds Mass. There is also a confessional, of sorts, for the Sacrament of Penance until the one we've requested from Rome arrives. Joseph insisted that Aileen participate, although it was easy to see her discomfort rise each month as the fourth Sunday approached. She became agitated and cross, taking to her room where she paced mightily. Joseph also hired a black woman to be with her night and day, a dark-skinned Negro named Mulay who was reared on Georgia's lower coast. Through some miracle, the woman could calm Aileen during her fretful spells, the bond between them something Joseph came to rely on.

He loves his wife deeply. He will not forsake her, I know.

There are details about that night I cannot relay, for as is so often the case, I was working the week in Lee County and so I wasn't there. Perhaps it is a blessing in disguise, for as many have said, I might have suffered injury. As it was, the hour was late—long after midnight—and Hagan Hall was empty. Without notice by either Joseph or Mulay, Aileen left the cabin and descended the hill. Then, for the second time in her life, she took a candle and set a heartbreaking fire, burning our little Catholic chapel to the ground.

It was Mulay who found her in the yard, her hands and arms badly burned. Uncle was beside himself with worry and also had great concerns that the wind might blow a spark toward Hagan Hall and cause significant damage. He sent Mulay to tend to Aileen's burns, and he spent the next dark hours throwing bucket after bucket of water on the dying embers.

At that time, of course, he didn't know just what had caused the fire. It was only later, with Aileen's crazed confession and Mulay's interpretation for him, that Uncle came to understand his wife was not the heroine of the story but its antagonist, the arsonist herself.

And so it has come to be that when Hagan Hall is completed, and I move there permanently, I will live on the property in that magnificent valley alone, but for the animals and the workers who will help me keep the place going. I have decided to run a number of ventures from there, including a farm and a grain supply, so Sulphur Springs will provide employment for a number of families. These will not be slaves, a commitment I have made to God and to my own conscience, for in truth it already carries this heavy load: I support the Confederates but not the Confederate cause. It is a laughable dichotomy, I acknowledge, for I hold no delusions that this war is not about economics and slavery. Still I will do what I can to demonstrate that there are other ways, better ways, to move forward out of this ancient, heinous institution. I will offer a reasonable wage to my workers, white and Negro, and I will provide schooling for their children. This in itself is not without risk and controversy, as the laws of the day prohibit any gathering to teach persons of color to read or write. Nevertheless, I hold this position on the matter: *Watch me.*

And so Uncle Joseph will not be here to be a part of it, and this saddens me, for he values education and enterprise with equal fervor. But I shall continue to do my best to make him proud, so that his investment in me—which has been considerable in every way—will have been a sound one. And I will continue my prayers for Aileen Whalen Hagan.

At forty-three years she is still that tormented Irish housemaid Uncle found serving soup in an elite Boston dining room, a damaged girl who stole his heart and to this day, holds it still.

WAR

CHAPTER TWENTY-EIGHT

———

20 March 1862

Dear Tess,

How can it be I am a soldier now? It is a question I ask myself over
and over. How is it I have left my home, my wife, and my child to
go fight in this war I don't even believe in. I did not expect it would
come to this and yet here I am, sitting in the cold, wrapped in an old
blanket worn and forlorn. Of course there was the promise that if
I signed as volunteer militia I would never be sent any farther than
the borders of Scott County. Which seemed a good decision at the
time, what with Conscription around the bend, and me ordered
then to join against my will. Ordered, and sent God knows where.

Nevertheless here I am in Russell County. I am with a portion of
Gen. Marshall's troops where we are waiting for orders since losing
Pound Gap. I do not know if you have heard the details and so I
shall tell them here best I can. It being my first week in the militia I
did not expect to go so quick into battle, a silly point since it is after
all a war. But as you know my heart, Elizabeth, I trust you with the
secrets there.

There was meant to be a collection of 700 Confederates at the
Gap where over time a small enclave has built up of log huts, com-
missary buildings, and a house that serves as headquarters. I say
"there was to be" because I don't reckon our numbers equaled half
that much. Gen. Marshall's boys had just returned from Prestons-
burg and Pikeville over in Kentucky. They hadn't had too good a
time of it under pressure from the Union and on top of that there
was a lot of sickness running through the troops like mumps and
measles. I hear from some of the boys it was an awful time and I am

glad I was not there. I do not want to upset you but there are not sufficient supplies for us to get by, much worse, even, than the reports you have heard. After the march into Kentucky a number of soldiers just walked away and headed straight to join the army of the North so they could eat and be warm. I can tell you I understand such a decision. I can't imagine what it would be like to be a 12-monther starved to the bone, worn out, longing so hard for home.

We were under command of Maj. J. B. Thompson with orders to hold the Gap against Garfield's troops who were marching close. A collection of our men proceeded to the Kentucky side where they spent time dropping trees and anything they could cut or drag across the road there. It was a pretty good strategy since the road through the Gap makes passage easy excepting for the deep mud there. It is March, after all, a season of cold rain and bitter snows, the combination of which makes a fine mess of the dirt paths that cross these mountains. The rest of us were meant to form a breastwork on the summit of Pine Mountain. (A breastwork is a temporary fortification. I did not know and asked.) Thank heavens Simon Rogers is here and has stayed close to show me the ropes. Do you remember Simon? He's the boy Billy Ray Rucker made get so drunk that night at Jennings Cove, a terrible trick I'm sure you would say. Billy Ray is here, too, and so is James Kelly who by the way married that girl Ruby he kissed on a dare that night. So I guess some good did come from our mischief even if it did land me in jail. Anyway, Simon has turned into a good soldier which is something I never would have guessed on account of him being such a timid person. But he believes in this cause and I guess that's what matters most when you're considering bravery, leastways it seems to me. I did not feel brave at all, I can tell you, and when I heard the command the Union troops were coming to Stand Firm I could feel my knees shaking.

I was there on that mountain wearing the uniform of a dead soldier because that is how my battle grays came to me. I should be grateful I suppose. There are men who have no uniform at all and I can't for the life of me understand how you don't have troops from both sides aiming for you when that's the situation. And I have a decent rifle—a minnie-shooting Enfield musket, thanks to Red Hopkins—which helps with the courage if anything can. You will remember at the time Red gave it to me all I could think was I'd never be able to take that bayonet and stab it into another man's chest. As it turns out not much stabbing goes on when you have a gun that shoots straight at long range, and mine does. I also have a good supply of bullets as it loads with the minnies made at Harper's Ferry.

Listen at me already talking like a soldier who's got used to fighting. But when you are <u>in battle</u> things change, that's the truth of it.

I was saying. I was standing on the mountain when the command came and everything in my body was racing. I held the gun close and the men around me rushed forward and I rushed with them, voicing the Rebel Yell like it was the most natural thing in the world. It is a funny thing to feel your body take over where your mind can't. I am telling you there was not one part of me that gave a single thought to that Rebel Yell but there it was exploding from me with the same sound as from the others, a holler from so deep down it's like every bit of hate you ever felt in your entire life is coming up and out, right through your mouth.

They came at us hard, their own hate showing, and their numbers so much greater than ours. I have heard it said 2,500 plus 100 cavalry. It only took a few minutes to know this was not a battle we could win. We fought for an hour or maybe more and were ordered to retreat and so we did. We scattered through the woods like buckshot, mountain boys looking to hide amid the thickets or to lay out low under a broad rock outcropping. You might of thought this was nothing more than a summer game but for those who fell left and right, their cries like an echo running round and round a cove. I will not describe it here because I do not want to plant it in your dreams like it has planted in mine. I will just say I felt a decent soldier, able to defend myself and my homeland. I am smart and strong and sensible and those are three things that help a man when he's facing down such an "enemy." You do not need to worry too much for my safety even though I know you will. I also know the love you have for me which is genuine and true, and that is the thought that sustains me.

Your loving husband,
Ben

PS: Write me every day.
PPS: Tell Jane her Daddy misses her something awful and give her a big kiss from me.
PPPS: I long to give you a big kiss too.

CHAPTER TWENTY-NINE

————

24 March 1862

Dear Tess,

I thought I knew cold but the past eight days we have walked a hundred miles or more in snow knee high and sometimes deeper. Do you remember it ever snowing so much in late March? Perhaps it is a sign from God Above this war is pure crazy, which is something I happen to believe.

First we marched from Lebanon to Abingdon where we weren't hardly settled in when Maj. Thompson got orders for us to go on to Big Moccasin in order to defend the pass there. That means we circled right around you and our home, the thought of which makes me ache through and through.

It is tough going, that's for sure, and us nearly all native to these parts. You'd think boys who've run these roads and paths their whole lives would not have such a time of it, but then none of us has ever been up and down and over these passes carrying an entire platoon of men with us, as well as the pathetic small load of supplies. If you want to count a blessing, I guess it's that there's not that much to carry.

Even in the snow the hills are alive, every spot you pass a blind opportunity for a mess of hid Union soldiers or a renegade guerrilla or two laying in wait to strike. We lost two men that way just Monday. We'd crossed Clinch Mountain headed for Abingdon and the column of us had made it nearly to the North Fork of the Holston when shots fired behind us. Three soldiers at the end of the line had stopped for a smoke thinking they'd not be caught by commanders, and just about the time they got lit up they were ambushed by a small troop of Unionists who happened to be passing through. In less than a minute, two Lee County boys were laying dead while one (who was from over on Indian Creek, I believe) outsmarted the Bluecoats by playing possum until they were gone.

I have been thinking of something on which I wish I could get your opinion, and that's of me becoming a Cavalryman. I like the idea not because of all the walking but because what they do mainly is ride on ahead to scout things for the approaching troops. They also accompany officers and I think that would be a much more interesting part of this war than the fighting. What I need to become a Cavalryman is a horse, and I am thinking of figuring how to get Buck if you would be okay with that as an idea. This is a big consideration because Buck is our main property and highly prized these days. There are so few horses that any man who can supply his own will be named to the Cavalry on delivery of the animal. Will you write to let me know?

For now I will end this letter. I miss you with an ache that never leaves, you are in my every waking thought and when I lay down my head and close my eyes to sleep, all I see is you.

Your loving husband,
Ben

PS: Love and kisses to Jane.
PPS: How is Mama and them?
PPPS: Write soon.

CHAPTER THIRTY

—————

Sweetest Tess,

The day of 3 April is one I will never ever forget even when I die, for the sight of you riding into camp on Buck is burned on my heart like a brand there to stay forever. I don't think the boys of Company E will forget, either, which has its good parts and bad for their kidding doesn't stop. I do not mind so much because I know they saw what I did, a brave, determined woman who for the sake of her husband took her own life in her hands and crossed this land, guerrillas and Billys and thieves be damned. How you made it here alive and home again (I hope) I cannot say. For it is nothing short of a miracle you were not shot and Buck taken. There is nothing quite so valuable as a horse these days but for cattle and even that I doubt, for the cattle would feed many and be gone, while the service of a horse will last as long as the animal is able.

Buck will do me well I know.

Your arrival did lift the spirits of my comrades for a time, which these have been laid low. We had not seen action at the Gap and there was no work to do around Camp. We have no tents, no blankets, no food to speak of but only a load of bedrolls that arrived (thankfully) on the third day. Maj. Thompson received a stiff reprimand for our retreat at Pound and that darkness hung in the air like bad news is wont to do. May I just say I do not understand how any high commander can think it is a smart thing to dress down a good leader who has had to make a hard call like that—we were outnumbered five to one <u>at least</u> and if we had <u>not retreated</u> but

continued in battle our whole battalion would have been lost—
hundreds left dead on Pine Mountain with no one to protect Big
Moccasin or Cumberland Gap or the road to Saltville or, dare I
say it, the people of this area. There was the loss of the Pound Gap
camp itself, a disaster I understand for the Blue Bellies burned every building, stole every provision and scavenged for any Confederate orders they could find. There were letters from Gen. Marshall
informing of Gen. Lee's plans as well as our next moves. All of these
were taken, so needless to say there has been some scrambling to
make adjustments. (That and your surprise bringing of Buck is
what brought me to Gladesville where I write this letter. More on
that in a minute.)

Anyway. There we were at Big Moccasin with nothing but
time on our hands. It is quite interesting to see a soldier create
ways to entertain himself in such circumstances, to while away
hours that if left empty will break you through and through.
There is a great deal of letter writing that goes on even among
those you think would not care about such a thing, and also
there is great whooping and hollering that goes on when mail
call comes, every soldier praying for an envelope with their
name on it. Some tear right in the second it is handed to them.
Others pull it close to their chest and walk away looking for a
quiet spot to read and reread and reread the letter.

I know about this because I have received two letters from you
to date, as well as one from Mama that was written in Aaron's
hand. Aside from seeing you on that horse, those were the happiest
moments of my Service so far.

There is a lot of card playing that goes on and a deck of cards
is a valued thing to be guarded, why if you are killed and your
belongings get rummaged a Union soldier will slide his hand in
your pockets and be as happy to find playing cards as a gold watch
even if they are made with Gen. Lee's picture. A lot of gambling
goes on, too, with poker and 21 and euchre if you have a joker.

In fact gambling gets attached to most everything here in Camp, like yesterday when there was a race between the lice that came from the heads of three men, the winner getting a sheet of letter writing paper from anyone in the crowd willing to bet something so valuable.

You are shaking your head I know. As Mama says, boys will be boys.

Things go bad fast though, with emotions running raw. It is not surprising that any time of day or night you are likely to see a fist fight break out between two men who would lay down their life for the other in battle. Maybe it has been this way since the beginning of time when men live in close quarters. I think of the stories I've learned of the days in Jerusalem when they were building King Solomon's Temple. This is part of the tradition of the Freemasons so I can't say much of it here. But I will tell you there was a great deal that went on. Like in this war, the stakes were high.

It brought me so much happiness to see you, I only wish it was for a longer amount of time. I do believe I could have figured a way for us to spend some time alone which I would have welcomed. But you were right, it would not have been fair to Will who came all this way with you, to leave him among the soldiers and him an unenlisted man. I know without a doubt it was his great love for you, his sister, that brought him in the first place. I am very grateful to him for accompanying you so you would have a horse to ride back home once you left Buck with me. I am very grateful to him for accompanying you so you were not a woman alone in this dangerous land. We did not get to talk much, so will you tell him that, once again? Will you also tell him I know what it cost him to stand as a free man amid these troops? To this very minute I question whether I made the right decision in volunteering. I understand him holding out even if I worry for him on account of the talk of Conscription, which I believe is coming soon. From this side of the fence I can see the need. We do not have enough soldiers on the Confederate side to hold our position much less make any advances. It is a losing battle as the saying goes.

At least I do have the comfort of knowing that as a part of the volunteer militia, I won't have to go beyond these mountains. At least I have that.

So now for the big news, I am officially a member of the Cavalry and am serving for a time up at Gladesville where I was sent to monitor the activity of the enemy and scout for the officers. I was guessing being a member of the mounted infantry would serve a man well and I was right. Conditions here are much better for me than on the Clinch where I slept with not even a tent. For the time being I am boarded with Morgan Tennessee Lipps, clerk of court, a kind man dedicated to this cause. I sleep in a barn with Buck, there being so little accommodations and Buck being too valuable to leave alone. I am fortunate to have a roof over my head even if it is a barn roof.

It's something what a man gets used to.

There are some others here and each day we plot our activity and coordinate it so we have this part of the county well covered from a scouting position.

There is one other bit of news I find happy, a little too happy some would say but you will understand. When Morgan Lipps learned I am a musician he brought me an old fife that I am learning to play. I miss my banjo something awful so it is wonderful to have something to fill that empty place. My first few notes on the thing were worse than cat screeching but it hasn't taken long till I've got the hang of it. The others around seem to enjoy my playing (now, not so much in the beginning) and it is a nice way to spend these long lonesome hours.

I will write more tomorrow as for now I am called away. It seems there is something brewing up near the Wise County Courthouse and Morgan Lipps has sent for me.

Write soon, my love, and every day. I miss you with an ache that takes me to my knees so I am happy to have work and Buck and this little fife to fill my time and occupy my mind. Otherwise I believe I would go crazy.

Hugs and kisses,
Ben

PS: Thank you again for bringing Buck. It is like having an old friend near.

CHAPTER THIRTY-ONE

PATRICK

MAY 1862

I KNEW THAT IT WOULD AND PRAYED THAT IT WOULD not, this passing of conscription for the drafting of soldiers in these Confederate states. Seven weeks out and already the proviso has proven disastrous. White men between the ages of eighteen and thirty-five now are *required* to serve, and the commitment is three long years. What did our lawmakers expect? Government cannot succeed when its overbearing will is placed over that of the people—and of all, one would think the body governing the states that seceded (on just such grounds) would see the immense folly. And yet! And yet, with these short-sighted leaders.

It has created chaos here in these mountains where now we face a new war, one far more violent and dangerous than a reasonable man would expect. Because in the midst of it all, our region has become a haven for dodgers and deserters. Men of character, some, but most not, men of both the North and South looking to escape, to hide, and doing whatever they must to survive. I have seen this myself as I am one who travels these mountains with great regularity, working on behalf of the Committee for Widows and Families.

Just yesterday I made the trip to Sinking Creek to see Louise Robinson. I'd received word her second oldest, Jack, had been severely wounded at Sitlington's Hill, and I wanted to prepare her for his return. Louise has borne more than her share since her husband died in a mill accident ten years ago, and I have represented her interests in trying to establish for her some stability. Her third son is one who finds trouble wherever he goes, but her youngest, Randolph, is bright, genial—a young man in whom I had taken a great interest before the war. I see a bit of myself in him, I suppose, for he is capable and curious, with a future that should be filled with promise. But with that clan of unruly brothers? Like me in those difficult days, Randolph Robinson always seemed to be standing in shadow.

I knocked on the door. I looked around as I waited for an answer, thinking of all I have seen over these last two years. War is doing some of its greatest damage to our families, to their homesteads and within our small communities that God willing will never see active battle. It's not just disrepair caused by despair or neglect, although there is gracious plenty of that. It's the marauding and plundering. The *taking of*, in whatever name is invoked. We are easy prey.

I knocked again, then called out. "'Tis Pat Hagan here, Louise. I've come with news of Jack." She was at the door then, a shotgun in her hand, and so I raised both arms. "'Tis I, Louise. Not here to cause harm."

Her fierce look held as she stepped out. "Jack, you say."

Something about the situation felt off, but I have come with information of sons and husbands and fathers often enough over this wartime to know the best course is to get to the point. "He's alive and coming home to you. He's suffered great injury, I'm afraid, but Jack is coming home."

Louise looked up as if to examine my face, as if to discover something I might be harboring there.

"He was shot in the thigh, from which he will recover. But the impact knocked him from his feet, and in the confusion of battle he was trampled. There was trauma to his shoulders and head, and he cannot be left on his own. He'll need ongoing medical care, as well."

She straightened, a swift intake of air adding a little height to her small frame.

"The field doctors believe he has suffered injury to his brain. We'll want a full evaluation when he gets home—they move so quickly with so many injured, the diagnosis is often a guess." I saw her sway backwards and I reached, afraid her legs were giving way. "Let's step inside, what do you say. Where it's cool. Where we can have a seat. There is so much to consider."

She didn't say yes and she didn't say no, and so I moved toward the door, a firm grip on her arm.

I'D NEVER BEFORE BEEN IN THE ROBINSONS' HOUSE AND I noticed it was clean, sparse but well kept. I might have expected it to be otherwise, there being so many boys, a rough-and-tumble air if nothing else, or perhaps a random ball or animal skin or mess of dirty tracks. Of these there was none, and I chalked this up to conscription—all four sons now gone—and I led Louise to a rocker and held it still while she situated. I took a seat in a straight ladder-back facing her, and with her gaze to the floor she began to rock.

"Louise," I said. She did not look up, but I continued. "Jack will be accompanied by a volunteer when he arrives here, for he is unstable and not able to travel unsupported. My recommendation is that we get him to Staunton as quickly as possible."

Her response was abrupt and immediate, her voice sharp. "To that lunatic asylum." Her words pierced with their reminder of Uncle and Aileen, six months gone from Hunter's Valley.

"For an evaluation, Louise. There are neurologists there, physicians who specialize in matters of the brain. We need their expertise to determine the best course for Jack. The best road for him, back to healing."

"*Pssshhhht*," she sounded, shaking her head. "They'll be wanting to lock him up and I won't have it. I'll look after him here."

"I understand your concern. But Jack needs to be seen by doctors who understand this type of brain trauma. And I've some contacts there that will make this possible."

"We take care of our own."

"Louise," I said. I reached and touched her hand, which was tapping fast on the rocker's arm. She jerked it away. "When Jack gets here, he will be heavily sedated. 'Tis necessary to manage his behavior, as due to his injury, he is uncontrollable. This is not a situation you can manage here alone."

"Well I can't pay for it. There ain't no money."

"I understand the challenge of this financially. But just so I'm clear. Your boys are diverting a portion of their war pay to you, right? Three dollars each, every month, as I recall. That should give you some to live on."

"Humph, maybe," she said. "Was it to come. Or maybe you ain't heard, but the South is running short of cash." She laughed, and it was not the kind of laugh that lightens a dark mood. "Nine dollars ever now and again don't go so far." She stopped, sat back, then commenced to rocking again.

Four sons. Three dollars. This didn't add up.

I moved closer. "I need you to be straight with me. Can you do that, Louise? Has one of your boys left the army? Abandoned his post?"

"My boys are good boys."

I thought this through. James, the oldest, the first to go in the earliest days of the war; Jack, now coming home; then Billy and Randolph, both subject to conscription. Had one not reported? Where was he now?

"Listen, Louise." I was concerned and naturally earnest. "I know you are not inclined to share, particularly as what you say could incriminate. But understand that I am not here on behalf of the military. At least not strictly so. I am here to support you and your boys, a family that is giving its all for the Confederacy. There's a mighty difference. You see that, don't you? You have sacrificed so much. And I need to know what's going on, so I can help you. Is it Randolph or Billy?"

"I do not know what you are talking about, Patrick Hagan."

It came to mind: *She doth protest too much.* I matched her expression, her distance, as before me a new plan formed. I knew how I could help us both.

"There might be a way, Louise, I can be of service to you in two ways. With Jack and his very specific needs. And also with this *other* situation, which at a minimum is risky and highly time sensitive." She glanced toward a door that was behind me and I pretended not to notice, even if I did project my voice a little more. "Whichever son it is, he will be found. And when that happens, the punishment will be severe. The Home Guard is going house to house searching, and the stories I've heard of what those soldiers do to evaders will make your spine tingle. Or if they follow the law and simply turn him in, punishment is severe—public humiliation, whippings, branding like cattle. 'Tis truly unconscionable." I paused, letting this sink in, then stairstepped my tone again. "And you, for hiding him? This is a dangerous situation."

A door creaked, and a voice came from behind me. "It's me, Mr. Hagan. It's Randolph."

"What...you..." Louise's teeth were clinched. Her head dropped. "Son."

"Stay where you are," I said. I did not turn to see him; instead, I got up to lock the door, to check the pull of the curtains, to retrieve the shotgun leaning inconspicuous against the far wall. "You can't be too careful, not knowing who is about."

This made Louise as angry as I'd ever seen her. "Then answer me this, Patrick Hagan. Why is it they ain't yet come after you?"

The comment stung, with all I'd done for her over the years; still I put up my hands in surrender. "'Tis a fair question, and I'll answer it honestly. The government has given any man the option of buying his way out of conscription. Three hundred dollars and you're done. And the truth is—I am a man who can afford it."

Mrs. Robinson "humphed" again, and before guilt could fully overcome me, I rushed to make my case.

"I also believe—and this is not inconsequential—I am of far greater value to the effort, and to the people here, when I am where I can offer support to those who are struggling. I have a great willingness to do what it takes to see that our families are not forgotten but instead are looked after. Taken care of. 'Tis what brought me here today." Louise and Randolph both were quiet, and in their silence I picked up my argument and went on. "But the point does raise the issue. For me to continue the work of the Committee for Widows and Families, I have to pay up.

Three hundred dollars to the government, like I said, or I can offer the army a substitute and pay that man directly for his service." Randolph looked to his mother, his face washed over in worry and relief, hopefulness and despair. For her part she kept steely eyes on me. "If you wanted to consider that, Randolph—you, too, Louise—I would pay you five hundred."

"Five hundred dollars?" Randolph said. "You would pay five hundred dollars for me to take your place?"

"Yes," I said. I looked to Louise. "'Twould cover costs for Jack and then some."

"But my boy is already marked, is what you said. He'd be punished."

"I could take care of that. Paperwork. I would have Randolph temporarily reclassified as exempt based on employment deemed necessary for the maintenance of a civil society. As a teacher, for instance. On my estate. A teacher in my school there."

"You have a school."

"Not exactly. Not yet. But I plan to, and I'm certain I could make that work. Paperwork, like I said."

"I've give them three of my four already. That ought to be enough."

I chose my words with care. "It ought to. But it's not. Randolph was obligated to report for duty, and he didn't, and now he's a hunted man. And when he is found, he'll be flogged and disgraced, and then forced to serve anyway. Or he may be killed right off. I don't like any of this either; in my opinion it's the government overstepping its bounds. But it's the way things are, and what I'm offering is an alternative. An alternative that allows you to be taken care of, Louise, and that allows you to take care of Jack."

"Randolph wants to go to college."

I turned to the young man and spoke directly to him. "You will go to college. I will see to it myself. You have a bright future, Randolph, and I'm confident you'll spend many years doing well by our fellow Virginians. You are a fine investment, and I will be proud to make it. Who knows, maybe you'll become a lawyer." I smiled. "Maybe you'll someday work with me."

"I'd like that, sir," he said.

"I've always believed in you, you know that."

"Yessir."

I looked to Louise. "Does all this work for you? If not, we won't do it. 'Tis vital we all agree."

"Come here, baby." She reached out to Randolph, and he moved to take her hand. "When would he go?"

"I'd need a day to get the papers in order. Let's say I'll come around Tuesday. It will be best if I deliver him to the division. Keeping everything above board, you know, plus keeping Randolph safe."

"And about Jack."

"I'll know more then. But with your blessing, I can go ahead and make arrangements for him to be seen in Staunton as soon as possible. Would that be all right?"

She lifted her son's hand to her lips and kissed it.

"Yes," Randolph answered for both of them. "And thank you. Thank you for what you are doing for our family."

"To you as well, son," I said. "I mean it when I say conscription is the government overstepping its bounds. But we are where we are in this war."

It was as true a statement as I'd ever made, if a disheartening one, and it served as a reminder that I needed to keep moving, as an endless round of visits stretched before me. "I will see you Tuesday," I said, and I left the Robinsons as I'd left so many families all around these hills, with a prayer for protection on my breath.

CHAPTER THIRTY-TWO

---

12 June 1862

Dearest Tess,

I am sorry truly sorry you have not heard from me in such a long time. I have written you every week and it seems for some reason my letters are not making it to you. I guess that is not so hard to believe for it's a wonder any of them are delivered what with all that is going on in these parts, I guess even the Mail Wagons have their troubles. I did get your letter of <u>21 April</u> but only of recent so I don't know what has become of Will and Amos who I know must now be or soon will be soldiers. Who would have thought when I saw you just last month the law for Conscription was only days away.

And what of Thomas? I pray he has been given Exception on account of him being a Merchant running your Daddy's store. Important work must continue even if it's just to keep moving the pitiful amount of inventory available to him. Something is better than nothing, I reckon, most certain in times like these. Also, as to Levi and Jonah, if you have any news of them ever good or bad please do write it, I do not hear much. I worry, as you know.

As to me. My focus has been Gladesville with an eye on Pound Gap. It is where this war started for me and it remains a pass of value to the Northern Invaders who now occupy it. The troops there are small in number I know because I have seen it with my own eyes, Buck and me on missions there to observe and report back to our commanders. But there came a more pressing matter that sent me to Lee County where Union soldiers have become numerous and so haughty they ride through Jonesville like there has been an invasion and they have won. Some say they are positioning for another attempt at the Cumberland Gap having 5,000 Federals on the Virginia side of the mountain and 5,000 on the Kentucky side, with Confederate troops guarding it from the top. Our troops are pinned in now, some of which are my comrades.

So a few others and I were sent to provide some protection for the good people of Jonesville. While I was gone, Union soldiers made a surprise raid on Gladesville and burned a great deal of the town. In particular they were set on the Courthouse and encountered Morgan T. Lipps and Commonwealth Attorney Alexander Smith. The two stood firm to protect the county's records and the Federals took them both as prisoners.

They released Smith in short order. But they rode away with Lipps, his wrists bound and his mouth gagged no doubt because he is a vehement and vocal supporter of the Confederate Cause. He believes it to be favored by God and he is not a shy man when it comes to politics or religion or anything else for that matter.

It is believed he is held now in Pikeville.

I did hear this story about his capture which I think you will find interesting. As it was a nice day and Lipps did some planting before he went to tend to his Courthouse duties, he found himself in shirtsleeves when they put him up on a horse to ride away in the care of a Federal Guard. Lipps expressed concern over this— the nights would be cold—and asked if they might first stop by his place just west of town so he could get himself a coat. Whether out of kindness or simply to quiet him down I do not know, but that's just what they did.

As for me, I was ordered back to Gladesville immediately, and so I am here now where I watch over the Lipps place and continue my military duties. Who would have ever expected it? Me, Benjamin E. Grubb, a member of Company E, the 64th Virginia Cavalry, and this frontier town we once called Big Glades a primary target for the Union Army.

There is also this I want to say. If I have to serve I am happy it is here. I stand guard on regular occasions in close proximity to the Virginia House Hotel, where you and I spent our wedding night. I am not a natural soldier, as you know, but I would not hesitate to take out a Blue Coat was he to attempt to set fire to the building. It is a sacred place for me, the site where we celebrated our union and first laid together as husband and wife. I remember every detail about that night, how shy you were, and how beautiful. I remember the candlelight on your skin and the smell of you, of lavender and us mingled, two become one. It takes my breath to think of it and so I only allow myself tiny bits and pieces, a little here and there so as not to become too melancholy. For that is the real battle of this war.

I do not know how long I shall be here or where I will go next, I don't even know if this letter will reach you. But I beg you to keep writing me, as often as you can, every day is not too much. Even if you don't hear from me. Even if you wonder if I have disappeared from the face of this earth. I have not and I will not. I am out here every second thinking of you and longing for you and for the day we are together again, your head against my shoulder, your breath in soft puffs on my chest, our hearts beating together in time.

Your loving husband,
Ben

CHAPTER THIRTY-THREE

———————

17 September 1862

Dear Tess,

It has taken me some time to write this as something has happened that has come as a shock and also broken my heart. Levi and Jonah are dead, both killed at Manassas. I ask you to be the one to tell Mama if she has not heard, go to her for you can be of comfort. Also, I have details about the battle, which most families never get. This is because Gen. Marshall, who I travel with some, and play music for—in kindness the general sent a soldier, Rob Clancy, to tell me. Clancy was there with Levi and Jonah and saw it all first-hand. I warn you some of this is hard to take, but I will not spare details for you are strong and of good judgment, and what Mama hears I will leave up to you.

I will start with this. Remember the day Levi came to tell us goodbye? And the letter Jonah left when he followed him? They wanted to fight together as brothers, and that's just what they did. They were under direct command of General Stonewall Jackson having come to be part of his Virginia Army early in the summer, something Mama may have known but I did not. I think it would be a great honor to fight for Jackson as he has one of the best minds in this war along with being fearless, which comes from his belief in God as his Protector. I have heard many soldiers' stories about him, in particular how he sits on his red horse called Little Sorrel and you can see his mouth moving as he prays, which I imagine is rather a sight to behold. I have also heard it said he is as comfortable in battle as he is lying in bed. This is all due to his Faith.

According to Clancy, Jackson and his 24,000 men had circled

back up above Manassas crossroads where they were between the Union Army and Washington, something the Northerners wouldn't expect. There was a farm there that offered the opportunity for a surprise attack. It had broad open fields and a deep ravine just behind the tree line, an abandoned railroad grade that ran along the edge of the property and down along the road. Jackson knew this was the route Pope's army would take, and it was under this cover he had his troops—Levi and Jonah and Rob Clancy among them—lay in wait. As Clancy told it there was a great thrill in the air, Jonah and Levi being side by side, and Jonah with a particular excitement about him, chatting on and moving about, shifting this way and that. Levi cautioned him a time or two to quiet down but it didn't do any good (you know Jonah). Then they heard boots coming and there was dead silence in the ravine, everyone holding their breath.

Out from the woods stepped a whole line of Union soldiers. Not a one of them was aiming a gun, they were just walking, not a care in the world, and Jackson let the whole platoon pass. His soldiers were lined up in the ditch—shoulder to shoulder, rifles aimed and ready—and what did Jackson do but wait. Another platoon came along and this one had greater numbers and was more organized. General Jackson rode right out in front of them, and high in the air he waved his sword, and he moved his mouth but no words came out. The red horse was doing big figure eights, and Jackson looked to be a mad man, nobody on either side knowing what he was doing or why. Then the general turned back toward his hid troops and trotted so casual he might have been on his way to church. He said so calm to his leaders: "Bring out your men, Gentlemen." And Jonah jumped like he was gonna run forward and Levi grabbed his coat and pulled him hard back into the ditch. "Don't do anything without me," he said and Jonah nodded, his breath coming hard.

It didn't take long until there was the command to fire. The smoke and bullets came from the ravine taking the Blue Coats by surprise, they could hardly see a Confederate soldier but still there was no doubt they were under grave attack. Another column of troops came from behind and another and another and for a time all our boys did was load and shoot, load and shoot. The air was dark with gunpowder but they could see bodies falling in the road and others, under command of Gen. Gibbon, running for the woods. Still those soldiers recovered faster than expected, they sent out skirmishers first and bullets came forward in big numbers. Then Gibbon ordered their front line into battle and unfortunate for us it was the Iron Brigade of 2nd Wisconsin, a fierce troop already known to the Confederacy, and in their tall black hats they stepped from the woods and began their imposing march across the field, guns raised.

Jackson's famous Brigade rose from the ravine. They stepped from the big cut and up onto the field opposite where they outnumbered the Black Hats two to one.

"I ain't never felt such a sense of thrill and doom," is what Clancy told me. "What could you do but watch? These were the bravest men of the war, North and South, facing off in a hellacious showdown. The Rebels said, 'Come on, goddamn you,' under their breath and at a hundred yards that's what the Black Hats did. They let loose such a wall of fire and artillery I ducked down in the ditch despite myself.

"Then it was all hell and fury, smoke and bodies flying and neither side backing down. The only difference was the greater numbers of the Confederates, so Gibbon ordered more men, and Jackson did the same, and when even that wasn't enough, Jackson sent for Trimble's line."

Levi and Jonah and Rob Clancy were still in the ditch, their unit had not been called. It was getting on dark and it seemed there would never be an end to the battle, just more and more troops entering the line and plowing each other down. That's when Jackson ordered all remaining men forward and Jonah jumped from the ravine, moving so quick Levi and Rob both lost sight.

"I'm going after him," Levi said. "Cover me if you can."

Clancy tried to follow, which was impossible due to the haze. He hadn't got more than a hundred yards when he caught his boot on the arm of a dead soldier and he fell to the ground. He pushed up, got to his hands and his knees and looked around. Then he saw Jonah, standing with his gun raised and its barrel trained on a Black Hat who had taken out the Confederate lying at his feet. The downed man was Levi.

The Black Hat twisted, raised his gun and fired. Just as his shot got off he jerked, his face and his hardee hat blown to bits. Rob ran to Jonah, who was still standing. "Have you been shot? Have you been shot?" he hollered. Jonah turned. The front of his jacket was drenched in blood. "I got the son of a bitch," he said. "Tell Ben it was me who got the son of a bitch."

Jonah fell to his knees, then he went forward over his rifle. Clancy got down and laid beside him, there being dead and suffering all around. Jonah's eyes were open and there was still some breath.

"You did good," Clancy said, "you took out one of the Union's finest and bravest. You got a member of the 2nd Wisconsin Black Hat Brigade."

Jonah didn't answer.

"I'll tell everybody what you did. I will. I'll tell everybody how brave you were for Levi."

It was a little while later when Jonah's spirit left him. Rob kept his arm across his back the whole time and when Jonah died, Clancy said the smile was still on his face.

I asked Clancy then about Levi.

"I waited for the shooting to stop," he said, "then I went to him. He was on his stomach and I turned him over, and I put my hand on his forehead and offered up a prayer. I checked his pockets, thinking if there was something in there I might could get it to his family some day. They were empty but for a letter."

He pulled the paper from his pocket and handed it to me and I saw it was from you. You wrote to Levi that you prayed for him and Jonah every day. And you included this scripture, do you remember?

Be strong and of a good courage; be not afraid, neither be thou dismayed: for the Lord thy God is with thee withersoever thou goest.

And so you see, dear wife, a letter from you was what Levi carried with him. Yours were the words that brought him comfort. He came into this war a boy with a romantic notion of what it was to be a soldier. Then he became his brother's keeper, marching across Virginia for hundreds of miles believing it was up to him to offer protection to Jonah. And what comes to me now is that excepting for you, I don't guess he ever received a letter of love and encouragement from anybody. It occurs to me now that Levi nor Jonah neither one ever got any mail, I reckon, but from you and possibly Mama, which is sparse due to her not being able to read and write. So thank you for writing him. And Jonah, too, I am sure.

Clancy says the fighting went on for three more days, and thousands died or were injured. I mourn for them all. Can I say that, if only to you? I mourn them all, the dead and the lame, and also the living, men of both sides with no choice but to rise up, take up arms, and fight like hell the devil that is at the heart of all this brutality. All this nonsense.

And now I hear Gen. Lee plans to continue the move North, the South becoming the Invaders as he launches the first battles on Union soil. Rob is headed for Sharpsburg and Antietam Creek while orders are for our troops, under Bragg and Kirby, to march on through Kentucky for attacks that coordinate with those to take place in Maryland. The boys of my Company are not happy about this as we all signed on with the agreement of the Confederate Army that we would never leave SW Virginia, as you well know. I wonder what will become of that fuss as many soldiers refuse to go.

As for me, I should tell you in spite of the agreement and my promise to you of the same, I am already traveling in Kentucky with Gen. Marshall. Before you get angry let me explain it is a decision that offered the promise of little battle and a lot of music, a covenant between me and the General himself. He heard me play at Gladesville and found my music lifted his spirits. His particular troops were moving into Kentucky to recruit soldiers there—something his unit badly needs—and he acquired a banjo from somewhere, presented it to me and asked me to be his personal assistant on this important mission.

There was another motive, I know now, as Gen. Marshall is as smart as a whip. He recognized music would be a good way to reach the people of Kentucky. Their hearts are like our hearts in many ways, so in truth of fact I am more a part of his recruiting effort than anything else even if he hasn't said so. I do not mind. I play for them, I play for him, I play for anyone who wants to hear and that is something that has brought me back to life.

There is another benefit and that is getting to travel with the General. As I write this I am at the residence of Alexander Barnes outside of Lexington. I do not have a place in the house, of course, but Gen. Marshall does see to it that I have blankets and enough to eat and that makes me luckier than anybody I know fighting in this war. Except for the commanders, and I wouldn't trade places with any of them, not for nothing.

And so we are off to Harrodsburg to join the troops of Bragg and Smith where our boys should see some action. They are anxious for this.

I will close now, my love. I have spent two days writing this difficult letter but as our communication has become less with all the moving about etc I wanted to be sure you know and can tell Mama of the fate of my brothers and their last hours as soldiers. I also wanted you to know of the importance of your letters to them, and to me, if any ever find me.

All my love,
Ben

CHAPTER THIRTY-FOUR

———

28 October 1862

Dear Tess,

Have you been getting my letters? Do you know what has been going on? Can you feel how hard I miss you? I have written every week but I have not gotten any word from you since long before Levi and Jonah died. It could be that with all my moving about your letters haven't got to me. I will believe this for <u>I know you</u> and <u>I know your love for me</u> so <u>I know you will be faithful to me and our marriage</u> even while I am off <u>doing my duty</u> in this hateful war. Do you know that as I wrote that long letter about Levi and Jonah, a horrible battle—<u>the most horrible battle yet</u>—was taking place at Antietam? Some say 25,000 soldiers are dead or wounded <u>just at Sharpsburg</u>. I don't know how there can be any men left, if we keep this up we will wipe them all out, North and South both.

<u>What is to become of our country?</u>

I don't have any news of Rob Clancy, I do not even know if he made it to Sharpsburg. Or if he did, if he lived through the battle.

<u>Are you getting my letters?</u>

We have moved throughout the eastern part of Kentucky but have not had success in recruiting here. These people are as sick of this war as I am, all they want is to be left alone. It is something I understand.

It is so cold I cannot feel my feet or even my fingers as I write this but only my heart which I fear is also on the verge of frostbite. Snow and sleet came early to these mountains so much that we are calling this Camp Snow, it is impossible to get warm. The men are starved and exhausted, calculations say they have walked more than 600 miles over these two months. Thank God I have a horse and can ride although keeping Buck fed is something that has become my biggest challenge. There is no feed, no fields, nothing but frozen ground all around. All I want is to be home by the fire in our little house with you. It is a mansion in my memory, a safe place, and I will never, not ever, want for anything more grand. Ever, for the rest of my life. I will be home and you will be there and I will have everything just being with you.

You are there, aren't you?

You are waiting for me. Right?

Are you?

Love,
Ben

CHAPTER THIRTY-FIVE

---

29 November 1862

Dear Tess,

I could not sleep last night for worrying about you and wondering if you are making it okay through this war which I do not know. It has been 4 months and 29 days since I last got a letter from you or anyone, even Mama. I do not know what is happening where you are, if you have food, if Jane is doing all right or God forbid has been taken ill with disease which runs rampant here and everywhere. I hear the instances of layouts and deserters are growing more every day as men hide out in every nook and cranny in our mountains of which there are plenty, the hills crawling with them now, Union and Confederate alike. We are all weary of this war, everyone is hungry and cold. Which makes a man do crazy things he wouldn't dream of, of a regular day. I hope you have survived okay. I am glad you know how to shoot a gun and pray that you have not hesitated to do it if you needed to, if you still have a gun at all, the Raiders likely to have taken it too.

I am sick with worry and that is the truth.

How is Mama? And Aaron? And Boo? What is it like for Boo who is not able to understand anything that is going on? How is your Daddy and Mama? And all?

It has not snowed today but is clear and cold so cold I don't know how we'll make it through one more night much less winter which is so clearly laying up against us now.

Your husband,
Ben

CHAPTER THIRTY-SIX

———

16 December 1862

Dear Tess,

Praise Jesus, as your Mama would say, my feet are back on Virginia soil and waiting for me were 22 letters, 16 held by Morgan T. Lipps in Gladesville and 6 others in a packet at Camp Fulkerson here in Abingdon. In addition I had 2 letters from Mama with news they are holding on okay all things considered which I know she is strong but I also know she does not want me to feel her sadness and worries given our loss of Levi and Jonah. I do worry, though, about her and about you, back in my homeland I find it is more ravaged than I ever expected to see it. I do not believe the battlefields at Antietam and Manassas can hold more sadness than this stripped land.

I am sorry to hear of the closing of the store, I know that has been a blow to Thomas and to your Papa.

And so they are all soldiers now, Thomas, Will, Amos, all but little Aaron. Damn Conscription. I can see how Thomas and Will might make fine soldiers but it surprises me about Amos who I always thought of as sensitive. Still I have to say our Confederate forces are filled with men and boys who were never cut out for fighting. Never ever and yet here they are. I will remember your brothers all of them in my prayers and I will look for them in my travels, although I do not move around so much these days, something that is just fine with me. And Lucy, too, how surprising it is that she found love in the midst of these troubles. And of this Union man, does your Papa like <u>him</u>???

My dear love, my sweet wife, how I miss you. How desperate

I am for you worse now than those long weeks I didn't hear from you. A tiny window into life at home is enough to rip the heart right out of a man's chest, it's like I see it beating on the frozen ground in front of me but still that is better than not knowing. It is. So I thank you for every word you write to me.

You are my beating heart, Elizabeth Young Grubb. You are my life.

Always,
Ben

CHAPTER THIRTY-SEVEN

PATRICK

IT WAS LOUISE ROBINSON WHO ALERTED ME AS TO THE situation with Elizabeth Young. "Don't look to be good and that girl's too proud to ask for help." Not that there is much for neighbors to share these days, two years of war and the sacrifice of our local families becoming increasingly, painfully clear. Children are starving, farms have been stripped by soldiers with no provisions, and looters have taken the balance with no conscience. Disease is rampant; there is little access to doctors and medicines or even a decent diagnosis. And the women who head these households—big-hearted women of strength and substance—have slid into survivalist mode, so worn down by loss and daily trials their only focus is making it through one more day.

And so it was as I made my way to the Grubbs' cabin. It was a journey that required great stamina as it was so cold one's breath froze in the air before you. There was ice and snow all around, so much so that after Danny slipped the third time, I got down, held the reins, and we walked together. We were both grateful it was not more than eight or ten miles.

I looked around as we approached. I was somewhat familiar with the property, but it looked desolate and forlorn in the cold, with not so much as a fence to keep it company. As there was no post I tied Danny to a tree near the front. I promised him I wouldn't be long.

"Elizabeth," I hollered. I rapped on the door with gusto. "'Tis I, Elizabeth, Patrick Hagan. I've come to check on you. To make sure you're doing all right in this dreadful weather." There was no response. "You *and* your baby. Did Marilee tell me she's her namesake? You named her Mary?"

"Jane. We're calling her Jane." It was harsh, this voice from behind the closed door, no resemblance to the young girl I remembered who'd been so spunky. "Mary Jane actually. But Ben wanted to call her Jane."

Danny was breathing loud behind me. He stomped twice, and the door opened slowly, but at least it was a start.

"Better come in," she said. Her voice and demeanor had given way to something gentler, or more exhausted, perhaps. "I'll get a blanket for the horse."

I stomped the snow and wet from my boots and crossed the threshold into the little house, a room, really, a bed pulled over by a fireplace with no fire. I could see a little girl asleep under the covers, her face red and her hair matted. There must have been five blankets over her and one pulled down at the foot. Elizabeth gathered it up to hand to me.

"You are very kind," I said. "But the horse will be fine."

"Take it," she said. "This blanket's the only thing I have to offer either of you."

I took it. "Could I bring in some wood while I'm out there? Stoke the fire a bit?"

She looked toward the hearth. "There's no wood. I've been planning to go out and chop some, but I haven't got 'round to it. Jane's been poorly and I can't leave her."

"You don't have a woodpile, then."

"I don't have a woodpile *currently*. Soldiers needed the wood and they took it."

"All of it? They left you with none?"

"I was happy for them to go."

I saw then that something was broken in her, something that chilled me. I headed outside to find an ax.

AN HOUR LATER I'D STACKED ENOUGH WOOD TO GET her through several days. It was old and seasoned, cut from a dead hickory I'd found in the woods. But the logs wouldn't burn until they thawed and dried. I could hear the baby crying and Elizabeth trying to soothe her, and I opened the door and went in without knocking. "You cannot stay here," I said, so abrupt it surprised me. She opened her mouth but I didn't allow room for protest. "I'll take you anywhere you want to go—is your family close by?" She didn't answer, but only looked at Jane, holding the child in her arms and rocking. "Are there relatives, Elizabeth?"

"I won't—" she started, but again I interrupted.

"Are there relatives."

She looked at me as angry and rigid as she'd been when I arrived. But this time I also saw tears. "There's nobody with less troubles than me."

"Well you can't stay here. Your baby will die. 'Tis that simple. Jane is sick, and she needs food and medicine. And heat, for God's sake. And so do you. You can't survive winter here with nothing."

She glared, no part of her showing the slightest relief I had come.

"Wrap up Jane the best you can. Do you have a coat? Does Ben have a coat here? Put Jane inside and then we'll wrap you both up together. If you won't go to family, I'll take you to Hagan Hall where Mulay can care for you and the baby. We've provisions and room. 'Tis a good distance, but we can keep you warm until we get there."

Five minutes later it was done. I'd held Jane while Elizabeth had gotten positioned on the horse. Then I lifted the child to her and wrapped them together in blankets, neither face visible. I took the reins and stepped ahead as together we began our icy trip across the mountain. *Come on boy, slow and steady*, I said, and for the rest of the journey Danny and I walked, as determined as the old-time Long Hunters who'd crossed these hills, as sure-footed as if it were summer.

SHE STAYED NEARLY TWO WEEKS. I GAVE HER PLENTY OF space, her needs tended to by Mulay. It was remarkable to watch the two of them interact; Mulay is a woman of few words and strong opinions, and she has a powerful way about her. She pulled the child into her arms the moment we arrived and doctored her with roots and herbal teas and balms. In no time Jane was running around the house, color and joy returned to her face, but her mum was another matter. There was an immediate, unspoken understanding between the two women that Jane was in good hands, and Elizabeth let go, sliding into the front bedroom's warm feather bed where she slept for two days.

Mulay woke her occasionally, insisting she eat proper meals. Elizabeth would comply, then she'd fall back into a sleep I could hear was filled with fitful dreams. Only once did I look in on her, as this was not proper, nor was it my place. But how could I not? She moaned in agony, and she often cried out. It was my instinct to help, but Mulay insisted we leave her be. "It she'own to do," I heard this again and again.

The fourth day, Elizabeth appeared downstairs. I was at the dining table reading the Abingdon paper as Mulay rolled biscuits and made fried eggs. We looked up together to see Elizabeth in the door, her hair a fright, her clothes worn and dirty. There was color in her face, but I hardly recognized the curious girl I had known just a few years before.

"I need to be getting on back home," she said. "I'm much obliged for your kindness, but we need to be getting along."

I folded the paper and laid it to the side. Mulay stood still, the spatula in her hands, and for a moment there was only the sound of grease popping in the skillet. It was Mulay who finally spoke. "You needs go, go'on. But da chile? She stay here. You go'on. Mulay tek care da chile." Then she turned back to the stove and flipped the eggs.

Elizabeth clearly didn't know how to respond; she stood there, her own arms wrapped around her torso. Mulay turned her head back toward Elizabeth. "Go'on," she repeated, her head nodding with emphasis.

"Or," I said. "Or you could sit down and have some breakfast while we think this over. Jane will be upset to wake and find her mum gone, so we'll need to think through what we'll do when that happens."

Mulay brought a steaming plate to the table and set it at the place beside me. "Dis you'un," she said to Elizabeth. "Seddown. Eat."

SHE HAD GAINED SOME STRENGTH BY THE SECOND week. I was gone much of the time tending to war duties and the needs of other families, but I intentionally brought my law work home, giving me the ability to see Elizabeth on the limited occasions she left the up-stairs bedroom. It was something I hardly admitted to myself at the time, believing it was simply a matter of doing the right thing on behalf of my charge. But I was also deeply curious about her, about the night-mares that haunted her, about the girl lost inside.

IT WAS TUESDAY EVENING WHEN I LOOKED UP TO FIND she was standing in the doorway. I was at my desk, absorbed in news the *Abingdon Virginian* was reporting—that there had been an ambush of the Virginia 63rd at their camp at Black Water. She spoke and her voice had substance behind it. "I was wondering if I could return this and borrow another," she said. She held a slim volume of poetry and I was surprised, something my face must have revealed. "Oh my. I guess you didn't send it," she said. It came as a quick little burst. "It was on a tray Mulay brought yesterday."

I knew nothing of the book but smiled at the thought. "Of course," I said. "My mind was elsewhere. I hope you enjoyed it."

"Yes. I did. Miss Kitchens...I mean, Marilee..." She stumbled over these words and I saw her blush. It was good to see color in her face again. "What I'm meaning to say is Marilee Kitchens, my teacher, as you know, Marilee made sure I studied the English poets. But since she has gone back home, it has been a few years since I've done much reading at all."

"Aah, yes," I said. "She does love Keats. And Byron. And Shelley, whom I must say I find difficult."

"All that carrying on about this and that. All caught up like prisoners of their own thoughts! Give me adventure over such nonsense any day."

"I see," I said, smiling.

"I guess you find that silly. Unsophisticated."

"I wouldn't say I do. I would rather characterize it as honest. And refreshing. A woman who knows her own mind."

She stared, unblinking.

"And a woman who speaks it." I gestured toward the shelves. "I've a large collection, as you can see. Why don't you come in and find something that interests you? 'Tis rather a shame to have all these books and only me to read them."

She stood a moment longer, her eyes locked on me. Then she stepped into the library and began to scan the shelves.

THE NEXT TWO DAYS I SPENT IN LEE COUNTY. I SHOULD have stayed another night but felt anxious to get home, and so I left after dark, arriving at Sulphur Springs just after midnight. I was worn and exhausted, and I climbed the back stairs eager for sleep. I'd just reached the landing when I heard a curdling scream and ran to the front, flinging wide the bedroom door. My lantern cast little light, but I could see Elizabeth was sitting up in bed, her legs pulled to her chest and her arms wrapped so her body made a tight ball. Her head shook back and forth and she spoke, although I couldn't understand any of the words she was saying. I went to her and put my hand on her shoulder and shook it. "Elizabeth," I said. "Wake up. You're having a dream. Wake up." I set the lantern on the table beside her.

She turned toward the light and said something, her eyes still closed. "Wake up," I said, more forceful. "Open your eyes." She did so, and I saw a look of such horror it still gives me chills. "'Tis I, Elizabeth. Patrick." Masses of hair fell across her face, and I swept the strands back. "Do you see me? Can you hear me?" She blinked, but there was no recognition. "You're at Hagan Hall. Jane is here, and she is fine. You are both fine, both perfectly safe. I am here. You're safe here, with me."

She reached up and wrapped her arms around me like a child, and I pulled her in close. She cried and I rocked her back and forth and I said, over and over, "You're safe. I am here. I am here, with you."

After a time the tears subsided and she pulled away. I stood to leave, embarrassed now, and when I reached the door I turned to offer an apology. She shook her head no, and so I didn't offer one.

"It's just been so—" She didn't go on.

"I've had a difficult few days myself," I said. "I'm going to the parlor for a whiskey. You'd be welcome if you care to join."

I POURED ONLY ONE, NOT BELIEVING SHE WOULD COME. Then there she was, properly clothed and wrapped in a quilt but also bare, somehow, in the firelight. I arranged chairs for our sitting and I angled them, their front feet near to the hearth: I would see her without looking. I handed her a glass and we sat.

I DID NOT KNOW IF EITHER OF US WOULD EVER SPEAK. I did not, and she did not, and so we sipped. Her legs she'd tucked beneath, her eyes she kept on the flames. The tumbler she held two-handed and it rested, absently, against her bottom lip. Light bounced across the angles of the glass, then moved over her face. Was she beautiful? Or was it the night and the whiskey, or the solitude of this sweet holy respite? For the war, for once, felt distant.

The turn of her head broke the silence and the moment. "How is it that you have all this?" I did not know what she meant, what she was asking exactly, and before I could conjure *blessings* and *good fortune* and *responsibility* she went on. "Men are dying. Their families are starving, and you have...all this." She raised her hands palms up, emphasizing her stabbing point. "You haven't been raided, you haven't been plundered. Your beloved estate. You have sugar and coffee and salt and heat and—" She looked at me now, and it was accusing. "How is it you're *here* and not off on some goddamn frozen field dying of dysentery? Your dreams gone, and your future lost. Like my husband. Like all the others. Like the rest of us."

I was blindsided, dumbstruck, rendered uncharacteristically speechless. How could she? How dare she? What she'd said, and the way she'd said it; there was vitriol.

She took a deep gulp. Then she held the near-empty glass before her, lifting it high and tilting it this way, then that, so that in the soft light the amber liquid shone rich. "I'll have another," she said. Then she turned toward me, downed the rest, and handed over her glass.

I did as she'd asked. Then I put a log on the fire and stood a moment, my back to Elizabeth, my self-esteem in search of a bolster.

"You know she's in love with you," she said.

"What?" I turned. It was one of my more brilliant comebacks, my training as a fine defense lawyer clearly on display.

"Marilee. She's in love with you. Surely you see that."

I considered; my surprised reaction was an honest one. Marilee'd been gone two years. No, longer even than that, and until I'd found myself standing at Elizabeth's door—trying to *save* her, no less—it'd been weeks since I'd thought of Marilee.

"I still hear from her, when mail reaches me, and every letter she mentions you. *Have you seen Patrick? How is Patrick? Any word of Patrick, by chance?*"

"How is she?" It was a sincere question, albeit one I wasn't sure Elizabeth would answer generously. She eyed me, sizing this up, sizing me up even as I stood tall before her.

"Fine. More than fine, actually. She's left Charlottesville. Did you know that? Gone to live on a sea island off the coast of South Carolina."

"*Our* Marilee? Are you certain?" This I could not imagine, and my disbelief delighted Elizabeth.

"*Our* Marilee, yes. She's a teacher at a school for colored children. Free colored children, the island being under Union control." There was a twinkle in her eyes, us both understanding the change in perspective this would have required of our friend. "I get the idea she might have gotten involved in the Underground Railroad, although she never outright said that. But I believe that led her to this work."

I had to sift these thoughts, my impression having been of Marilee as a supporter of slavery, having been reared in a slave-owning household. But it was a liberal upbringing nonetheless, and lord knows she could make an argument from any side. Marilee a vigilante? Marilee risking it all in the fight for freedom and rights? I liked this new version of her. I liked the thought of a Marilee with gumption.

"She's found her passion, Patrick. That's all you can figure. She was a woman in search of passion, and now she's found it."

I took my seat, and I considered. I sipped. "I don't think she was in love with me," I said, the statement sounding less sure than I'd meant it.

"Then you are not as smart as people say you are."

I looked at Elizabeth. I felt her eyes on me and I turned to meet her, face to face. "As to your earlier allegations, I would like the opportunity to respond. I would ask the benefit of your listening with an open mind. Hearing me, if you can, with an open heart."

She did not react, her eyes did not waver. And so I summoned every skill I have in logic and persuasion, and before Elizabeth Young I began to make my case.

"I understand how all this must look to you. I have so much, and as you said, so many have lost everything. But the reality is that my commitment to the people of this region is of far greater benefit if I am *here*. I have unique circumstances that allow for that—my experience and offering of wartime services as an attorney; my connections in both the judicial and government sectors—locally, yes, but also regionally and nationally; my understanding of the devastation of the challenges people here face. And yes, as crass as it is to say it, my wealth. My considerable wealth, which yields far more power than it should in the previously mentioned arenas, and which allows me to personally provide what I can, where I can, to whom I can, when appropriate. All of which takes a great deal more consideration and forethought and finessing than one might imagine."

Her skepticism did not waver.

"I could be a soldier. I should be a soldier, it is not lost on me that this is what you are thinking. But I found a substitute, and I paid my way out. 'Tis true, and all very legal, and even so I will not divulge details, as that would prove disrespectful to the young man who stepped up in my stead. I will simply say that it was a situation as desperate and dangerous as any I have seen, and I believe my involvement lessened the war's horrific hold on that family—at least as much as was possible, given their terrible circumstance."

Her glass was empty, and she set it on the floor. "And what of this place, Patrick? Tell me how your *magnificent* mansion has stayed—I don't know—protected. Safe, when no other place seems to be."

"Well, it is guarded, for one, by men I pay to perform that task."

"Slaves," she said.

"Negroes, yes, for the most part. But none are slaves. They are in my employ as free men who are hired hands. That's how they consider themselves, and that's how they are considered by me."

"I should like to speak *to them* about that." This she said under her breath and still I challenged her.

"I invite you to do that. Anyone on the estate. Anyone in the house. Or simply ask Mulay. You've seen for yourself that neither I—nor anyone, for that matter—could get her to speak anything but the truth."

"Her own truth."

"Aye, but truth nonetheless."

Elizabeth considered this. I wondered what she was thinking, having been brought back to health by Mulay, having given over her daughter to Mulay's capable, if unconventional, ways. "It's like she sees things. Like she *knows* things." She said this, and I understood that her resolve had relented some, as if for the moment we sat together on the same side of a fence. She looked to me, her deep brown eyes searching. "How is it I find that *comforting*?"

"Perhaps it is because Mulay's intentions are for good."

We sat quiet. I noticed how warm the room had become, the fire burning hot, if low, our glasses empty. Should I toss a log? Should I offer another drink?

"Me and Jane are doing okay." It came from her as a pronouncement, a declaration, and somehow I had the presence of mind not to respond. Still it felt as if I'd challenged her. "We are. I was. For all those months. I kept Jane fed and clothed and happy. I took care of the garden. I put up what I could, looked in after my mother and father, Ben's mama, Aaron and Boo. I did a good job of it."

"You did," I said. "I know."

"And then those…those goddamn *bushwhackers* came through and—" Her voice cracked, and she turned her head away from me.

The nightmares, then.

She got up from the chair, her back to me. Her arms were crossed and her head hung low as if scanning the floor for something she'd lost. She rubbed her right foot over the bricks and as she did this, she talked, quiet and slow.

"I was out back looking to see if there was something to find in the garden, an old leaf of fall kale or a shoot of winter greens. There was nothing, of course, the ground stripped and me having looked ten times already. The only thing my mind held was the thought of what on earth was I gonna make us to eat. Then out of nowhere, there they were. I was down on the ground before I even knew what was happening. Two of them held me while the other lifted my skirt. I kicked and screamed and he put his filthy hand across my mouth. With everything in me I bit hard as I could into it. Then I heard the blast of a rifle and his head exploded all over me, my face, into my mouth, bits in my eyes. He came down heavy on top. The other two ran, and with all my might I pushed the body off, I pushed it hard, and it flipped and fell over on its back. It looked up, dead, and I ran for my gun and for Jane. She'd been sleeping but the shot woke her, and when I got to her, she was standing on the mattress and crying.

"I shoved everything I could find in front of the door. I looked a fright, I knew it and I knew it scared Jane worse. Still I went to her. I wiped my face with the back of my skirt and I picked up my screaming child and held her close, blood and guts and all. I didn't know who was out there, or where the shot'd come from, and I was afraid to leave the baby so I didn't go out for two days. On the third I locked her inside and went out to figure what I was gonna do with a goddamn dead body. Which I knew, by then, would be disgusting. But when I got around the corner of the house, nothing was there. No body, no blood. Nothing." She looked at me now, her defiance returned. "And before you ask, no, I did not contact the sheriff. I never told anybody, and that includes Ben. What good would it do? He can't help, and he'd want to, and no telling the lengths he would go to. No. This is my war. This is my scar. This is—"

"But you didn't—"

"Don't. Just don't."

I accepted her demand with the same finality she'd made it, and in that moment I accepted the secret as one that, for the rest of her life, Elizabeth would carry alone.

THREE DAYS LATER WE PACKED THEM UP IN THE WAGON, and along with stashes of food Mulay pulled from so many hidden places I can't imagine, I drove them back across the mountain. We'd struck a bargain before we left Sulphur Springs that I could help get them more stabilized but only with her help. That meant I could chop a more sizable stack of wood and do a little work to secure the house only if she were there, working alongside me. It turned out she was more than capable, and with Mulay to look after Jane, these were tasks that didn't take long. Along about dark we said goodbye, and Mulay and I drove away, leaving Elizabeth Young Grubb to her own life.

CHAPTER THIRTY-EIGHT

———

11 March 1863

Dear Tess,

There has been a lot of talk among the troops about Lincoln's Emancipation Proclamation, mostly nobody understands how he can free slaves in Rebel states when he is not even our President. Of course, there is no love lost for Lincoln around here anyway so it doesn't much matter when you get right down to it. We are not seeing much battle, that is a good thing, and we are not seeing any food or provisions either. There was a few days when some Union Troops stirred it up over around Little Moccasin Gap. There was some fierce fighting, then the Federals stomped around a bit before we ran them back into Tennessee. I've heard it said they found our terrain to be too difficult to manage, something that gives the boys here a bit of pride. It's something that's needed since they mostly just sit around and pass the days complaining about Lincoln. From time to time I get an order to ride over to Lee County or Abingdon to check on this or that, or to deliver something from one officer to another. I am happy when those orders come because it gets me out of this hellhole and gives me some time on my own. I ride along old mountain trails and day-dream about a life I can hardly remember. I also dream about you and the next time we will lay together. And I wonder about Jane who is no longer a baby but a little one toddling about probably talking up a storm. Can she say Papa? Does she know who I am? I love you, Elizabeth, and I try to remember every detail of you.

I am so afraid of forgetting. I am so afraid of our good memories together being replaced by this war, by boring days and some so horrible I can't even speak of them.

Ben

CHAPTER THIRTY-NINE

———

21 April 1863

Dear Elizabeth,

I have just got word from Red Hopkins telling me of your Papa's death. I am on my way to you. I don't know how I will get there but I am coming. I am posting this letter in the event I don't make it and the Confederacy labels me AWOL. I am not a deserter. I would never ever want you or our daughter to remember me that way. I will be seeing you soon (I hope).

Love,
Ben

CHAPTER FORTY

———

Dear Tess,

The black cloud of this war is over me and I am wrapped in a dark state like I've not known. I close my eyes to shut it out and all I see is Jane's face, a child I would not recognize but for those few days at home. The desire to be with her and you overcomes me, this war pulling me under like a thick slide of mud. Why did I come back? There is nothing good here. Our brigade is so forlorn they've taken to fighting among their own, causing so much trouble Gen. Marshall has made a curfew. A curfew for grown men soldiers. There is also a camp police force within the unit that has the right to shoot on the spot and I mean permission for one soldier to shoot another within his own brigade. I guess this is what war does, makes men behave in ways you can't hardly imagine.

Hundreds, I guess thousands, have just walked away. I leave for the first time in a year—for my father-in-law's funeral—and when I come back I am punished "as an example" to the others. Gurney had the whole platoon gather around when he put the brand to my hip, a "D" the Confederacy believes will shame me to my grave. Instead I will wear the thing goddamn proud. I will wear it in testament to the fact I did not cry out but thought of my daddy Stoley Grubb and your Uncle Ruck and Red Hopkins who said Do What Is Right. I will wear it proud, a reminder they did not take me down. You were right, it was a dangerous choice to make and still it was worth it to see you and hold you and love you—a decision I would make a thousand times.

Our home barely standing, that was a shock even though I

expected things to be bad. I do not know how you made it through winter. Thank goodness for the kindness of Patrick Hagan and for his friendship with Mary Lenore Kitchens which I believe has resulted in special consideration for you. I know you don't agree, you think he is a good man who has worked his fingers to the bone to be sure all widows and women and children left behind are taken care of best he and the County can. But I believe there is more to it, and I am grateful. He brought you enough to get you through this frozen winter, and while some husbands might find this to be a man overstepping, I believe it saved Jane's life. My only question is why you didn't tell me about it at that time. <u>Do not think I cannot take worrisome news</u>. I can. It is worse, far worse, to not know what is going on and to wonder what you are going through with me here and you there. <u>Tell me the truth</u> Tess and <u>all of it</u>. Promise you will do that.

It's my thinking I should just leave here for good and return to you. If I had done it before, I would have had the chance to prove myself to your Daddy and to make him see <u>I am a good man</u> and <u>I will always take care of you</u>. As it is he died without us coming to terms and this is something I will regret to my own dying day. I know your Mama was so overcome with grief as to hardly see me there but it was worth it to help your family. Our family. To hold your hand through the long night of Sitting Up and to make the Tree Coffin, which what would have happened without me there to do it? There are no men left so maybe she was grateful there was me to make a coffin at all, Will and Amos off fighting and Thomas in that hospital in Roanoke. I did not know he had lost a leg. It will bring him home soon, that is the good news I believe.

The pain of this war shows on Lucy but there is a light in her eye, the light of love, and it did my own heart good to hear her talk of her Rollins, her eyes bright. He is a Cavalryman like me and it is strange to hold the thought if we met on a battlefield we would be on opposite sides of this war, two men intent on wiping each other from the face of this godforsaken earth.

I know your heart is broken. Just remember you were the Apple of your Daddy's Eye. He is not struggling, in that we can rejoice. He is with the Lord where he has found his voice again and I bet he is Up There telling everyone about you and that eulogy you stood up and gave at his funeral, a very proud moment for me and for him, I am sure.

I will close now since I have night drills, something they have started up here of late, I can't even say why. Look in Jane's sweet eyes and remind her her Daddy loves her. Her Daddy loves you too.

Always,
Ben

CHAPTER FORTY-ONE

---

30 May 1863

Dear Tess,

I have learned of your Mama's passing. I can't say as I'm surprised it happens so much when a husband dies the wife follows or vice a versa. I cannot come, I know you understand why. Still it is taking everything I have not to get on my horse and ride through the night to be with you and Jane. And also Lucy who I expect is taking it hard. I could be of help if only I was there. I pray Thomas will be home soon.

Love,
Ben

CHAPTER FORTY-TWO

———————

16 June 1863

Dear Tess,

You are <u>EXPECTING</u>? I guess there is one good thing from me coming home for your Papa's funeral. Maybe we should name him Daniel then all our life we can tell him I got his initial branded on my hip. <u>Take care of yourself</u>. I will see you soon I hope one way or the other.

Love,
<u>D</u>'s father Ben

CHAPTER FORTY-THREE

---

8 August 1863

Dear Tess,

It gets more awful the news of this war. I cannot fight my way out of the cloud that is Gettysburg black with sadness and waste. More than <u>50,000 dead</u> in just three days and God knows how many wounded, how many arms and legs amputated and lying now in piles filled with flies and maggots. I guess it will not be over until we all are dead, maybe then the politicians will be satisfied. I lie down at night and what comes is the thought this is the rapture, the end of days. For what could be worse? Young men and old men and boys attacking each other with so much venom their mission is to wipe each other off the face of this goddamn earth. He is not a vengeful God and so I can only think now he is an angry one, the Pennsylvania land he made so gentle and rolling scarred for time eternal. Our thanks for the gift of creation.

There are so many lost. And so many of them boys from home even though we don't know who. And will we ever, with so many dead and bodies so mangled they can't even be identified? How many mothers from the South and North both will learn they've lost their sons at Gettysburg simply because they never come home? I am in a black state, Tess, and cannot write anymore. Perhaps tomorrow will be better.

Ben

CHAPTER FORTY-FOUR

---

10 August 1863

Dear Tess,

I owe you better than my last letter for you have your own struggles and do not deserve the weight of my anguish. I will do my best to give you news that will make you know I am better off than most, alive at least and I will come home to you in time. We will build a life, us and Jane and Baby D., a life we will every day be grateful for.

We are back in Abingdon so it's familiar stomping grounds at least, Camp Fulkerson my home away from home. There has been talk of some upcoming action so we were surprised to move. But then who knows why we do anything these days, there is so much confusion and so little information you can count on.

There has been a raid on Gladesville, this one bigger and more troublesome, 120 Confederates taken prisoner and only by the Grace of God am I not one of them. The luck of the Federals is something to behold, after all these months they waltz into town just at the perfect time, so many soldiers gathered more or less in one place, the situation <u>unusual</u> to say the least. I know because I was there even if I find my own story one hard to believe.

Troops in these parts was feeling down, the pressure of marching and waiting and moving about weighing heavy then layered on that the sadness of every worsening Gettysburg report. It has got so bad some of the men decided to take matters in their own hands, organizing a <u>Ball</u> in an effort to lift spirits. It is something we all deserve, I think you can agree even if Col. Benjamin Caudill, who is a good man and a Baptist preacher, did not. But the boys would not back down. So everyone gathered in Gladesville on Saturday night, people from miles around and before you know it things were lively and loud and it felt like a good break from the fighting and sadness. There was enough to eat for once and plenty of whiskey, where it came from I cannot say. But all night it flowed. And when the sun rose men were laid out all over town, officers and soldiers alike bedded down in homes and yards throughout the village. That's when the Federals rode in like Satan's Fire and surprised us all. It took no time for them to kill twenty or thirty and round up another hundred or so, officers included, which straight away they marched them right out of town. I don't believe any townspeople were hurt or killed, that is a positive. I was not among them on account of me staying at Morgan T. Lipps's place.

This is what I think about when I consider the embarrassment of the entire event. Would it have happened under command of Gen. Marshall? I think not, but I am not in the majority in my respect for him, especially since his resignation in June. How I have missed him, not to mention I am now considered a regular member of the Cavalry, available for battle like all the men here who have been holding that duty for such a long while.

Well the party did serve to lift spirits for a period of time including mine and for that I am grateful, particularly since right at this moment I am not one of those marching across Kentucky with a gun pointed squarely at my head.

Your loving husband,
Ben

_____

CHAPTER FORTY-FIVE

15 August 1863

Dear Tess,

There is a lot of carrying on about the possibility of us moving to Jonesville, there's reports a large mass of Federal troops is headed for the Cumberland Gap and losing it would mean losing Saltville, which if that got cut off some think it could very well spell the end for the Confederacy. For now we are still here in Abingdon with nothing much to do but wait and speculate.

I hope you are feeling well, I guess you are in your fifth month now? Hopefully you are not so tired but I know it is difficult with me gone and you there with a two-year-old to chase after plus everything else to tend to.

I will write more as soon as I know it. I can say this only to you but after these many months I feel afraid at the thought of battle. I am a musician, not a soldier, that is the honest truth. Since that first day at Pound Gap I haven't been called on to shoot a Federal, and I picture myself standing with the 64th looking over the Gap at a mass of approaching Union Johnnies and I wonder what I would do. I guess I would do like all the men, Load, Aim, Fire. So many are hit, Tess, I wonder what it's like to have a bullet or a minnie ball rip through your arm or your leg, what goes through a man's mind. I guess what would go through mine is how much you mean to me so don't you ever forget it.

Always (and forever),
Ben

CHAPTER FORTY-SIX

———

17 August 1863

Tess,

I want to get this to you before we head out. Gen. William Preston has issued a Special Order for Col. Slemp's troops to move to Jonesville where we will be not more than 10 miles from the Cumberland Gap. Cavalry is going first so I will have to close this letter now. We will be under command of Col. John Frazer, if you get any news about Frazer's troops.

Ben

CHAPTER FORTY-SEVEN

———

5 September 1863

Tess,

I don't reckon this letter will ever get to you but just in case I wanted you to know we have been ordered to defend the Cumberland Gap <u>at all costs</u> and are <u>ready to do it</u>. We figure to have the upper hand as we know these mountains inside out and backwards and nobody is as good as we are at maneuvering over and around them.

This is a new experience for me as I am not serving as Cavalry but rather am positioned with my comrades as Infantry. We spent the day digging trenches to give us a position of strength when the attack comes. We do not expect it to be long away as there are already masses of Federal troops posted all along the Gap's northern border. It is dark now, and so we have retreated to a small camp which is what allows me to write this letter by lamplight. It is exciting, I guess, in a way, all this waiting with anticipation. But it is also terrifying. Just the thought of fighting right here on land I know so well. It is also maddening knowing it is land I am willing to fight for, knowing my duty might be to give up my life to protect it. I wonder about my courage at the moment of battle, still I do. But when the time comes to charge and something pushes me forward I believe it will be your love, and my own love for these mountains, that will do it.

Always,
Your husband Ben

CHAPTER FORTY-EIGHT

———

7 September 1863

Dear Tess,

Several brigades of Federal troops have moved in along the South and we are pinned between them and their comrades to the North. There was some shooting but it didn't lead to much. They cut off our food supply a day or so ago (measly to begin with) and now they've cut us from Gap Springs, which is our water. At dark we hear battle drums which I swear they use to taunt us. Everyone knows we cannot last long under these conditions. Col. Frazer has called a Council of War no doubt to decide whether or not to surrender. There is no good choice to make. Engage and the outcome is certain, we are outnumbered 10-1 and surrounded on all sides. The result would be 2,000 Confederate dead and in spite of it, Federal control of the Gap. On the other hand, if Frazer surrenders, we will forever be known as the troops who gave up the Cumberland Gap without so much as a fight. Humiliated for all eternity, but alive, that's the truth of it. I guess tomorrow will tell.

Love, your husband,
Benjamin E. Grubb
64th Virginia Infantry
Company E

CHAPTER FORTY-NINE

Patrick

September 1863

HER SWELL WAS EVIDENT FROM ACROSS THE FIELD THE day I first came with news. I was still some distance away, and there she was in silhouette—one hand shading her eyes, the other at her waist, her skirts pulled tight across her belly. She was not expecting a visit, as I did not make the ride to Turkey Branch often. Not that I didn't want to. I did. But I resisted the urge to constantly check in on Elizabeth and instead put her on my regular war service rotation. Even so, Mulay always seemed to find a little something extra to add to the meager war rations in my pack: a jar of green beans, a slab of striped bacon, a tiny wooden toy. I chose a book from my library to take to her each visit, a decision I gave an inordinate amount of consideration. I presented the offerings with little fanfare and she accepted them in the same way. It pleased me, I must say. It was heartening to believe the deliveries made a difference in her life, as bleak and difficult as I knew it to be. The news I carried this day would only make it more so.

"Come, let's sit on the porch," I said. I'd just dismounted Danny, and she eyed me curiously but followed. I saw that Jane was holding a flat rock she was using to scrape along a small patch of dirt, piling it up, smoothing it out, then piling again. She seemed content to continue her work, allowing us to talk. "Have you heard from Ben of late?"

"Yes. He's been sent to the Cumberland Gap." Her face then clouded. "Is there news?"

"There is."

She grabbed my arm, her fingers pressed deep. "What is it? What's happened?"

There was so much I didn't know, and as I spoke I chose my words carefully to convey the information properly: His unit had been surrendered at the Gap; the decision to surrender had been made beforehand; there was no battle, and the soldiers, on command, simply laid down arms.

"That's good. Right? Nobody was hurt or killed. And the whole thing is over."

"Yes. But there's something else. Two thousand soldiers were taken prisoner. Ben is likely among them."

Elizabeth constricted, and her body tightened. "My husband's a prisoner. Of the Union Army."

"Yes, perhaps. Probably."

"And if he's not? Is he dead? Is he missing?"

"There are tales of soldiers who ran rather than surrender. These are just anecdotes, you understand, stories in circulation for which there are no military reports. So there's no way to know—officially—who was among them. If it happened at all, which I cannot confirm. My opinion is it would have been a very dangerous action to take, given the proximity and power of Union troops on that mountain, and it's far more likely Ben is a prisoner. It might even be the safer option."

She stood, she walked away, she turned back to me. "When will I know something? When will somebody with actual information come and tell me?" She kicked at a rock and I, too, looked to the ground, feeling the crush of the truth I needed to deliver. "It's too much to ask. It is, isn't it, Patrick? It's too much to ask of the Confederate Army who, by the way, takes and takes and takes. It's too much for their government— which is an *embarrassment*, to say the least—it's too much *trouble* to let a wife know where her husband is. To know if he is alive or goddamn dead."

All I could manage was to look at my feet, knowing it was true, feeling her pain and that of every wife of every soldier in this war. It would be months before records were compiled and released, and even then, the information would not be reliable. And if Ben was not among the prisoners, he could be anywhere, alive or dead, hidden away or on the run. These were going to be long, difficult months for my friend. It was my desire to help, of course, and as head of the Committee for Widows and Families, it, too, was my responsibility. "Perhaps I can find someone who was there with Ben. Perhaps I can find someone who can confirm what happened on that mountain."

The look on her face changed. "Could you? Would you?" She came to kneel in front of me, hands on my knees and her eyes searching mine. "You have so many contacts."

"And I've a rank now, Colonel, honorary though it may be." Her response was dubious, which I'd expected. I shrugged. "Perhaps it will help."

She nodded and moved to sit beside me. We sat in silence for a while, watching Jane lift high the rock then tilt it, the wind blowing powdery soil hither and yon. Elizabeth's hands were clasped, her fingers fidgety, when without a thought, she moved them to her swell.

"So you're expecting," I said.

"Yes," she said. "I've been meaning to tell you."

I nodded.

"It's a miracle. In the middle of all this hell, it's like my own little miracle."

Her smile was slight, but genuine, and I wanted to share this small hope but instead I ached. What was to come for her, my Eilís, this woman grown of the plucky young girl who'd pushed and questioned and challenged me from the start. I looked toward the horizon and felt my blood rush, and my face flush, as my heart pulled to hers with a gravity I had not expected and for all the world had not seen coming.

CHAPTER FIFTY

———————

3 November 1863

Dear Mrs. Grubb,

Col. Patrick Hagan has reached me with a request that I tell you what I can about your husband, Benjamin E. Grubb of the 64th, Company E. I was not alongside him and his regiment, still I assume with some confidence he is now a Prisoner with the others, held in Louisville, Kentucky. My expectation is he is receiving humane treatment and reasonable nourishment, and given the starvation he likely faced as a soldier he may be better off. There has been a great deal of Prisoner trading throughout this war, so there is a chance he may be released before too long. When that happens he will have quite a distance to travel, some 250 miles. But there has been plenty of walking in this war already and he is no doubt accustomed to that. And so keep the faith. If any word comes to me, I have told Col. Hagan I will pass it along.

Col. Campbell Slemp, Commander
64th Virginia Infantry

CHAPTER FIFTY-ONE

13 December 1863

Dear Mrs. Grubb,

Sources tell me your husband Benjamin E. Grubb spent four weeks at Louisville where he received humane treatment and where there was consideration of a swap of prisoners North and South. This action would have freed him but as final details were being negotiated a band of Federals entered the Camp and took the men of the 64th and many others to the train station at Louisville where they were boarded under heavy guard. They traveled for three days before arriving at Camp Douglas, a Union camp just outside of Chicago, Illinois. I do not know firsthand of Camp Douglas so I will not offer any specific details here. But I suppose you should know it has a reputation for being harsh both in the living conditions and in treatment of its prisoners. Officials are at work behind the scenes to get our men released but I do not know of anything as yet that sounds promising. I do know there is an agreement that Prisoners on both sides be allowed to write home and there is the expectation that those letters will be delivered regardless of the state of the war. So it is my hope that you have heard or will hear from your husband soon and you will read, in his own words, of his situation. Until then I can only urge you to stay strong and believe in his fortitude. As I mentioned before, I do not personally know your husband, but I do know a great deal about the nature of the soldiers of the 64th Virginia, and men of stronger will I have never encountered.

Col. Campbell Slemp, Commander
64th Virginia Infantry

CHAPTER FIFTY-TWO

———————

PATRICK

JUNE 1864

IT HAD BEEN JUST BEFORE CHRISTMAS WHEN LUCY
Young appeared at my law office, asking my assistance in getting Elizabeth back to the family's farm. She'd reached her wits' end, she said, her sister holding on to stubborn hope Ben would be back any minute, that she would spot him walking up the lane or crossing the frozen field and she'd be there, waiting. Elizabeth would not risk him coming home to find the little cabin empty or his wife gone. I understood this. Lucy did too, but there had been no word in three months, and it was winter now, and Elizabeth was great with child. And so I hitched up a wagon and off we set, headed for Turkey Branch. We would not leave without her, Lucy and I agreed, although we knew Elizabeth would not come willing.

There was a standoff, of course. So after a time I pulled Eilís away and suggested to her that it was her sister who was most in need. I reminded her of the loneliness Lucy faced having been caretaker and their parents now gone; the heartache so palpable I'd felt it when, on our ride to the farm, she'd mentioned a soldier. There was Jane, there was that; did she expect her daughter—at three years old—to be the one to attend to her when it was time for the new baby to come? Elizabeth stood stone-faced and distant but, in the end, did partly relent. She would stay through Christmas, she agreed, and through the birth, but then she and her children would return promptly to their home. I was relieved with this compromise, and so was Lucy, and we exhaled as Elizabeth stubbornly climbed into the cart, even if she refused my arm in doing it.

It was late the last night of the year when Elizabeth started to feel she might be laboring. The child wasn't expected yet, still Thomas set out for Jenny Mae Grubb who got to them in time to bring another healthy—if tiny—baby girl into the world. It was also Jenny who persuaded Elizabeth that it would be best if she and the children stayed put for a time, there at the farm. Jenny was the only one, according to Lucy, who could ever talk any sense into the girl; and when Elizabeth agreed, it provided a welcome relief to everyone who would have worried over her so, including Lucy, and Thomas, and me.

In early spring, the first letter from Ben arrived. It was followed by a second, and a third, and I can't imagine how Elizabeth would have managed had these notes come to her in that little cabin alone, nothing but the children for comfort. As it was her family enfolded her, held her aloft as the days moved on, as war carried on, and as the news contained in the letters soldiers sent home became more and more dreadful.

CHAPTER FIFTY-THREE

————

February (I believe)

Elizabeth,

I do not know if any of my letters made it to you but I do not think so since your last one said you didn't know if I was alive or dead. I write when I can which is not much because of guard ridicule for missing your wife. I have bribed one this time in hopes you can at least find out I am here and you will <u>wait for me</u> to come home. It took two months to get what I needed for the bribe and if this gets to you it was worth it.

They do give us some letters to keep us in line. Write me, Tess, you are my hope.

There is a great deal of sickness, so many piled in with each other and there not a proper latrine area we can get to. I have watched many strong men die, their bodies give out with so little food and that which we get not fit to eat. It is colder than you can dream, thank God, for if you imagined it in your sleep you would not likely wake on account of freezing. There is at least 15 inches of snow and ice now and if we complain we are made to stand out in it until we beg or die whichever comes first. There is also the Mule, a two-inch beam raised 4 feet off the ground men are made to straddle and <u>ride</u> in the snow and ice, their clothes taken. For all my life I will hear those screams and feel that pain burning inside me.

Minute to minute I do not know if I can go on and then I make myself remember you and our daughter and the baby inside you who I guess must be born now. Is it a boy? Did you name him Daniel? I will get home somehow. I will see you again. That is my promise.

Ben

CHAPTER FIFTY-FOUR

———

April

~~Elizabeth~~ *Tess,*

If you do not recognize the handwriting it is because I have asked my comrade Priv. James B. Barkley to write this to you. They are my words I am telling him. I am in Camp Hospital suffering from infection. I have been here three weeks. I joined some boys trying to escape through a tunnel under their barracks. Some got free but most got caught. We spent time in White Oak Dungeon. Are you all right? Did the baby come yet? Maybe you wrote to say but sorry I can't remember some things.

Your husband,
Priv. Benjamin E. Grubb

PS: This part is from James. I am doing my best to watch over Ben but it is hard under these circumstances. He has been mighty sick but is some better now.

CHAPTER FIFTY-FIVE

———————

10 June 1864

Mrs. Grubb,

I expect by now you have been notified of the death of your husband Ben Grubb here at Camp Douglas. I do not have details other than he was very sick which you know because he had me write a letter to you. This is a difficult place to be but then you know that too. I found the enclosed and thought you would like to have it. My sympathies to you for there is not a better man than your husband Ben Grubb.

Sincerely, Priv. James B. Barkley
64th Virginia, Prisoner at Camp Douglas

WAR SONG

I left out from home, a promise was made
I'd never lose sight of these hills
Rocky and rugged they crisscross the place
A boy can get lost in his will.

Wearing the gray but feeling so blue
I shall come home to you
Tess of the day,
Tess of the stars
I shall come home to you.

The enemy came, I charged up the hill
Around me my comrades, they fell.
My courage it came, or could it be fear
Rifle drawn, heart beat, Rebel yell

Wearing the gray but feeling so blue
I shall come home to you
Tess of the day,
Tess of the stars
I shall come home to you.

Then September, over a time
The feds, they laid us a trap
Surrounded, and starved, they sure worked their way
Our give at the Cumberland Gap.

Wearing the gray but feeling so blue
I shall come home to you
Tess of the day,
Tess of the stars
I shall come home to you.

Here I am now, so far from home
This war, this camp, this mistake
So strong is my promise, the love I've for you
My will nor my heart will they break.

Wearing the gray but feeling so blue
I shall come home to you
Tess of the day,
Tess of the stars
I shall come home to you.

I shall come home to you.

by Ben Grubb

PART FOUR: 1864–1866

HOGMANAY

———

CHAPTER FIFTY-SIX

RED

THERE WAS SO MANY LOST IN THE WAR IT'S HARD TO say one was worse to take than the other. But Ben Grubb dying in a prison camp was one hit me hard. I couldn't get it off of my mind how he joined up with the Home Guard believing he'd never leave these mountains. Then him ending up a thousand miles away plus lord knows what he went through. And Elizabeth—why she had that little girl, Jane, and then the other one born 1 January 1864. Which that should of been a happy time, the baby coming a sign of things changing, of good days ahead. But that ain't what happened. That weren't the case at all.

Ben's dying broke Elizabeth down. She was twenty-three years old and already a widow. I was real glad she had Lucy and Thomas to lean on, plus Jenny Mae who I have to say shared ever' bit of her pain and still would not let her give up. And Boo, sweet simple Boo, who couldn't of understood none of it and still somehow saw straight through. She'd get right up at Elizabeth, right in her face, those fat little hands one on each cheek. "You not my Bit," she'd say. "My Bit smile. My Bit laugh. Where my Bit?" I seen this myself, and I'll tell you it's what first caused me to think there might be situations that goes beyond the Brotherhood. That even if what'd been held from Elizabeth might not solve her grief, maybe there was some measure by which it could help soften some of it. Because Ben died and days and months of the war went on, and that girl sunk to the earth like it was the only thing big enough to hold her. This caused me great worry having saw what'd happened to Jon. Oh, she didn't carry anger like him, quiet and stubborn as it was, nor the bucked-up rage of Ruck. She done different, disappearing almost, her will resigned. This was a dangerous thing in those days what with war wreaking havoc, with things so off kilter. People everywhere was bearing such loss, nothing was familiar, it was like hellfire had let loose and twisted and turned and wiped out all that was good, all we'd come to stand on as truth.

We was mourning, too, for those we lost and for the old way of life we had to let loose of. It was a gut-wrenching task born of the very mountains that held us. No longer was we living in a place all our own, where the quality of a man's life was made of pride and hard work and fierce loyalty. War'd took that. And it left us ravished and exhausted and threadbare. You will call me crazy but I swear you could feel our ancestors turning in their graves, our pride near gone and it taking everything we had just to make our way from one day to the next. There was so little left. There was so much change ahead.

I was thinking of these things the day I stopped in at the Youngs' farm. I wanted to check in on Tess, it being near four months to the day of Ben's death. She was out back, Lucy said, and I went 'round to find sure enough there she was, sitting under Jon's apple tree, her back up against the trunk and its fruit hanging low amid a flame of red leaves.

"Hey, girl," I said. She looked up. I believe she tried to smile, but despite the effort she did not succeed. She had that little worry bird which I noticed she wasn't rubbing but just holding in her lap, her hands loose around it. "I was thinking maybe we could take a walk, you and me. There's some things we need to talk through." I held out my hand but she did not take it. "If this requires I come down there where you are, that's what I'll do. But I'm telling you right now, Elizabeth Young, my old knees ain't gonna be happy about it."

"I can't take a walk, Red. I've got the girls."

I looked all around, then I removed some of the kind from my voice. "I don't see your girls. Which means they're being looked after just fine. So come on. Get up."

Elizabeth did not protest, and again I reached out. It was begrudging, but this time she grabbed on and let me pull her to standing.

WE DIDN'T TALK AT FIRST, WE JUST MOVED TOWARD the barn which I could tell somebody'd been working on. There was some patching to the siding even though I knew there wasn't any animals to corral. "Ever go in there?" I asked her.

"No," she said. She didn't offer more, which why would she? We'd got several hundred yards past when I decided it would be best to go on and lay things out.

"This here's what we're gonna do," I said. She bristled up, and I felt it rise but I kept up our stride. "We're gonna get to that fence gate there—" I pointed as if I needed to make clear which, like there might be more than the one, like it wasn't the one upon which she'd climbed a thousand times, a little girl giggling *Push me, Mister Red. Push.* "When we get there, I'm gonna talk some, then you're gonna talk some, and between us we're gonna get some things straight." She stopped then, clearly unwilling, and so I stopped too, equal in my unwilling to let this go. "You're gonna tell me what's going on with you here"—I tapped her head—"and here"—I tapped her heart. She tried to turn away but I grabbed her arm and held it. "I care about you, Tess. And I can't sit by one more day watching you fold in on yourself the way your daddy did. I won't have it."

She jerked her arm and bucked, her voice holding more substance than I'd heard in it in months. "I am not like him." I raised my eyebrows and tilted my head and that told her what there was to say about that. "And I ain't talking about it, Red. Not with you, not with anybody."

"Oh but you are. And I'll tell you why. Because I'm gonna give you something in return. I'm gonna tell you the full story of the secret you've been chasing your whole life. There's been missing parts, you've been right about that, and I'm willing to fill in ever' blank, answer ever' question you had then and ever' question you have now about what went on between your daddy and your uncle, to the very best of my ability." The saying of this was all it took for the hold to break, for the burden of the decades to lift and lighten and, for the first time, for me to understand the full telling of this tale might do as much for ol' Red as it would for the girl in front of me. I looked to Elizabeth ready for a nod, waiting for a smile in grateful agreement but instead it was just my offer that hung there, a clump of dangling crab apples not picked yet and neither willing to let go and drop to the ground. "There's things Jon never knew, Elizabeth, not over the whole of his life, things nobody knew but for me and Ruck. Which means now—I'm the only one who can ever tell you." It was hard-hearted the way I said it, how could I be so cold what with loving her so much? Which, I reckon, is the reason I was able to go on with the hateful thing I said next. "It's a one-time deal, Tess. Now or never. Take it or leave it."

She eyed me, sizing things up, and I did not so much as blink. Then she turned to walk down the hill. I let out a big exhale and followed. By the time I got to the gate, she already had the thing unlatched and had passed through, so I did too, stepping quick to catch up. We were headed in the direction of the river, and we'd only got a little ways when she started.

"I don't know what you're looking for me to say, Red. My husband's dead. I've got two babies that now I will be raising on my own. I think I have earned the right to be sad. And I'm not sure why you or Lucy or whoever put you up to this has a question over that."

"Nobody put me up to this, Tess. I care about you, is all."

"There's more to it," she said. Her look reminded me I needed to stay in truth.

"I—" I what, exactly? "I've come to believe I failed your daddy. I failed Jon. I meant to be a good friend to him, a faithful friend, and I've come to realize I wasn't. I can't do nothing about that now, but in the least, I owe it to him to not make the same mistake with you."

"You failed him *how*?"

I searched for an answer, I got ready to speak it when *Oh no girl, you ain't turning this on me* was what come out. "We'll get to all that. But first you're gonna talk and we're gonna determine how I can help, what it's gonna take to bring you back to your life. You have them babies to consider, and it's not like you, Tess, to—"

"I know about the babies, Red. Godamighty, I am aware of the babies. They are mine; I will be taking care of them the rest of my life. Me alone. Me, without Ben. Which, by the way, he is the one who wanted a family to begin with. Did you know that?" She looked at me, accusing. "Do you know what I wanted? I wanted out. I wanted to leave this godforsaken place...this *hellhole*, which, by the way, *before* the war was a terrible place for a girl like me."

I thought she might cry, but she didn't. She just shoved hands in pockets and kept walking. I hastened to keep up, anger having stretched her stride and pace plus what she was saying was not what I'd expected.

"A girl like you," I said, trying not to sound breathy.

"A girl like me," she repeated. She slowed, then stopped. Everything about her softened. "A girl with hopes. A girl with dreams. A girl who wanted a different life, a *bigger* life—" She paused, and she laughed even if nothing about this struck me as funny. "A girl who really believed she could have it."

We stood together on that road, me not having words and her resigned to the silence. I was wondering what I could say to this since over the whole of my existence there had never been a time when I, my own self, had ever wanted for more than I'd been given. How satisfied I had been with this life right here.

Tess, is all I could think to say; "Tess," is all I said, and that girl broke wide open and emptied out with such a breathless mess of sobs and tears all I could do was reach. I pulled her close, I rubbed her head, I said over and over, "It's okay, girl. It's all gonna be okay."

AFTER A TIME SHE COLLECTED, AND WE WALKED ON. WE got to a place where there'd once been a bench, its seat made from an old split log that'd been cut flat and sanded smooth. It'd got a lot of use over time, being near the road and next to a pond, and people passing by would stop sometimes, water their horses, sit for a spell and look toward the ridges in the distance. That bench was long gone now, ripped out by somebody who believed they had a better use for it than the rightful owner. Neither of us said this, it being sad. We just stood there and took in the view. Then we turned and headed back to the farm. I knew Tess was waiting but I didn't rush. A light wind had picked up, and over the field you could see the goldenrod and the Queen Anne's lace sway.

SHE SURPRISED ME WHEN WE GOT TO THE GATE. SHE reached for the top and pulled herself up, setting one foot and then the other on the bottom rail. I give the thing a push and it swung, giving the girl a familiar ride. She didn't giggle the way she'd done as a child, but I thought I might've saw in her a little spark of joy. I laid my own arms across the top of the fence and I clasped my hands and leaned in, letting the boards and pickets hold me.

"So here it is," I said.

Elizabeth looked up.

"With what all went on with your daddy and your uncle them many years ago, there is, in fact, more to that story. You figured so, and I aim to tell it to you now."

Am I doing right? I considered one last time. *Am I doing right in telling?*

I took me a very large inhale.

"How I know is because Ruck told me. It was a requirement, you see, of joining the Freemasons. Each and ever' candidate has to come clean about any questions of character. As I was the one done Ruck's Examination, it was in that context that he shared. Which made this a confidence I was bound to by oath. It is a confidence I am bound to, still."

Elizabeth nodded, but she did not comment. And so I went on, taking my time in the telling.

"I MIGHT AS WELL START WITH THIS RIGHT HERE, BEcause it's the one fact that sets up everything that was to follow. Ruck loved Tilly first. Your daddy might have been the one that married her, but it was Ruck who loved her first." Elizabeth didn't give no reaction, so I carried on. "They was an unlikely pair, I'll give you that. Tilly was a preacher's daughter, and also a girl more timid, more shy. Whereas Ruck—well, you know Ruck. He was the kind of man women *always* seemed to like—"

"Handsome and confident," she offered. "Wild, and all up front about it."

I seen Tess smile and it reminded me *this girl had loved Ben Grubb.*

"Point is, Tess, of all them women—and Ruck sure had his pick—it was sweet Tilly Perkins who took hold of his heart."

Elizabeth seemed touched and satisfied both.

"Now them becoming a couple was something not generally known. Ruck never did like people in his business, and as Tilly's daddy was a preacher, he only allowed them to court there at the house where he and the Missus could mostly keep an eye. They went on that way for some months until after a time, Ruck earned their favor."

I shifted, getting ready.

"Then early one morning there come a knock at Ruck's door. He was hardly out of bed when he opened it to see, of all people, the Reverend Horace Perkins. The Reverend hemmed and hawed a bit, but his point was that he'd got caught up in some dirty business; that he owed a great deal of money; that was his gambling debt not paid by Monday, collectors would be coming after Tilly."

"After Tilly," Elizabeth said.

"And that ain't all. The money the good reverend had lost? He'd took it from the church."

It dawned on her, you could see it come across her face. "He needed Uncle Ruck to win it back."

"Yes," I said. "And more specific, he needed Ruck to go off somewhere to do it. The bunch Horace had got caught up with was local and also was oversaw by Wildcat Sims, the meanest gambling head around."

She stepped from the gate. She fiddled with the lock. Then she looked to me. "He did it, didn't he, Red. He did it for Tilly."

"He did," I said. "He took right out, headed for the eastern part of North Carolina where he knew of a high-stakes ring. He played for five days and nights and accumulated an impressive sum. He hadn't quite made enough to cover the entire debt, but time came to go, so he left, facing the problem, now, of making it alive with all them winnings strapped to his body. He rode like hell. He never slept. He reached Rye Cove around midday on Monday, where he went straight to the church and found Horace and Wildcat Sims waiting there, together.

"They struck up an unusual bargain. On account of Ruck's reputation as an even-handed gambler, Sims agreed to let the shortfall go. But there was a catch. No one could ever tell nobody about the debt or the deal. It would ruin his business, Sims said, if people was to find out he'd 'gone soft.' And if him or his boys ever caught wind this was ever spoke about, at any time, to anyone at all—the consequences for Tilly would be bad. Worse, even, than before."

"So they agreed not to tell anybody," Elizabeth said. "Which seems like it works out nice for the reverend as he wouldn't want any of this known in the first place. But what does it have to do with Papa? It's not like him and Tilly got married while Uncle Ruck was gone."

My bushy red eyebrows raised like a question mark.

"They got married while he was gone?"

Oh, did I have her attention now.

IT'D BEEN THIRTY-FIVE YEARS SINCE I'D HAD THIS CON-versation with Ruck, and my thoughts went back like it was yesterday. He'd got Wildcat paid; he was wore out and starved; he'd went home to get something to eat. He'd fell asleep and time he woke up he rushed to see Tilly. She wasn't there; she was already at the farm, with Jon.

Elizabeth shook her head like she was a dog throwing off water.

I said this next thing plain as I could, as it was the heart of the decades-old secret. "Tilly was with child, you see, and she'd been afraid to tell Ruck. When he up and disappeared, she thought he'd figured it out and had took off because of it."

"Let me guess." Elizabeth did not hesitate. "Tilly went to Papa. And Papa—who always, *always* believed the worst of Uncle Ruck—Papa agreed that's just what'd happened."

Loyalty to both brothers rose in my chest, and I shrugged, letting the statement be.

She kicked at the gate.

"Look here," I said. "This is what's important. This I want you to remember." She crossed her arms but at least she looked my way, considering. "For good or for bad, your daddy thought Ruck was long gone. I really believe that. And Tilly was standing there in despair and Jon made a decision—an *admirable* decision, is what I'd say—to do what was honorable, what he believed was right, on behalf of his brother."

"Yeah, well, I guess," she said. "Maybe." She kicked the gate again, harder now, and it slammed shut with her on one side and me on the other. "But surely all that changed when Uncle Ruck came back, when he explained where he'd been."

"He couldn't tell them, sweetheart."

"Well then, when they told him about the baby."

"They didn't. Rather, Jon didn't. What was the point? Him and Tilly was already married, and nothing was gonna change the fact of that. Time he realized Ruck didn't know about the child, he figured it would only hurt him was he to find out. Jon was wanting to protect his brother, that's what I think, and Tilly, too, not wanting to let anything loose that might make for a scandal, that might ruin *her*. I can see how, in Jon's eyes, this was what was right. And so when Ruck showed up, what Jon said was this was a decision the couple had freely made and that he hoped Ruck would accept it. That he should respect Tilly's choice, for she had made one."

"Yeah, well. I'd have punched him," Elizabeth said.

"Maybe he did." I give Tess a gentle wink, for that is, in fact, what had happened. Ruck had gone into some detail about the satisfaction of the hit, about Jon falling to the ground, about him leaving his brother there and walking away, intending never to return to the goddamn farm.

"In any case," I went on. "Ruck left Jon and Tilly to their lives. In a few months he learned they were having a baby, and the picture in his mind was of the two of them as a happy couple starting their own family. He never got over it, is what I know, but he sure enough showed his love for both of them by leaving them be, just as Jon'd asked."

It was Elizabeth's arms that hung long, now, over the fence, and I waited, watched, wondered if, to her, the matter was put to rest. I should've known better.

She raised up.

"So Red. What about the night Tilly died?"

"What?" I said.

"You know, when Hester sent you to go get Uncle Ruck and bring him to the farm. The night with the lightning bugs."

Her calling up of that tender memory touched me, still I didn't know how I could go on with the end of this story. "Humm," I said.

"I guess what I'm wondering is did Uncle Ruck ever learn the truth. You know, that Mary Rose was his daughter."

It was flooding over me then how Ruck's demeanor had changed as he moved to the last parts of this story, how his hands wrapped tight around a cold mug, its coffee long since finished. He'd been talking quite a while by then, and he'd done so in earnest. Still, when he reached this part, he kept his eyes down like he was seeing a final act play itself out.

"I left you and Hester and ran for the stairs," Ruck had told me. *"I got to the top and there was Jon, wild with sorrow over losing the baby and crazed at the thought Tilly wouldn't make it through the night. It was clear he was willing to do anything to keep me from her—his whole body was blocking the doorway, his arms and legs spread wide to fill the space. I begged him to let me pass, I pleaded with him to please just let me through. Tilly heard, and her weak voice called my name. Jonathan's legs give way and he sank to the floor and I stepped right over him. I stepped over Jon so I could get to Tilly.*

"She was so weak, Red. So thin. She reached out and I pulled her soft up against my chest. My arms was around her and my face and hers was touching and she whispered she was sorry she had lost our baby, our Mary Rose, and that she would love me to her grave.

"I held her while I tried to understand, tried to figure how to tell her I never knew she was expecting, that I never for a single minute left her. But then Jonathan came into the room and he was so overcome—so distressed—my heart couldn't take it. I couldn't do it, I realized then, I couldn't do it to him. So I laid her back against the pillows, I kissed her forehead, and with everything in me, I stood to walk out. And I left them there in that bedroom, Jonathan and Tilly, together."

The memory of all this near brought me to tears. I thought of Jon and Ruck and the fine men they were and the sacrifices they made, each in their own way. I thought of all it cost them. I looked at Elizabeth, their beloved, standing right there in front of me, and I smiled at her as one last time I considered what was to be gained and what was to be lost in the way I answered her question.

"I don't believe he ever knew," I lied.

She thought this over, and I let her be while I let my own gaze rise toward the heavens. Put it to rest, I prayed, let it end right here.

"So Papa was right, and Uncle Ruck was right. That's the truth of it, in your eyes."

"Yes," I said.

"And still they never found their way back to each other."

"No," I said.

"It doesn't seem right. Seems like it all should have sorted out, one way or another, in the end."

"I suppose," I said.

I pushed open the gate and walked through as, side by side, Elizabeth and I started for the house. In no time here come Jane, breaking loose from Lucy and running wild down the hill. "Mama, Mama," she hollered, and Elizabeth caught sight, and she opened her arms and the child ran straight into them. "Twirl me, Mama, twirl me!" And Elizabeth did, and they giggled and twirled, and twirled and giggled until all of us—me and Lucy included—got caught up in the laughing so much not a one of us could catch our breath. I bent to touch my knees, and time I raised up I seen Jane was reaching into her mother's pocket, coming out with that ol' worry bird and holding it tight in her little hand. Tess give me the sweetest look, and she put Jane down to where the child said, "March, Mama, march!" and off they did go, right past me, right past Lucy, all the way up the hill.

CHAPTER FIFTY-SEVEN

PATRICK

SO THIS IS HOW IT ENDS, I THOUGHT, *ANNIHILATION AND humiliation, one great city at a time.* My head was down, my attention focused on yet another horrific report of the war. Atlanta had been surrendered, and Confederate troops had been forced to march away, leaving the city under Northern control. General Sherman had then expelled Atlanta's residents, forcing them to abandon their homes and property. He ordered all military and government buildings burned.

"Patrick," I heard. I looked up to see, in my doorway, Elizabeth Grubb. Her face was drawn but her stance was determined.

"Eilís." I rose, and my face flushed at this use of a name that suddenly felt too intimate. I stepped around the desk. She did not come closer and so I stopped, holding some distance, constraining an overwhelming desire to sweep up my friend and offer comfort.

"What brings you—how can I—is there something—"

I did not have words, and with no change in her demeanor she broke in to say, "I'd like to volunteer for the Committee for Widows and Families. I believe I could be of some service. These are struggles I am familiar with."

"Yes," I found my voice. "There are so many in need." Her eyes were vacant, and as she leaned absently, I was glad that in the least my door could hold her in support. I did not offer niceties to inquire as to her state; that much was obvious. "How are the girls?" I asked instead.

"Good. Fine. A handful." There was nothing more to be found in her response. Then she added, "Thank God for Lucy."

I smiled at this, hoping she'd do the same. She did not.

"She said she'd look after them while I do the committee work, if that's what you're asking."

"Oh. No. I'm not—it's not—I'm just aware they've been through a trying time. You also."

She stared but made no response.

"So," I said. I stepped back around the desk as if we had some serious business to cover. "When would you want to start? What would be your availability?" I picked up some papers and flipped through them as if one might contain information I needed, a schedule or a list of priorities, something related to the question. Nothing like that existed, but it did give my hands something to do. I looked back up.

"I can start now. I can work as much as is needed. As much as you want."

My face registered surprise, so I turned my back to Elizabeth to hide it. I set the papers on the credenza, shuffled a little more, then returned to her. "Well. That is good news even if I can't find what I was looking for." I waved a hand dismissively. "No bother."

She stood straighter, looked firmer. "Was there someone else you wanted me to speak to? Other volunteers you are coordinating. I don't—"

"No, no. Nothing like that." My smile rendered sheepish. "There is only me, I'm afraid. Which means your kind offer has doubled both our forces and our efforts." She might have offered a fleeting grin, or maybe I imagined it; either way, my heart responded with a leap. "There is a matter to consider, though, and that's your safety. We will want to coordinate what we are doing, you and I, so that any calls that need to be made, we make together. I am not comfortable with you traveling about alone during these dangerous times."

"You needn't worry. I can take care of myself."

"'Tis regulation." (*Regulation?* Did I really just say that?) "Also, we'll want to travel via horseback. Be able to move quickly, nimbly. Horses are more practical than a carriage, given the circumstance and the geography, which I'm sure you understand."

Her head tilted, her hands clipped to her hips. "Who do you think you're talking to, Patrick. A carriage? Seriously?"

I blushed, a bumbling boy. "Then horseback is fine for you. Good."

"Yes. I don't have a horse, but other than that, yes."

Of course she didn't have a horse. Who did anymore?

"I was thinking I could work with people closer to the farm, you know, places I can walk," she said. "I'm not opposed to walking. Then you can do the others, the ones farther away from me. We can make a map and mark it off, so we'll know who's doing what. You know, based on where people live. What they're needing."

I tried hard to look as if I was considering this.

"I can help in other ways, too: keep up with records, that sort of thing."

It was rather pointless, this line of discussion. I appreciated her willingness but this work covered an area of more than five hundred square miles. How to do this, and Elizabeth with no mode of transportation? There were records to keep, yes, but they were centralized here at my law office, and this was at least eight miles from the Youngs' farm. Still, in the last few minutes as we'd discussed it, I'd seen my friend return to herself. I'd glimpsed the fire I'd so admired in Elizabeth the student, Elizabeth the girl.

"I'll tell you what," I said. "Give me tonight to work this through. I'll figure a way. We'll find a way. So many people need you, Elizabeth. You can be a resource for them, and also someone who provides insight and comfort in a way that I can't. There is so much value in that."

"Thank you," she said. She nodded, her business here complete, and she turned to go. It occurred to me then, and I hollered after her.

"So how did you get here today?"

Her head swiveled, but her body continued forward. "I walked. How else would I get here?"

I grabbed my jacket and took out after her, intent on seeing Elizabeth home. I knew vehement protests were to come and come they did, her attitude bordering on belligerence. In time I relented, and she set out. Still I worried for her safety, so I quickly saddled Danny and at a distance followed. The next day, I decided then, I would make the ride again. I would arrive with a surprise delivery—a horse for Elizabeth, to be her very own.

CHAPTER FIFTY-EIGHT

ELIZABETH

FEBRUARY 1865

IT WAS HAGAN'S HORSE I RODE WHEN I RETURNED TO our empty Turkey Branch cabin, a mare named Sugar, the one after these many months he still insists I consider my own. I have not. I will not, no matter how great the desire. For she is a horse to love, no doubt about that, gorgeous and strong, a will to match my own. Still this is a work arrangement, something about which I remain clear even if he does not. And once this dreaded war is over, and my committee assignments are done, I shall return Sugar to him—her service, and mine, complete.

I slipped from the saddle and she stood with me, both of us taking in the sight. A year had passed and our place looked as if we had never been there, the porch overrun with summer vines now stripped and brown in winter's cold. The patching we'd done to the chinking held, but new spots crumbled. At least the chimney stood. I knew not to consider for long; I could not let my emotions get the better of me. So I tied Sugar's reins, straightened my shoulders, and like a soldier toward battle marched determinedly across the front field to the door. I opened it and walked in, moving quickly to the hearth. A loose floorboard sat firmly where it belonged, just to the right of the stones, and I raised the wood to find, yes, there was the tinderbox—I wondered how in my despair I had ever had the presence of mind to hide it there. I lifted the box out, opened the lid, and struck flint to steel, creating a spark.

I MIGHT NEVER HAVE KNOWN, FOR THAT WAS HIS PLAN; I might've lived a lifetime thinking what Ben, too, had believed to be true. Because this was a secret meant to be kept from us both. How had Patrick let the details slip? How had he not been better at concealing? We were arguing, he and I. Or rather I was arguing and he was simply Patrick being Patrick, maddeningly logical, maddeningly reasonable. A woman I'd met had needed help with a land deed, as there were questions over a tract after her husband's death. I had questioned Patrick's memory of the situation, and he'd sent me to the courthouse to confirm a detail in the record. And that's how I happened to find it.

WHERE TO START, THAT WAS THE QUESTION. I LOOKED around the room. As if by divine guidance, a stripe of light crossed the far wall where the old library had been. The shelving planks long ago sanded by Ben were gone, pilfered along with every remnant of life that had remained when I moved out of this cabin. But the ropes still hung, old and worn and dry. I walked across, I held the tinder, I raised the flame and lit them, one by one.

DEED AFTER DEED: *A TRACT OF 50 ACRES; 275 ACRES hereby sold; property of Patrick Hagan, these 325 acres northward, southward, running along the creek; Patrick Hagan, owner.* Then map after map, some surveyed, some hand-drawn, all indicating his purchase or acquisition. It was astounding to me, all the land he owned in western Virginia—it must be thousands of acres. Tens of thousands. And there it was. Among Patrick's holdings was a drawing of Turkey Branch and the land for miles around. I flipped the page to see an amended map with a new deed attached. *Bequeathed to Benjamin E. Grubb these five acres and a cabin at Turkey Branch, Scott County, Virginia. Free and clear, by Patrick Hagan, 2 August 1860.* And there was Patrick's perfect signature. And there was the place for Ben's, but the line was empty.

I STAYED INSIDE THE CABIN LONGER THAN I'D MEANT to, long enough that my lungs burned with smoke and I had to gasp for

air. Three walls were in flames by then, the roof at one edge beginning to
cave in. I thought of the neighbors, distant though they were, what if the
meadow caught fire, or an ember flew, settling in the woods and ignit-
ing the underbrush. It was winter-wet, I rationalized, and let the worry
go. By the time I made it back to Sugar she was in a state, kicking and
thrashing, wanting to run. I didn't blame her. I pulled loose the reins
and set her free. Then I, too, walked away, the heat at my back pushing
me on.

I turned around to look, but only once. "I'm sorry, Ben," I said, and I
felt the regret of youth rise in the air, twist in the wind, marry with flame
and smoke, then vanish.

I CONFRONTED HIM. I MARCHED STRAIGHT TO HIS LAW
office where, as usual, Patrick was knee-deep in files and details. I'd taken
the record without asking, just slipped it into my sack like it belonged to
me, which I reckon in some ways it did.

"What's this?" I asked, pulling the paper out and shaking it in front
of him.

He looked up. "What is what?"

"This deed. I mean, I know what a deed is. I also know where this
property is because I lived there. Turkey Branch. See? Right here?" I
pointed to the map, which Patrick didn't look at. He just stared at me.
"What I don't know is why you saw fit to give the land to Ben. To just
sign it over, and then to lie about it, about how it came to him, using his
daddy's good name. Using Stoley Grubb. The very idea."

I was too mad for even the sight of Patrick Hagan and I turned my
back to him. I waited but he didn't answer. He didn't say a thing, which
required me to twist again, and that made me madder. "Yes?" I said,
shooting the word toward him in question.

"Yes," he said, but he didn't go on.

"Why'd you do it? Did you find you owned *too much* land?" I
laughed, this next thought coming to me in perfect comparison. "Like
those awful English Lords? The ones who came into Ireland and took
all the land with any value. *Outsiders* who then made the local people,

'peasants' I think you said in Miss Kitchen's class, they made *peasants* work that land even if they would never again own it." Patrick looked stricken and I was glad. "Or maybe it was just how sorry you felt for Ben, him being a lowly musician. Feels good, I guess, always doing for others. I mean, you've got plenty, so why not help out the poor mountain folk." I shrugged, throwing up my hands in disgust. "Buy up all their land. Then come riding in like a savior."

I was worked up: Every bit of pain and sorrow and anger I'd felt over all these years had boiled up and boiled over and boiled out. I stared at Patrick and tears came to my eyes and what did he do but wait, he just watched me and waited like this was a storm he knew would pass.

"Why did you do it?" I shook the paper, I shook all over. "Why did you sign this over to Ben?"

He did not answer right away. He regarded me and considered. He looked to his polished shoes, then raised his head and spoke. "I did it for you. For your happiness, Eilís. I did it for you."

"Did Ben know?" I asked.

"I took papers to Jenny and indicated the property had belonged to Stoley. I told her he had left it to Ben. She never knew different."

"Did Ben know?" I repeated louder, like maybe he was hard of hearing.

"No," he said.

"You had no right." I said this through gritted teeth; I punctuated every word.

Patrick didn't say anything, and that made me even madder and so I took the deed, I threw it on the desk, and I got up in his face so close our noses nearly touched.

"*Colonel* Hagan," I said.

IT WAS EASY ENOUGH TO GET AWAY WITH, PEOPLE FIG-
ured the fire to be started by a ne'er do well or drifter, or a deserter hiding out. People were kind about it too. Mister Red came soon as he heard, offered how it'd be nothing to rebuild, how he'd help and he'd see to it my brothers and Ben's brothers helped, too, as soon as the war was over.

A couple of people came by the farm and brought food like this was a death or something, which I guess in some ways it was.

"YOU'RE NOT WRONG."

I didn't expect this from Patrick, and it took me aback, which I refused to let show.

"A little harsh in your judgment, perhaps, but not wrong. I owned that property, yes, and I signed it over under false pretense because I knew that was the only way Ben would accept it. He loved you, and you deserved a home, and so I created that possibility for you."

I started to protest but he overrode, his voice suddenly louder and stronger. "Marilee was not one to gossip. You know that. But it was clear to me she worried that you might be...let's say...*stymied*, at home, living with your parents, particularly given the hold created by your father's illness."

Marilee? Was there no end to—

"She never knew about any of this, let me be clear. I never told her. I had this property, it held a cabin, and as you've noted—what difference did this small tract make in my overall holdings? So I gave it to Ben. I did this in a quiet way, to ensure he would accept it. But then he owned the property free and clear. There were no strings attached."

"And what made you so sure I would live there? What made you so certain I would marry him?"

"Well, Marilee, I suppose. Although I'm not sure she ever said that."

"Sounds like to me the real reason you did it was for her, not me. Which I don't actually understand because she loved you like crazy and as we have previously discussed, you did not return the favor."

He got a funny look, one that held confusion and uncertainty, both of which were uncharacteristic. "I couldn't love her, Eilís, because you were..."

He did not go on and I was glad. I did not want to hear more. I stepped back, I needed space. I took it.

"I have always understood the situation," he said. "I have always accepted it. I accept it now."

How dare he, I thought, "How dare you," I may have yelled. And then I fled. I was out the door, out to the street where, without looking back, I bunched my skirts and threw my leg across the horse and together we took off, Sugar and me, both of us running for the hills.

CHAPTER FIFTY-NINE

PATRICK

APRIL 1865

I DID NOT BELIEVE SHE WOULD EVER COME AROUND. And so I tried to make peace with that reality, knowing if I spent the rest of my life with no wife at all that would be preferable to settling for someone I would never love as much. It was not easy, I will admit that, even as I know I am not the kind of man in want of a woman to make me feel whole. I have God for that, and the work before me. It is the core of my faith that I am greatly blessed, and it is my privilege—aye, my responsibility—to honor those gifts with a contented life.

And so I did my best to rest assured that all would be well. For if it should prove to be God's will that her heart never recovered or her resolve never faded, I would spend the rest of my days loving Elizabeth Young Grubb the only way I could: from afar.

THERE WAS GRACIOUS PLENTY TO HOLD MY ATTENTION. The war raged on, although the Confederacy teetered perilously close to defeat. Gen. Tecumseh Sherman had taken it as his personal mission to march across Georgia—Atlanta to the coast, stealing everything he could and burning the rest to the ground. It was a path of destruction that cost the South dearly both in infrastructure and heart; by the time he reached the sea, Savannah had been militarily abandoned and its gentrified ladies, so as to avoid the annihilation of their beloved city, simply handed it over. Sherman then presented Savannah to President Lincoln as a Christmas gift.

He set his sights then on South Carolina, marching north to the capital city of Columbia. It, too, was surrendered, but in the aftermath was burned nonetheless. Many people believe this was an egregious and despicable act of retaliation on the part of the Union, punishment for the state's role in leading the secession movement. I find it another heartbreaking chapter in the awful story of this war. I had visited Columbia in the spring of 1856 and I found it to be a charming city, one of notable architecture and a spirited, welcoming population. Reports of the damage done there, along with the pain inflicted by that devastation, left me heartsick.

Which leads me to the most disconsolate news of all. On April 14, at ten o'clock in the evening, President Lincoln was shot by John Wilkes Booth as he watched a performance of *Our American Cousin* at Ford's Theater in Washington. It was Good Friday. Five days earlier, General Lee had surrendered his Army of Northern Virginia to Grant at Appomattox, a sure sign that the war was soon to be over.

CHAPTER SIXTY

Elizabeth

MAY 1865

I HAVE HEARD IT TOLD WHEN WORD SPREAD TO THE North that General Lee had surrendered, church bells rang out across the land and people danced in the streets. That is not what happened here. Whether you came down on the side of victory or of defeat, in our mountains we were so worn out, so broken down and used up, there was simply no celebration in us.

I cried when I got the news, bent in two and sobbed until my body gave out. I cried for Ben, and all those lost, every wife left behind. For every mother, father, daughter, son. For the ragged soldiers coming home, and to what? Lives they wouldn't recognize in a world they wouldn't understand. Because change was the enemy now. All of us—soldiers and families—had a past that must be dealt with, hateful differences to be mended following a brutal civil war. It had to be reckoned before we could move on, something that wasn't possible yet, something you may not realize. Because we were in ruins, the South and her people, burned out and hollow, crumbling.

The future was patient, I'll give her that. She sat off to the side and waited. We moved through our days washed out and gray while tomorrow watched, quiet, confident. Knowing full well time would come around and we'd do the only thing we could, the single choice left, the one thing we knew how to do. We'd pull on our boots, we'd get to work, and we'd begin again.

I DIDN'T SEE PATRICK MUCH IN THE WEEKS AFTER THE
Surrender. There was a lot to do in sorting out the affairs of the soldiers,
which I have to say were surprisingly complicated given the bare nature
of the last months of the war. He worked night and day to straighten
out records, identify the dead, locate those still missing or in hospitals
sprinkled all over the South. He practiced law, too, representing soldiers
and families with problems of different kinds. They would be a while
settling—the handful with a real case—but most times he just listened,
offered a commonsense look at whatever their issue was, and sent them
back home, satisfied.

I spent my time with the widows. We felt a mighty connection,
women pulled and held together in a pool of suffering so thick and so
deep couldn't none of us see our way out. You might find this morbid,
but I promise you it was not so. We held each other's pain like water
holds a boat, gentle but tight, our grief collected and made into its own
willful force. I could not bear the thought of carrying on alone, and
those sisters were the solace. For each of us had suffered the same great,
undeniable truth: It is love, not war, that does the most damage of all.

CHAPTER SIXTY-ONE

PATRICK

JUNE 1865

IT WAS LATE IN MAY WHEN I ASKED ELIZABETH TO AC-
company me for a ride up on Buckner's Ridge. I made no bones about
my intentions, stating for the record it was not meant for business but
for courting. I had not been this brazen before, but recent weeks had reminded me life is delicate and uncertain. And I am a man of thirty-four
years, after all.

She would surely turn me down. That was my expectation and the
outcome for which I planned. So when she answered "I suppose. Yes,
all right," I should tell you I had to scramble for words and hold myself
tight to refrain from embracing her.

The journey turned out to be less romantic than in my mind. For
one thing, the route was tricky and, due to the prior night's showers, the
ground was a slippery mess. Then partway into the ride the rain started
again. It was gentle at first, then more sure. We'd both dressed for the
weather but decided to stop for a bit at a clearing marked by a large rock
outcropping. There was plenty of room for both of us under the ledge,
and for the most part the ground beneath it was dry. So we took refuge
and sat huddled, close in proximity but not touching.

We were accustomed to speaking of our work, I realized, our conversations centered on problems we were trying to solve. Absent that, I felt
awkward, self-conscious, as if anything I might offer would sound boyish.

"I'm happy you decided to come," I said finally. "I didn't think you
would."

She didn't respond.

"There are things I've wanted to say...I want to say...I want you to know. 'Tis best to get it all out in the open, so you'll be clear on the intention." The rain was pouring now, and I had to speak louder just to be heard. "I will do this only once. I will accept your position on the matter."

My heart was pounding as I searched for words.

"You're not ready for this. For me. For us. I know that. There are a thousand reasons. Good and important reasons for you not to move on." I turned toward her, her face in profile. "I honor every one of them. I do, Elizabeth."

My heart was breaking for the pain she felt, for my role in collecting her sorrow and wrapping us in it, in this cave.

"I know how deeply you love Ben. I feel the depth of your loss, I swear on every grave, I do."

She shook her head yes. It was nearly imperceptible, but it was there.

"But that doesn't change how I feel about you. If anything, it makes me care more deeply. I know what you are capable of, how strongly you hold your convictions."

She took in a deep breath, then released it, slow and measured.

"I want to marry you. That is what I need you to know. I want to marry you, to spend all our days as partners, as friends, *mo ghrá*."

We sat silent for a while. Then boldly, I reached for her hand.

"If you do not love me or cannot love me, I will accept that. I will. And I will leave you be. But if you share these feelings in any way at all, if there is even a chance, I ask you to tell me."

The rain was slowing. I watched it dance on the puddles before us as I waited an eternity for her to respond.

"It's not that simple, Patrick."

"I know. You are right, there is nothing simple about this. So help me see it all from your point of view."

"There are my girls to consider."

"I will love them as my own. I do already, Eilís. And I will provide for them. I have the means, so they will never want for anything. They can attend the best schools, travel, whatever it is your heart desires for them."

"That kind of life is unfamiliar to them. To me. I can't picture it, Patrick."

"But I can," I said, my heart pounding. I knelt in the dirt before her and took both her hands in mine. "It will be whatever you want it to be. You will spend your life doing just what you want, moving about the world in whatever way you choose. We will have a hundred children. Or none at all, if that is your wish. Just you and me, and Jane and Sarah Kate, a family complete."

She nodded, but her eyes were still distant.

I squeezed her hands. "Look at me, Elizabeth. Look in my eyes so you can know it is true." I held on tight. "I am in love with you. I love you with all that I have and all that I am. We are meant to be together. In all the chaos of this war, that is the one thing I am sure of."

"I don't know," she said.

"What other explanation is there?" I shook her hands again and brought her eyes back to mine. "I'm a lad from Ireland. Why am I not there? Or at least Boston? Or Richmond? A thousand circumstances conspired to bring me here, to you. How can you possibly explain it except to say it is God's plan? That is what I believe with every fiber of my being. It is God's plan that we be together, and ours is a union He will richly bless."

She pulled away from me and stepped out from the rocks onto the path. The rain had stopped, but the world around us was wet and dripping.

"I am a widow, Patrick, a widow with a heart that is damaged beyond repair."

"I don't believe that," I said. "This war, your loss—these things have only strengthened your resolve. Your intention. Your ability to love. I've seen it with my own eyes."

She turned to face me. "I am a simple girl, let's at least be honest about that. I've never been beyond these mountains. I've hardly an education and certainly no mind to go toe to toe with yours. You'd be bored to tears within a month."

"Eilís—" I started.

"You should've married Marilee. She is the match for you. She always has been."

She turned her back to me. I stood to walk toward her, then thought better of it and stopped. "I've heard from her. There is news."

She twisted in my direction.

I reached inside my coat to the pocket and pulled from it a letter. "Here," I said. I nudged it toward her. "Go on."

She took the paper and unfolded it. Then she stepped away, turning her back to me once more.

May 16, 1865
St. Helena Island, South Carolina

My dearest Patrick,

It has been too many months since I've written, so much has happened that I hardly know where to begin. I will dispense with commentary about the war and its horrors; I have been sheltered from much of it here on this island and for that I am grateful. Still I am as hopeful as anyone about the promise of being one nation again. There is the hard work of healing to come, certainly, and that will take time. May I say it is a process I know something of.

I could write volumes about all I've learned in my three years here, and someday perhaps I shall! For now I will just say it has been my privilege to work with the free Negroes who call this island home. Schools were set up to educate them in the early days of the war—Saint Helena has been under Union control since the plantation owners fled in 1861—and I was brought here as a teacher, which you know. But I have also had some involvement in the Port Royal Experiment. Do you know of it? We are seeking to model the integration of these former slaves into their own free society. It is heartening to see so many of them now landowners who are fully self-sufficient. They are proud people who work hard, love their families, and are eager to learn. It is a pleasure to serve under such conditions.

And now to the reason for this letter.

For more than a year I have been involved in a serious romantic relationship. I am not writing to tell you we are to wed; Frederick and I can never marry for a number of reasons, and we keep our relationship quiet (although it is certainly no longer much of a secret). This is a reality we have accepted, and while inconvenient, we are both blissfully happy to have found each other, contented to know that that which binds us together is love.

I know, without asking, you rejoice at this news. You have always encouraged me to find my purpose, and it is here where the people are filled with hope and have the fortitude to make their dream of true liberation come true. Their path is education, as it is for all of us, and to be a part of that in some small way is gratifying beyond measure. To have found love in the midst of it—even if that love does not resemble anything I ever imagined for my life but is, in fact, more beautiful—well, it is nearly more than my heart can hold.

And so I want to thank you, Patrick, for all you have meant in the long journey that brought me here. From the night I met you all those years ago, I have known you were an important part of my story, and that is as true today as it was then. You are a friend in the truest sense.

And if I may be so bold as to ask this of you. Put your arms around my precious Elizabeth. She has suffered mightily and needs rescuing even if she fights the notion. You are a knight of the noblest kind, after all.

Take care, my sweet Patrick, my compatriot, my friend. I pray we will see each other again in time, and when we do, we will rejoice together at the fulfillment of our respective destinies.

Love, always,
Marilee

When Elizabeth had finished, she carefully refolded the pages and gave a great long sigh. Then she turned around to face me.

"And so you think I need rescuing," she said. "Both of you."

"I think I am in love with you," I said. "And I think we have Marilee's blessings."

The world was silent in that moment, not a single bird chirping nor raindrop falling leaf to leaf. I walked toward Elizabeth and took her in my arms, just as Mary Lenore Kitchens had asked. And then I kissed her, long and slow and sweet.

CHAPTER SIXTY-TWO

RED

THEY HAD THEIR WEDDING 19 SEPTEMBER, IN THE YEAR of our Lord 1865. It was a mighty nice day for a celebration, it being early autumn in the mountains. Patrick had wanted him a big wedding with everyone invited, people from Scott and Lee and Wise County, all of which he served as a lawyer. And others from miles around, him believing it could signal a new day for us all. But Elizabeth, she had another thought and so they settled on a small gathering of mostly just family. That made twenty people or so, not counting the children, these being the ones I remember:

Lucy

Will

Amos

Thomas, who give her away

Col. Campbell Slemp, who stood up for Patrick

His new wife Nancy

Boo, who dropped rose petals

Jenny Mae

Mulay

Other people who work for Patrick at Sulphur Springs, there being about seven in all

Two judges from over in Lee County

Abijah Alley, who did the marrying in spite of Patrick Hagan being Catholic

I MIGHT AS WELL START WITH THAT.

First I will tell you they was big compromises Patrick had to make in marrying Elizabeth, the biggest one him being Irish Catholic and her not. Things took some sorting out. For instance, there was the breaking of the forever bond between Elizabeth and Ben, which some in the church might of made a hint at, but which Elizabeth did not like. Patrick had tried to make her understand this did not mean what it seemed, that her and him and the children would always remember and honor Ben and their union and his Sacrifice. Still he couldn't get her to make the switch over to the Catholics. For her part, she did agree any babies they had would be raised up as little Catholic children, even if she didn't exactly say this about Jane and Sarah Kate. But she didn't not say it, neither. And so all that, and some other things I won't go into, is how it come to be when Elizabeth and Patrick got married their wedding was not a Catholic one.

This is also why it took place not in a proper church but right on the lawn at Hagan Hall.

As to how it worked out that Abijah Alley was their wedding preacher, here's how that come to happen.

For one thing, he offered to do it. He heard about the Catholic vs. Not Catholic thing and he came right on over to Hagan Hall suggesting he could do a ceremony satisfying both, more or less. This was tricky business as the Catholics don't mess around with this sort of thing. But you know Alley. He laid out a compelling case, and Elizabeth, once she heard about it, liked the idea, in particular the thought of the Little Band playing for the wedding. Patrick said he wanted *Ave Maria* and another *Jesu* song which the Little Band did not rightly know but which Alley offered they would learn. They would be right pretty on dulcimer and guitar, all three agreed.

And so it was something that come to work for most everybody, Patrick's Uncle Joseph excepting. He had no love lost for Alley, as you know, and he was even more Irish Catholic than his nephew if that's possible. When Patrick asked if he'd do the honor of standing up for him at the wedding in spite of the aforementioned compromises, Joseph politely declined. "I am overjoyed you have found love, nephew," he said. "I will honor that love and your union by not complicating things with my disapproving presence."

Patrick accepted his uncle's position.

And that's why Col. Campbell Slemp was the one stood up for Patrick at the wedding, the very same man who was on that ridge with Ben Grubb and who wrote to tell Elizabeth about the surrender. And that is how Elizabeth first met his new wife, Nancy, a belle from Kentucky and a Union sympathizer to boot, a delicate thing who, in the last days of the war, had proved to be brave as a soldier. (I will try to remember to tell you more about her later, and you'll see.)

But let me tell you now about Lucy and her Cavalryman, Parker Rollins, which in my opinion is the bright spot of the war if there even can be such a thing. Because he was right there with her on the lawn for her sister's wedding, even if it was a surprise to everyone, him and her included.

We was all gathered 'round, the ceremony beginning and the Little Band playing the *Jesu* song just like Alley'd said. The late summer sun was bouncing off ever' leaf on ever' tree in that whole valley. It was a pretty place for a wedding, I'll give Hagan that, what with Stone Mountain rising up in the back and the land at the house laying so gentle. There wasn't quite yet the full colors of autumn but it was like any minute there might be—that time just before something special happens when you can feel it coming and which is sometimes even better than the real thing. That's how the leaves looked and everything else including the bride, Elizabeth Young Grubb. She come out of that house and stood on the porch looking around that valley and toward her groom with a face like the promise of a new day. She was beautiful and happy, nothing about her nor anything putting on airs. She put me more in mind of a wheat field, in fact, her wedding dress not white but instead that soft color wheat gets, and all tied up with a gold ribbon. Or not gold, really, but something else, more like that wildflower, goldenrod I guess you could say. And lord that Patrick. He was looking at her with them blue eyes wearing a dark suit that looked for all the world like it had been cut out and made just for him, which I reckon it was. You ain't never seen nobody so pleased.

Elizabeth took her a step toward the stairs, and Thomas, who was waiting at the bottom, moved up. He was holding on to a wood cane carved head to toe with dogwood blossoms, something Patrick had made for him by the man who made the banister, just after Thomas come home from the war. He shifted that cane to his left hand and extended his right just as the bride reached him. He was wearing his fake leg, and while he still wasn't too smooth walking with it you would have to say he did just fine, them two coming together toward Patrick and facing all of us on the lawn. When they got to him, Thomas give her a kiss on the cheek and stepped away, and Patrick and Elizabeth turned back toward the house and there was Abijah Alley in that fancy robe of many colors smiling like the cat who got the canary. He raised his arms and Lucy, looking so pretty in a dress the same color as laurel leaves, and Col. Campbell Slemp in his Confederate Officer's uniform, both of them come forward to stand for the wedding party.

It was just about then that Lucy turned to face Elizabeth, and the valley road beyond, where she seen somebody come riding up it. This was a tall man on horseback who, when he realized they was a gathering going on and not wanting to disrupt the proceedings, stopped and dismounted. How she knew it was him from that distance I cannot say. But what did she do but holler out "Parker, Parker," then she picked up the skirt of her dress and took off running towards him.

You might think this would upset Elizabeth the bride or make her unsure about what to do next but that is not what happened at all. Why soon as she realized who it was, what did she do but clap her hands and say, "He's come for her! Lucy's love has come for her after all!" Then she, too, grabbed at her skirt. "Let's welcome him. Let's all welcome Parker Rollins to Sulphur Springs!"

For his part, Patrick just smiled and said to Abijah Alley, "I suppose this wedding can wait another few minutes. But don't go far."

First thing Capt. Rollins did when Lucy got to him was lay on her a kiss so big it would make a hussy blush. She was all caught up in it, then stepped back to catch her breath and wipe the back of her hand across her forehead like she might faint or else die of embarrassment, it was hard to tell which. This didn't faze Capt. Rollins, who said to Elizabeth in particular and the rest of us in general, "So sorry to interrupt things, but it's been two years and I just couldn't wait another minute to see this pretty lady here." He threw his long arm out around the small of Lucy's back and pulled her so close there wasn't no daylight between them at all.

"We're so pleased you're here," said Elizabeth. "Now this day is perfect."

None of the other folks at the wedding had come down, like Elizabeth had said to, so they was still standing on the lawn looking toward the valley road wondering what on earth was going on. This included Mulay, who had Sarah Kate up on her hip and Jane by the hand, all three of them confounded by it all. Jane broke loose of Mulay's grasp and took off after her mama, and then Boo followed, a trail of white rose petals flying behind her.

"Mama, Mama!" Jane yelled, now in a full run. She reached the bride, who leaned over, give her a kiss on the forehead, and said, "Capt. Rollins, if you please, would you join us? We have a wedding to finish."

"It would be my honor," he said, extending his arm to Lucy who took hold of it with both hands like she weren't never gonna let go.

Elizabeth looked to Boo. "Can you lead us all back to the house?" she said, which is just what that little girl done. Boo out in front, walking right up that long cobblestone path, more petals falling; then Elizabeth and Jane following hand in hand; then Lucy and her Capt. Rollins. The Little Band struck up *Jesu* again, and this time there was more pep and less reverence. Patrick Hagan stood right there, God love him, looking over the whole thing, him and Col. Slemp both smiling big as they watched the happiest, most unusual wedding procession I reckon there's ever been.

Everybody got re-situated and Alley got the whole thing going again. "Dearly beloved," he started. "We are gathered together..."

There was some scripture, and the Rite of Marriage, then Alley nodded and the fiddle players, brothers, played a slow duet of *Ave Maria* that would bring you to your knees. Elizabeth turned toward Patrick and he took both her hands and kissed them, and for that whole song they just stood there looking at each other like they was the only two in the world. It was so moving, there might of been a tear or two on my own cheek, I'm telling you what's the truth. Alley pronounced they was husband and wife, and they did the kissing, and the Little Band struck up and played the happiest song you ever heard, one they had made up special for this very occasion.

Then there was dancing and carrying on and food like you can't believe, all of us celebrating together, judges and children and housemaids alike. Capt. Rollins told his story over and over, how during the war he was in the area on a solo mission and he happened upon the Youngs' farm. It was desperate cold and he needed warm shelter for the night. So he went right up to the door and knocked to ask if he and his horse might stay in the barn. Lucy was the one come to the door—her papa was mighty sick by then and her mama wouldn't leave his bedside—and the moment their eyes met, they both knew something was up between them.

"I knew how dangerous it was," Lucy said, "letting a Union soldier stay. But how could I say no? He was so polite about it all. And it was raw, rain and sleet and snow all mixed in together. So I told him to go on out to the barn but to stay out of sight."

"She brought me food and blankets," Rollins added, winking at Lucy. "And then she stole my heart."

He come and went from there for close on three weeks before being sent on deep into Kentucky. That's the last they seen of each other until this very day.

I should also mention Jenny Mae Grubb and the single round of buck dance she let loose, later in the afternoon. Everybody there just stepped aside, known, like she is, as the best flatfooter around. She looked light as air, back and up, back and up, like all that tapping didn't take no effort at all. Still I reckon it did. She was happy about the marriage, I do believe that, but for obvious reasons she chose to sit out the dancing most of the day. And so I took it on as my business to keep my eye on her, to see she was comfortable and had something cool to drink, to provide for her whatever it was she might find herself needing.

CHAPTER SIXTY-THREE

ELIZABETH

YOU MIGHT THINK THE BEST PART OF MY WEDDING WAS it being there in that pretty valley or having my most loved ones around or Capt. Rollins showing up, which was a great surprise I would never have imagined. But there was something else, something big that started later, and of all things it has to do with Mister Red.

I was so happy he was there. He'd been important to me all my life, and to Ben, too, him being a friend to Stoley, and then their own relationship growing close through the Freemasons. It was like a circle closing is how it felt, so me and Patrick had ridden out to see him before we settled on a date to make sure it was one he could accommodate. His place looked a little sad, which surprised me—Mister Red always being such a strong-willed man. But I guess it missed a woman's touch. It was clear there was some things Red just hadn't kept up with in the years since he lost Salley Belle: the flower beds grown wild with weeds, the front porch leaning left like it might just give out.

I guess that's why it pleased me so to see him give attention to Jenny Mae at the wedding. They are good, decent people, both of them, and they have a lot of living still to do. If it worked out they did that together I would be mighty glad of it. For one thing, I figured Jenny to be lonely now that Aaron was off working in Tennessee. For another, Red would get him some grandchildren, them being my Jane and Sarah Kate, and my children would get a wonderful granddaddy to love.

Him and I danced twice, and both times he told me how happy he was I'd married Patrick, that it would have pleased my papa so. The third time he started down that same road, I looked him in the eye and said, "Red Hopkins, something is up with you. What is it? What's on your mind?" He looked sheepish then asked if I minded stepping around to the side of the house, as he had something for me that was better delivered in private.

I took him away from the porches and people. "So?" I said then, waiting. He pulled from his jacket a man's pocket watch that he put in my hands, cupping both of his around mine like he was giving a blessing. "What is this?" I asked.

"Consider it a wedding present," he said.

I opened my palms to see the round gold cover and noticed some engraving there. I tried to make out the letters. R...R...Y. "RRY?" He nodded, and that's when it came to me. RRY. Rufus Randall Young. It was Uncle Ruck's.

I held the watch close to my chest, and tears filled my eyes. I think they might've filled Red's too, for he looked up at Stone Mountain, blinked twice, then brought his gaze back to me. "He wanted you to have it."

"You've held it all this time?" I asked. "Why, Uncle Ruck's been dead—what, fifteen years?"

"Open it. Go on."

I turned the watch over, looking for the latch. It clicked, and there tucked tight inside the cover was a small round photograph. It was a man I didn't recognize. He reminded me of Papa, but wasn't. "Who is this? Why do you—" Like a bolt of lightning it came to me. This was Uncle Ruck, Papa's twin, now an old man. "But Red. He was hanged in the gallows in Estilville. I saw it. There were hundreds of witnesses."

Again Red nodded, but this time it was sort of a yes and sort of a maybe.

"He's alive? Are you telling me Uncle Ruck is alive?"

"I'm telling you he sent this watch with instructions I should give it to you on this, your wedding day. He sent a message as well."

I couldn't speak, couldn't understand this at all.

"Ruck made you a promise. It was years ago; last time you seen him, I believe."

"I visited him at the jail."

"You remember what he told you that day?"

"He said he was gonna keep his eye on me."

Red nodded. "He's kept his word, Tess. He's done it. One way or the other, during ever' trial you've faced, Ruck Young's been close by."

I tried to think back, think through, but it was too much to take in.

"He's a man of some age now, and he ain't getting around like he used to. Staying put in a place where he can live out his years. Quiet, out of the way. Can't nobody know where that is. I don't even know."

"But Red," I started.

"This here's his message: You're in good hands with Hagan. You won't be needing him like you used to."

"But I want to see him. I want to know how all this happened. How could he survive a hanging? What's his life been like? I have so many questions."

"There ain't no more I can tell you, honey. I'm sorry about that, really I am. But I promised Ruck years ago, and I am a man of my word."

"But Red," I said again.

"It's your wedding day, Tess. Let it be enough. Let it be enough that Ruck's alive and that you know it."

I nodded yes and wrapped my arms around his neck, hugging hard, thinking I might break down and cry. Just then Patrick came around the front corner of the house, and I slipped the gold watch back to Red, for safekeeping.

"Aye, there you two are. Jenny Mae is dancing, and it's something you'll want to see."

"You are right about that," Red said, letting me go. "Better get ourselves out there quick." He winked at me, gave Patrick a hefty pat on the back, and headed toward the front lawn.

Patrick reached for my hands and held them, standing squarely in front of me. He searched my eyes. "You all right, *mo stór*?"

"Yes," I said, my fingers feeling the warmth of Uncle Ruck's watch, of my husband's sweet love. I gave them a little squeeze. "I am so very good."

He lifted my hands to his lips and kissed them, one at a time, his eyes never leaving mine. Then we turned and walked together, following Red to the celebration.

CHAPTER SIXTY-FOUR

PATRICK

IT WAS CHARLESTON, SOUTH CAROLINA PAPERHANGER Harry Smith who opened my eyes to the truth. He was known to be an artist and a craftsman, and I'd hired him to come work with Elizabeth in making whatever changes she wanted to the house.

"It is a lovely thought, Mrs. Hagan putting her own mark on your grand home here," he said as he stood before me, his hat in his hands. "But if I may speak candidly, sir. She gets no enjoyment of it. The entire exercise comes as but a chore."

I did not understand; how could this possibly be? "But she can have anything she wants. Money is no consideration. I should think a wife would find that thrilling."

"That has been my experience. But Mrs. Hagan? She is far happier when she is with the gardener, up to her elbows in cabbage and dirt."

I nodded, trying to understand.

"And there is one other thing, if I may. She spends a great deal of time in that cabin, the one tucked up in the woods, there, behind the house. Perhaps she finds it more...comfortable." He was referring to the simple home Uncle had constructed before he and Aileen moved to these mountains, one much too small for a man of his means and yet a size he thought better suited to his wife's needs. It had been vacant since their departure for Staunton. Elizabeth spent time there? How had I failed to notice?

"I hope I have not overstepped my bounds, Col. Hagan. It's just that I work with many, many women, as you might imagine. I find Mrs. Hagan to be quite different. Refreshing, in fact. I have grown quite fond of her."

"Thank you, Harry. Thank you for your candor. You have done me, and Mrs. Hagan, a great favor."

He nodded, then left the room.

THAT NIGHT AFTER DINNER I SUGGESTED WE GO FOR A walk along the creek. It was cold but clear, the moon bright. She slipped her hand through the bend in my arm and together we set out. For a long time neither of us spoke. The frozen leaves crunched beneath our boots and with each step our breath formed small white clouds. We walked past the giant oak, the feed silo, then rounded the bend that parallels the west fence line. After a time, I asked. "Are you happy, Elizabeth?"

"Good heavens, Patrick. What is there to be unhappy about?"

We walked on a bit, a thousand night stars twinkling high above the valley road.

"You are at home here." It was tentative, unsure. "What I mean is... all of this is yours, Eilís. The house, the land, the animals. It is something you realize, *an aontaíonn tú*? Sulphur Springs belongs to you as much as it does to me." We'd made the turn by then, the one that crosses in front of the great lawn. "Nonetheless, there is something your heart desires. What is it, m'love? *Inis dom.*"

There was a quick puff as she exhaled into the cold mountain air, and we stopped, facing Hagan Hall together. "It is beautiful and impressive and exactly what you deserve, Patrick. But I don't fit here. Can't you see? I'm trying. But this is a world I don't know how to live in."

I felt the weight of a hundred thousand bricks, each fired right here on the property.

"I know what this place means to you. I do. I'll figure it out." She turned and took my face in her hands, her palms against my cold cheeks. "I just need time." She gave me a quick kiss, our cold lips barely brushing.

"What can I do?"

"Understand that this is something you can't fix."

I started to speak, and she put her finger up to quiet me.

"It's a good thing in a strange way. I am used to battles. And I am a woman who needs to do her own fighting."

JUST WEEKS LATER WE STOOD TOGETHER AGAIN, ELIZA-beth's eyes covered for a Christmas surprise. She had planned the whole of the holiday, and other than this moment, I had not dictated a single detail.

First, the house was to be filled with family. This proved to be more complicated than it sounds, as the Youngs had scattered hither and yon in the months following the surrender. Making good on a wartime pledge, Amos had gone West with four members of his battalion. Aida had taken a nursing job with the Lynchburg Hospital. Even Jenny Mae and Boo politely declined, as they were hosting Red Hopkins at their place, something that made Elizabeth very happy. Still, Lucy and Capt. Rollins were here, Will and Thomas were here, and, to my great joy and surprise, Uncle Joseph made the trip from Staunton and was to stay with us three days.

Second, we were throwing a festive party on the last eve of the year for the families of the people employed at Sulphur Springs. It was Eliza-beth's most ardent wish that it be a night they enjoyed, and so she spent a great deal of time considering every detail. The house was too formal, she decided, so the celebration would be held at the cabin, remov-ing much of the furniture and decorating every windowsill with pine boughs and candles. Customs of all those gathered would be honored: fireball tossing; the prayers of Watch Night; Hogmanay, or First-Foot, with gifts for every man, woman, and child. I was to read a portion of *A Christmas Carol*. There would be music and dancing and food and drink—the entire evening meant to be a joyful, heartfelt demonstration of appreciation from our family to theirs.

But first there was Christmas.

"I can't see a daggone thing with this blindfold on. Who's here? What are you up to, Patrick Hagan?" Thomas and Will were closest to Elizabeth, the two of them holding the large wrapped sign between them. I removed the covering from her eyes.

"Open it, Mama!" cried Jane.

"What on earth?!" Elizabeth said. Thomas's grin was so big and genuine, I let go a bit of my trepidation. "Help her, Janie," he said, and off came the covering. The room was quiet as she took it in.

"What...is this?"

Thomas looked to Will, then to me. I nodded.

"It's the sign for our building. Young's Store. We're reopening Papa's Mercantile."

She shook her head, confused. "That can't be. The building's in awful shape. And there's nothing to sell. There's no way to get inventory, and no money to buy it if there was."

"We have an investor," Will said.

She looked to me, defiant. I shook my head no.

"Will somebody please tell me what the dickens is going on?"

"'Tis I," Uncle said, stepping forward. He was speaking softly, his tone uncharacteristically unassuming. "I have always believed in this region of the Commonwealth. The majesty of the mountains. The strength—or shall we say *stubbornness*—of the people." He smiled. "It is a good investment."

Elizabeth turned to her brothers. "You're going to run the store? Together?"

"We are," they said in unison, and in the joy of the moment we all laughed.

IT WAS A GRAND GESTURE, YES. BUT UNCLE MEANT IT when he said he considered the backing of the store a *business* opportunity. Recovery in the South would take years. Decades, even, the economic system in ruins, the railroads destroyed, and cities and farms and plantations burned to the ground. But here in these ancient Appalachians, people were used to hardship. They were fiercely independent and bootstrap-strong; it didn't hurt that self-sufficiency was the way of life. So a mercantile offering a small selection of carefully considered items—seed, tools, hardware, cloth—with enough capital to allow lenient terms? Uncle was betting that this was just the engine an area like this needed.

It was just what Elizabeth needed, in any event, and her brothers. I considered all Joseph Hagan had meant in my life, how time and again he had shown me what it means to hold to a standard and give with generosity all the same; how a man of heart and wealth can use both, in full service to each other.

CHAPTER SIXTY-FIVE

ELIZABETH

OUR HOGMANAY CELEBRATION WAS EVERYTHING I'D hoped it would be. Yet here I sit at this bedroom window looking out into inky dark. Mulay's prophecy keeps me from sleep; her words circle 'round like flies I can't swat.

She'd whispered from behind me as we'd collected for First Footing. "Deh be de chile," she'd said. "Deh be de chile in you."

"What?" I'd said, turning.

"An seb'n mo to com."

The door had opened and on a blast of cold air, Patrick had ridden in. It was midnight, 1865 slipping into the past and all of us stepping together into the bold promise of a new year. His arms were loaded with gifts, and children jumped and giggled and pulled on his coat; his own smile was bright. I'd looked again for Mulay but she was gone, her back to me as she moved through the crowd.

How could she have known? I hadn't told anybody, not even Patrick, waiting to get used to the idea of this baby myself. *Seven more? Is that to be my place here at Hagan Hall? A lifetime spent raising children?*

Surely there is to be more to my story.

I LOOK THROUGH THE GLASS TO SEE DARKNESS IS FAD-ing. The sun is still below the ridge, but just above, light is rising. Streaks of purple and orange stretch wide across the sky, then I watch as dark gives way to blue, clear blue, bluest blue; a blue that is honest. It's a peek through to heaven, I think, or maybe it's an offering: a promise of a peace that's to come for all who suffered so during the long years of war.

Or perhaps it is both. Maybe heaven *is* peace, struggles ended, every question answered.

I think of Ben, and Papa. And Mama, with her worrisome ways. Levi and Jonah and all the lost boys. The dead of the widows. And I think of Uncle Ruck—my protector Uncle Ruck, who I will not see again lest it be in heaven. Are they gathered around me now, their pain relieved, their differences reconciled? Are their souls at rest?

Patrick stirs, and I turn toward the bed.

"There you are, my love," he says. "Up to greet the sun, I see."

"Yes," I smile.

"Does the day ahead look to be a pretty one?"

"It does."

"Aah, good now. There's so much that's needing to be done."

I turn back to the window. The sun is just above the mountain now, its long rays stretching thin and bright. The icy snow shimmers. All is quiet, and as I look out to the fields beyond the back valley, I feel my husband watching. He speaks again.

"Why don't you come here first, *mo ghrá*?" He puts his hand on my empty place in the bed. "The needy world can wait."

EPILOGUE

From the *Bristol Herald Courier*
March 30, 1917

We rejoice in the remarkable life of Elizabeth Young Grubb Hagan, Sulphur Springs, Virginia, who at the age of seventy-seven has gone to meet her Lord and rejoin her beloved husband of fifty-two years, Col. Patrick Hagan, who preceded her in death just one month ago. Mrs. Hagan was married previously to Private Benjamin Grubb, an infantryman with the 64th Virginia, who died in service to Scott County in the War Between the States.

Mrs. Hagan was known to all as a kind, thoughtful, energetic person who devoted her life to her family and to the successful oversight of their vast holdings. Col. Hagan considered her to be his partner in all ventures and she took an active role, stating it was her intention "to be sure our mountains and our mountain ways are respected and protected as we move forward in the name of progress." It was a battle she fought with might, particularly as railroads, logging, and the discovery of vast reams of coal and minerals began to change the face of Southwestern Virginia.

She served as a gracious hostess at their grand estate, Sulphur Springs, where she and Col. Hagan welcomed royalty, political leaders, and famous entertainers, always with an eye to introducing them to our area's mountain culture. They frequently invited neighbors, friends, and strangers as well, becoming most known for an annual gathering held every September 9th called Gray Day, honoring Civil War widows and their families.

Mrs. Hagan was involved in the founding of two schools, one on the Hagans' property that, until the advent of our public school system, was used to educate the children of the estate's many employees, as well as the Boo School for Exceptional Children, founded in the name of her sister-in-law, Suzanna "Boo" Grubb, who died in 1875 at the age of twenty-six.

Mrs. Hagan is known for testifying as a prosecution's witness in the famous Daniel Dean murder trial in which her husband served as the Defense Attorney. The case was tried three times in Scott County and finally at Virginia's Supreme Court, where the earlier conviction of Hagan's client was upheld. It was the first and only time in Virginia history a case was decided purely on circumstantial evidence, something Col. Hagan continued to renounce for the rest of his life. His client, Daniel Dean, was hanged, and Hagan never practiced criminal law again.

Mrs. Hagan was the daughter of Sarah Jane Carter and Jonathan Young of Fort Blackmore. Her father's family was killed in the last known Indian raid in Scott County in 1793—all but Jonathan and his twin brother Rufus—who was convicted of murder and hanged in the Estilville gallows in 1850.

Mrs. Hagan was the mother of nine children and grandmother to twenty-nine. She was of the Methodist persuasion until converting to Catholicism in 1875 when the Hagans' marriage was first recognized by the Catholic Church. She remained a practicing Catholic for the rest of her life.

At a celebration marking the renaming of Osborne's Ford to Dungannon in honor of his homeland, Patrick Hagan asked his wife to say a few words. She stepped to the podium and looked out over the crowd. Then she raised her arms to the Clinch River and Clinch Mountain beyond, turning toward Long Hollow, Poor Valley, the Cumberland Gap, Fort Blackmore, and Hunter's Valley. She lowered her arms, settled back in front of the gathered crowd, and said:

Unlike my husband, I have not been a great adventurer. I haven't traveled the world. I haven't stood in awe at its Seven Wonders. Instead I've spent my whole life right here, content to be where God surrounds me with more beauty and grace than my soul can hold. Most of you understand this; it's been your life, too, born here as I was, our family lines reaching back for generations. Others of you have come to these mountains more recent, brought here by luck or by fate.

In either case, the point I'm making is the same.

These ridges and rivers and valleys, they become part of you. They test you. They strengthen you. And lord knows they humble you. It is their wildness, I think, a spirit that sets in your bones and remains no matter where life takes you. Because once this is your home, once you have surrendered your heart to these mountains, they will not let you go.

You are theirs forever.

AUTHOR'S NOTE

IT IS MY PRIVILEGE TO TELL THIS STORY OF THE PEOPLE
of Southwest Virginia and the challenges they faced during a tumultu-
ous nineteenth century. Many of the characters are real people of the
era and place, and like many of the Civil War battles and incidents
represented here, they are rooted in historical records both official and
from family and genealogical records. I spent ten years researching and
writing this novel, and today I remain as interested in—and fascinated
by—the lives that inspired it as I was in those very first days.

Patrick Hagan is the character who first found his way to me. His
reputation as an attorney of great faith and conviction, his decision to
step away from criminal law following the guilty verdict of a client based
on circumstantial evidence—the only murder trial in Virginia history to
be decided on such—and more drew me right in. I learned of the grand
mansion and the vast estate he'd established at the base of Stone Mountain, which is just over "High Knob" as we call it, the peak most familiar
to us on the *other* side of the mountain, where I grew up. How had I
never known Hagan Hall existed? Or the (by all reports) remarkable
man, Patrick Hagan? The wealthy, successful, sophisticated Irishman
was a mystery to me, and the more I learned, the more I wanted to tell
his story.

But then something amazing happened. As I continued my research,
along came Elizabeth—**Elizabeth Young**, our heroine—and I knew
this was a tale best told from her forthright, unvarnished, *local girl* perspective.

I'll start with Patrick, though, as a great deal more has been docu-
mented about his life. This comes as no surprise given the fact he was,

of course, male and a man of means and influence. The most extensive profile I found with regard to Patrick was in *The Virginia Law Register New Series*, Vol. 2, No. 12 (Apr., 1917), pp. 881–884, which outlines his immigration to America at sixteen; his subsequent travels to New York, Philadelphia, Norfolk, and Richmond; his studies in English, Philosophy, and Latin under his uncle, Joseph Hagan; his reading the law in the office of Col. Joseph Stras in Tazwell County, VA; his practice of law in Estilville (now known as Gate City) and later, Lee County, where "he rose rapidly in the profession and within a very few years after he was admitted to the bar was recognized as one of the leading lawyers of the southwest." The journal further states he was a relentless prosecutor, one of the best criminal lawyers in the state, and a specialist in land titles, a branch of law in which he gained a national reputation.

I giggled—I'm sure I giggled in delight—when I got to these sections:

His arguments before courts and juries sparkled with choice passages from classical literature. In common conversation he most frequently illustrated his point with some beautiful literary quotation. He was fond of quoting poetry, especially to young folk.

He was a man of commanding personal appearance. He had a natural dignified bearing, a deep and mellow voice, a decidedly rich Irish brogue, so he was easily distinguished as a man of mark among any body of men.

Oh, Patrick, I thought, *you are a charmer.*

And so a great deal of what I wrote of Patrick Hagan is based, at least in theory, on actual records. But I did take liberties. I changed his birth year from 1828 to 1831 and created, purely of my imagination, the backstory of his escape from both the Potato Famine and an oppressive, abusive father. Records indicate Hagan was a Democrat in his political leanings, although all commentary of his interpretation of those particular terms and beliefs—his position on the presidential election of 1860, his view of the Kansas-Nebraska Act, his attitudes with regard to slavery and the Civil War—all are purely my own creation. One would expect Patrick Hagan was most certainly a slave owner; the sole note I came across was in a profile that appeared in the *Kingsport News*, Sunday Magazine section, November 9, 1952, which states, "Hagan had a large colony of Negroes on his farm and provided a school and church for them." In the narrative, I chose to include the reference to the school.

I do not know anything specific as it relates to Patrick Hagan and the Civil War. I assume that if he'd become a soldier or officer, his service would have been noted in one of the handful of profiles I found, and it was not. I do know at some point he was bestowed the rank of Colonel, and my assumption is, as I wrote in the novel, this was an honorary designation. The Committee on Widows and Families, and his work thereof, is purely mine as a component of this fictional story.

As to Elizabeth Young. As mentioned above, I found very little information about my beloved Elizabeth, and therefore, I had the great fortune (and a rollicking good time) forming her, and the people in her family, primarily from my imagination. This includes Uncle Ruck, who in my mind's eye is as tender and kind as he is rugged and strapping. The story of Uncle Ruck was informed, however, from a document I found on the Scott County Historical Society website, in an article titled "Hanging Sheriffs of Scott County," by historian Omer C. Addington. It suggests the "fake hanging" in 1858 of one Baxter Pate, a man who'd been held in the Scott County jail at Estilville for committing a murder in the upper room of the old Compton Hotel. As Addington reports it, Pate was "hanged" then placed in the casket alive by "brother Masons" who drove him to the Tennessee/North Carolina border and released him. Pate then headed for Texas, where he lived out his life "and prospered."

I also know that Elizabeth was married to **Benjamin E. Grubb**, and that he became a soldier in the 64th Virginia Mounted Infantry, Company E, via its precursor unit, the 21st Virginia Infantry Battalion, on 8/6/1862. ("My" Ben enlists earlier, so as to take part in the Battle at Pound Gap.) Military records show Ben as AWOL on 3/20/1863 and taken POW on 9/9/1863 at Cumberland Gap. Following Frazer's surrender of his troops there, Ben was, in fact, sent to the horrific Camp

Douglas where he was held until he died 5/30/1864 of "heart disease," according to military records. He was twenty-seven years old. He was buried in grave 1149 in Chicago City Cemetery. I don't know anything of Ben's family or brothers, if he had brothers, although there is a record of a **Levi Grubb** who enlisted on 2/1/1863 in Lee County. There is no death record for this Levi Grubb (who in my story dies alongside his brother Jonah at the Battle of Second Manassas, also called Bull Run). Instead, records show Levi Grubb as having deserted 6/29/1863.

Of course, the war itself is an important part of this novel, and the officers and battles depicted in its pages are born from research while here and there I have taken liberties in the interest of the story. **Col. Logan Salyer**, **Col. Campbell Slemp**, **Brigadier General John Frazer** (who was later stripped of the commission due to his surrender at Cumberland Gap), **Alexander Smith**, **Morgan Tennessee Lipps**, **Gen. Humphrey Marshall**, and others who appear in the novel's pages are real people. Among other sources, I relied heavily on Luther F. Addington's *History of Wise County, Virginia*. I will point out that while the scenes in this novel involving the colorful Morgan T. Lipps may read like tall tales, according to Addington, the stories are indeed true. Further, I referenced multiple volumes of Civil War history written by Jeffery C. Weaver, all of which demonstrate significant discrepancies even in the reports of those who were there for the battle of Cumberland Gap. These include multiple points of view as to the effectiveness of Frazer's leadership as well as a generally accepted fact that Col. Campbell Slemp not only escaped capture at the Gap but then led a band of Confederate soldiers as they ran, rather than follow orders to lay down arms and surrender. All of this to say: While based on actual records, the version of the Battle at Cumberland Gap in this novel is a composite of viewpoints I found, and the details as presented are strictly of my choosing. I also regularly reached for Robert M. Addington's *A History of Scott County Virginia*, first published in 1932, for information about the daily lives and habits of people of the area in the nineteenth century.

As a character, **Abijah Alley** is far too wonderful not to have been born of an author's most ambitious dreams. And yet Alley was a real

person with a history and legacy fully his own. The man did have a striking presence and a long white beard; he did fancy himself a prophet; he
did write and publish a book of prophesy that foretold of the southern states seceding and of the resulting Civil War and its outcome. He
visited the Holy Land and returned to Scott County to build a replica
of King Solomon's Temple on his property in Long Hollow. He also
created his own religion. While I found little describing its doctrine
and beliefs or its style of worship, I do know the followers of Alley's
church were called the "Little Band" (which is the name I used for Alley's musicians). Much of this and more was noted in a profile of Alley
that appeared in *The New York Times* in 1897. Also, to my complete
delight, there is a page about Alley in a volume of genealogy written by
my grandmother, Rita Kennedy Sutton, and published in Spring 1973
by the Historical Society of Southwest Virginia. In *Early Osbornes and
Alleys with Notes on Allied Families*, my grandmother wrote:

> *In his more mature years, Abijah Alley became a man of many ec-
> centricities. He wore a full beard, which extended to his waist. Many
> stories are told of his absent minded ways. Often, he went to mill,
> but forgot to take the grain; or returned home, only to discover that
> he had left the meal.*
>
> *He was the founder of a religious sect called "the little band"
> which has a small following, after 150 years (1941) of precarious
> existence. Abijah was the principal contributor to the construction of
> a church in the Long Hollow Community of Scott Co. This strange
> preacher frequently began his services at midnight or several hours
> before dawn; and large congregations did attend these services.*
>
> *The minutes of the Primitive Baptist Church on Copper Creek
> record that, on January 15th, 1853, Abijah Alley was invited to
> preach. His text was from Matthew 24th chapter, 12th verse; and
> he closed by repeating some poetry.*

And so I imagined the scene in my novel, taking great joy in having Abijah Alley preach from that very verse. It was one of those magic

moments a writer of historical fiction lives for—finding a juicy nugget, then in doing the writing discovering just how much kismet is sometimes involved! I simply could not have chosen a more fitting verse for the story I'd created than the one Alley, via my grandmother, handed me.

Mary Lenore Kitchens is a character who formed easily before me, and she is purely fictional. As is Mister **Red Hopkins**, although I suppose he is more a compilation of many salt-of-the-earth Appalachians I've known, as his is the voice I hear most clearly.

As mentioned above, prior to researching this novel I'd neither heard of nor been to Hagan Hall, but it most surely was the grand showplace I did my best to bring to vivid life in this novel. There are colorful descriptions to be found online via family and community remembrances, including the *Kingsport Times* article previously referenced, and four articles I found via the Scott County Historical Society including "Remembered: Hagan Hall" from The Scott County Herald-Virginian, July 2, 1980; "Preservation Movement Rolling" by Brenda Taylor; "Hagan Hall," by Dawn Scott; and "Hagan Hall in Scott County" (no author noted). The details, as I've described them in the novel, are accurate according to the sources I found, including the seventeen rooms, a fine library, the mahogany banisters carved with dogwood blossoms, indoor plumbing with hot water, and all the rest. As part of my research, I visited the site, which remains private property and stands in ruins today. Still, it was not difficult to imagine the estate's grandeur in its heyday— an experience I called upon when writing the scene in which Marilee imagines herself living there. Even the detail in a later chapter in which the Charleston painter and paper hanger, Harry Smith, appears—it was noted in a profile of the estate that the man's signature was found on an uncovered plaster wall in the mansion's pretty front bedroom.

I'd like to offer a word about geography, as well, for the ridges and valleys of this region are a significant part of this story as my characters crisscross the land in their day-to-day lives and as troops move over and around during the long years of war. From the beginning, it was important to me that I get the geography right. I did loosen that expectation a bit as it became clear I did not have near the working knowledge that was required to achieve perfection, particularly as these are characters who mostly travel on horseback or on foot. I do hope the people who know these lands and places well will forgive me that indulgence. Also, I attempted to be historically accurate in my naming of towns: Gate City today was once Estilville; Jonesville today was once Mump's Fort; my own hometown of Wise was once known as Gladesville, or Gladeville, depending on the source.

Apologies, as well, to any Freemason who may read this story and recognize any details that are not in keeping with the fraternal organization's specific traditions. There remains today a bit of mystery regarding the secret society, but I did my best to stay true to the spirit of the brotherhood as I understand it, for it is one I have come to hold in reverence.

Also, to the people of Scott, Wise, and Lee Counties who see their histories in these pages, who perhaps even see their kin. It's my great hope you feel the novel honors that which we, of these old mountains, have always held dear—our land, our families, our proud heritage. That was my intent with every word I wrote. That is my reason for writing this novel, still.

Cathy Rigg
10/22/24

ACKNOWLEDGEMENTS

WRITING THIS NOVEL HAS BEEN ONE OF THE GREAT JOYS of my life—the fulfillment of a dream I've had since working a high school summer job at the Lonesome Pine Regional Library in Wise, Virginia. (Yes, it was the best job *ever*.) The year was 1975, and I was shelving books when I came across Lee Smith's *The Last Day the Dog-bushes Bloomed* and pronounced "I want to be a writer. And I want to write books like this." That library not only served up Lee Smith to me but, as a social and educational center in our small mountain town, brought many wonderful writers to our area. How thankful I am that the library—and my mother, with her fierce love of and dedication to that library—exposed me to the works of Lee, Clyde Edgerton, Kaye Gibbons, Robert Morgan, and so many more at such an impressionable age. I further had the chance to study with Lee Smith at the Key West Writers' Workshop in 2015, when I'd written the earliest pages of this novel. As every Appalachian writer knows, she is not only the queen of Appalachian literature, Lee Smith is also its most generous benefactor. Her support for this book has been unwavering.

I, too, bow to the incomparable Adriana Trigiani, who also read early and called to offer "You got it, Cath. You're the real deal," in that very Adri-way. At every stage, she has been a guiding force, and I could not be more grateful.

The folks at the Appalachian Writers' Workshop—faculty and attending writers alike—have molded and championed and cheered…I do not exaggerate when I say it is a supportive community like no other. Patricia Hudson has been a failsafe wonder, never letting me give up or misstep; Amy Greene got the manuscript to Turner Publishing with such a lovely stamp of approval it might have made me cry; the folks in each of my AWW-formed writing groups—Matthew Kingesly, Tamela Rich, Loren Crawford, Kristi Walker, Rachel Holbrook, Chelyen Davis, Erin Reid, Jennie Miller—read pages and offered insightful notes and made the writing fun.

Every editor made this book better: Thank you to Leslie Rendoks, Amanda Chiu Krohn, Ashlyn Inman. A special thanks to Amanda Chiu Krohn for loving this book and taking it under her wing, and to the entire team at Turner Publishing/Keylight Books: I so appreciate your guidance and faith. To Ryon Edwards, the designer I spent my career working alongside, your passion, talent, and generosity inspire me. Thank you for always, always being there.

I cannot *not* thank the vast network of friends and coworkers and my immediate and extended family who have continued to cheer and celebrate the publication of this novel with me: the Wise Women, the RP crew, the Clemson gals, all my beloveds in Columbia, Wise, and on Cats Mountain. A special shoutout to Lisa and Randy, Suzann, Christina, Cris, Leslie, Teresa.

To my daughter, Eliza, who amazes and inspires me everyday; to Preston, who makes her world bigger; and most especially to Tim Monetti, my husband, who has taken on a thousand daily tasks and cooked a hundred thousand meals to create the time and space for me to devote to this novel—it is an embarrassment of riches. I adore you all. I am forever grateful.

THAT WHICH BINDS US
DISCUSSION GUIDE

———

1. The novel is written from the first-person points of view of five primary characters: Elizabeth Young, Patrick Hagan, Marilee Kitchens, Ben Grubb, and Red Hopkins. Why do you think Rigg chose to tell the story this way? What does each character bring, in terms of narration? Which character is your favorite?

2. A central conflict in the novel is set up in the earliest pages, regarding the relationship between twin brothers: Elizabeth's papa, Jonathan Young, and Elizabeth's uncle, Rufus Young (Uncle Ruck). What purpose did this conflict serve in the story? How did you feel about each of these characters in the first half of the novel? Did your feelings change by the end of the book?

3. The teacher, Marilee, tells Patrick she believes she can help "the poor unfortunates" of the area through education—a comment that doesn't sit well with him. How did you react when she said that? Why do you think he feels the way he does?

4. The novel features a triangle of religions with distinct differences between their doctrines and faith practices: Primitive Baptist, Roman Catholic, and Abijah Alley's "free love" faith. Why is this important in the novel? Which characters' motivations or actions are driven by their beliefs?

5. Marilee quickly falls for Patrick, seeing him as her equal in "a barren land." He regards her as a good friend. Although their relationship never progresses much beyond that, she hopes against hope, remaining devoted to him for years. Why do you think she did that? Do you fault her for it? Why do you think Patrick *didn't* fall for Marilee? Do you fault him? Have you ever hoped against hope for something?

6. Another thread throughout the novel is the brotherhood of the Freemasons—the world's oldest, largest, and most well-known fraternal organization. Membership is based on your own "free will and accord," and in the novel, Ruck chooses to pursue membership while Jonathan does not. Why do you think each of these men made the decisions they did regarding the Freemasons?

7. In Part Three: War, we never hear directly from Elizabeth. Instead, we learn of her situation in bits and pieces through Ben as he responds to her letters, as well as through Patrick, who has some interaction with her through his work on behalf of the Committee for Widows and Families. Why do you think Rigg chose to write the war years in this way? How does this inform Elizabeth's character even though we aren't hearing directly from her?

8. Patrick Hagan buys his way out of military service and conscription, making the case that he is far more valuable to the community and to the war effort if he is at home doing the work he is doing. This was a real option during the Civil War based on The Enrollment Act of 1863, which provided that a draftee could pay a substitute $300 (about $5,000 in today's terms) to enlist in his place. What do you think of this policy? Do you believe Patrick's rationale for making that choice? Do you believe that his intentions in doing so were for good?

9. After Ben's death, Red Hopkins tells Elizabeth the full truth of the secret of what happened between her papa and her Uncle Ruck—a story only he can tell. He fills in details up to the very end, but when she asks if Ruck ever learned the truth about his daughter, Red lies. Why do you think he kept this one detail to himself? Do you think it was the right decision?

10. After she learns that Patrick gave Ben the tract of land before Ben and Elizabeth were married, Elizabeth burns down the home she'd shared with Ben. Why do you think she did this?

11. As you consider the novel and its conflicts, what are the things that tear us apart? What are the things that bind us together?

ABOUT THE AUTHOR

CATHY RIGG was born and raised in the Appalachian Mountains of Southwest Virginia where her people, on her mother's side, go back generations. She moved to South Carolina after college and founded the brand marketing firm, Riggs Partners. Rigg's fiction and poetry have appeared in *Litmosphere: Journal of Charlotte Lit*, *Still: The Journal*, *Clinch Mountain Review*, and other publications. She and her husband divide their time between Columbia, SC, and Burnsville, NC, where they stare at the view and obsess over the bears on a ridge high above Asheville.